KITTENS AND KILLERS

An Isle of Man Ghostly Cozy

DIANA XARISSA

For Mom – it's been a while since I dedicated a book to her.

AUTHOR'S NOTE

This marks the eleventh book in the Ghostly Cozy series. I'm enjoying spending time with Fenella and her friends more and more with each title. Mona may be my favorite character, but don't tell the others. If you haven't read any of the other titles in the series, I suggest you start at the beginning and read them all in order, but each story should be enjoyable on its own, if you prefer not to do that.

Fenella grew up in the US, so these books are primarily written in American English. Characters who are British or Manx use British terms rather than American ones, however. I try to make sure that I've done this throughout the book, but I'm sure I make mistakes. If you find any, please let me know so that I can correct them.

I could (and do) talk for hours about the Isle of Man. This unique UK crown dependency in the Irish Sea was my home for over ten years and still holds a very special place in my heart. I don't think there is anywhere else in the world quite like it.

This is a work of fiction. All of the characters are products of the author's imagination. Any resemblance to actual persons, living or dead, is entirely coincidental. The shops, restaurants, and businesses in this story are also fictional. The historical sites and other landmarks on the island are all real. The events that take place within them in this story are fictional, however.

If you are interested in keeping up with all of my new releases, all of my contact details are available in the back of the book. I have a monthly newsletter as well as a fun Facebook page. I'd love to hear from you.

❧ I ❧

"**J**ack is leaving tomorrow, isn't he?" Shelly Quirk checked as she and Fenella started their morning walk down the Douglas promenade.

"He is. He has to be back in time to recover from his jet lag before classes start back up again," Fenella Woods confirmed.

"Are you going to miss him?" was Shelly's next question.

Fenella took a deep breath. "I am, actually, which I wasn't expecting."

Fenella and Jack Dawson had been a couple for over ten years when Fenella had been living in Buffalo, New York. It had been a good but unexciting relationship built on mutual respect and admiration rather than passionate devotion. When Fenella had inherited her Aunt Mona Kelly's estate on the Isle of Man, she'd welcomed the opportunity to cut her ties in the US and move to the island. Jack had had difficulty accepting that the relationship was over. Many months after Fenella had moved, Jack had come to visit her, seemingly determined to rekindle their relationship.

"He's given up on the idea of you two getting back together, hasn't he?"

"He has. Truthfully, he's almost a different person now. If things

I

were different, I might almost be disappointed that he's not still interested in me."

Shelly laughed. "I never thought I'd hear you say that."

Fenella nodded. She'd never expected to think such a thing, but the trip to the island had changed Jack in many ways. She wasn't sure if his new attitude toward life had come about because he was more confident now that he'd traveled abroad for the first time, because he'd found himself caught up in a murder investigation, or if there was something else going on entirely, but she found herself liking the changed man a great deal.

"He'd probably still welcome the thought of you two getting back together," Shelly suggested.

"I'm not sure he would, but I really don't want to try again. I would hate trying to have a long distance relationship and I've no interest in moving back to Buffalo."

"Jack could move here. He seems to like it here."

"We'd have to get married in order for him to get a visa. Just because I like him a lot doesn't mean I want to spend the rest of my life with him. There are other complications, too."

Shelly chuckled. "Like Donald and Daniel."

"I'm not sure what I'd call Donald," Fenella sighed.

Donald Donaldson was a very wealthy man who pursued Fenella whenever he was on the island. Because he traveled a great deal, managing his businesses, the pursuit seemed to start, stop, and then restart almost constantly. His daughter, Phoebe, had been in a bad car accident in New York City some months ago, and Donald had been by her bedside ever since.

The last Fenella had heard, he was planning to move his daughter to London soon to continue her treatment there. Fenella wasn't entirely clear on his intentions with regard to herself, though.

"How is his daughter doing?"

"As well as can be expected, apparently. The last time I talked to Donald he said that she has good days and bad days. He has her doing a dozen different therapies and he thinks they're all helping, but no one can say at this point what the limits on her recovery might be. Once they're settled in London, Donald wants me to come over and spend some time with him. I'm not sure what I should do."

"Do you want to see him?"

"Yes and no," Fenella said. "We had a lot of fun together when we went out, but there were always difficulties."

"Like Donald's reputation as a player, and Daniel."

"And the fact that he's rich, and I felt intimidated by that."

"Except now you know that you're just as rich, if not richer."

"I still haven't really managed to get my head around that," Fenella told her closest friend. "I never imagined, when I inherited Mona's estate, that it would be worth as much as it is."

Over the course of her long life Mona Kelly had managed to accumulate dozens of properties all over the island. She also owned stocks, shares, bank accounts, an expensive red sports car, the luxury apartment that Fenella now called home, antiques, jewelry, and goodness knows what else. Fenella had been delighted with the apartment and the car. Everything else felt like a huge bonus, one that she was still coming to terms with in her own mind.

"Well, you don't have to decide anything today. What are you and Jack going to do with his last day on the island?"

"He wants to have one last drive around so that he can take a final look at it. He's hoping to come back one day, but he has a long list of other places he wants to visit now that he's actually tried traveling. I expect I'll be getting postcards from all over the world soon."

"Good for him. I feel as if I should be doing more traveling," Shelly told her. "The island is pretty special, though, and I'm retired, so it isn't as if I need a holiday from my life."

"I know what you mean. The first thing I thought about when I found out I had money was traveling, but I still haven't gone anywhere. I don't really like beaches or heat. I don't ski. As a historian, I should want to visit museums and historical sites, but I keep putting it off because I'm still enjoying seeing the sites around the island."

"Maybe we should go somewhere together," Shelly suggested. "Let's talk about it another day."

The pair had walked from one end of the promenade to the other and were back at their apartment building.

"Yes, let's," Fenella agreed. "I think we'd have lots of fun together wherever we went."

"I should be visiting interesting and exciting places to use as settings for my books."

"How is the writing coming?" Fenella knew that Shelly had been trying to write a romance novel for a few months now.

Shelly shrugged. "Slowly. I set this first book on the island, but I think I'm going to have to find a more interesting setting for the next one. It isn't that the island is boring, exactly, but it isn't as exciting as a cattle ranch in Texas or an island in the Caribbean."

"You only feel that way because you live here. I'm sure Americans will love reading about the island. Most of them have probably never even heard of it."

"I keep thinking I should change the protagonist, as well as the setting. I've made the heroine an older woman who was unexpectedly widowed, but maybe I'd be better off writing a more traditional story about a younger woman."

As Shelly herself had been unexpectedly widowed just over a year earlier, Fenella suspected that she'd modeled the heroine on herself. "I think you should write the story you want to write. You don't have to worry about making a living from your writing. It's just for fun, right?"

"It is just for fun, but I'd love it if it became a big success, not for the money, but because that would mean lots of people would read my book."

"Maybe you should focus on getting it written before you do anything else," Fenella suggested. "My friend who makes her living self-publishing her work told me that she wrote about half a dozen books that she'll never publish because they're so awful. She reckons it took her that long to get good enough to try her hand at self-publishing."

"Half a dozen?" Shelly echoed. "I don't think I can write half a dozen books, let alone wait until the seventh one to actually try to do anything with them. I was hoping to self-publish this one if I can't find an agent or a publisher, or whatever I need."

"As I said before, you should probably focus on writing the book for now. All those other things come later."

"In that case, I'm going to go and write," Shelly told her. The pair had made their way up to the sixth floor while they'd been talking. Shelly gave Fenella a quick hug and then disappeared into her apartment as Fenella dug around for the keycard that opened her own door. It was always in the bottom of her bag, but she found it eventually.

❧ "I'm back," she called, startling Katie, her tiny black kitten, who was asleep on one of the chairs in front of the floor-to-ceiling windows that showcased the promenade and the sea beyond it.

"You don't need to shout," Mona said sternly as she walked into the room.

Fenella looked over at her and sighed. Mona looked younger than ever today in a long gown that showed off her slender figure. Although the woman had been over ninety when she'd died, the Mona who wandered through Fenella's apartment looked no more than thirty. Fenella could barely remember Mona from the very occasional visits Mona had paid to the US during Fenella's childhood. It seemed, therefore, that the woman in her apartment truly was Mona's ghost and not a figment of Fenella's imagination.

"Jack is leaving tomorrow, isn't he?" Mona asked as Fenella headed for the kitchen.

"Yes, he is," Fenella agreed. "I'm not sure what you've done to him, but he's going back to Buffalo a changed man."

"I told you I didn't do much, just made a few small suggestions to his subconscious, that's all. Let's face it, the man needed the help."

Fenella couldn't argue with that, even if she did feel slightly uncomfortable with the idea that Mona was manipulating Jack in some way.

"Once he's gone, you'll have to have Daniel over for dinner," Mona told her. "I'll make sure I'm out that night."

"Why does everyone keep bringing up Daniel?" Fenella demanded. "Daniel and I are just friends."

"Yes, which is why it's time to start trying harder."

Daniel Robinson was a CID inspector with the Douglas Constabulary. He was an attractive man in his late forties, with light brown hair and hazel eyes. Fenella had met him after discovering a dead body, and their relationship had developed from there. When he'd recently gone away to study for some months in the UK, they'd put everything on hold.

Once Daniel had returned to the island he'd admitted that he'd met someone else, but that circumstances meant that they couldn't be together. Before Jack's arrival, Fenella and Daniel had discussed giving their relationship a fresh start, but with Jack visiting they hadn't seen much of one another. While Fenella really liked Daniel, she was apprehensive about what the future might hold.

"I'm not ready to start trying," Fenella protested.

"If you don't hurry, someone else will grab him. He's gorgeous, or hadn't you noticed?"

"I've noticed. He's smart and funny and great company, too, but I'm not going to start chasing after him like a schoolgirl."

"I should hope not. I expect you to chase after him like a sophisticated woman. Invite him to dinner. Make him feel special. Make him feel as if he can't live without you."

"Is that what you did with Max?"

Maxwell Martin had been Mona's fabulously wealthy benefactor from the time Mona was eighteen until his death. He'd showered her with expensive gifts, but the pair had never married, something Fenella still didn't quite understand.

"Oh, Max couldn't have lived without me," Mona told her with a throaty laugh. "He needed me for so many reasons."

"Such as?"

Mona shook her head. "I haven't time to go into all of that right now. I'm having a small party later and I need to get everything ready."

"A party? Tell me more." As soon as the words were out of her mouth, Fenella was sorry she'd said them. Mona seemed to love telling her things about the ghost world, knowing full well that Fenella could never be sure what was true and what wasn't. The sly grin on Mona's face told Fenella not to believe a word of whatever Mona was about to say.

"I'm just having a few friends over for drinks," Mona told her.

"Over? As in here? In my apartment?"

"It was my flat first, and it's still my home. Where else would I have guests?"

"What if I don't want them here?"

"You won't be able to see them and they won't bother you. Why should you care?"

"Maybe I'm just slightly uncomfortable with the idea of sharing my apartment with a bunch of ghosts, all of whom are total strangers."

Mona shrugged. "There are ghosts everywhere, you know. Well, maybe not everywhere, but we're around in a lot of places. Most people just ignore us and get on with their lives."

"I never thought to try that," Fenella muttered under her breath.

"If you're going to be difficult about it, I'll have my friends meet me in the ballroom instead," Mona told her. "That will disturb Max, of course, but I don't suppose you'll mind disturbing an old and slightly confused man, even if it's only through his generosity that you can enjoy this flat and everything that goes with it."

"Have your party here," Fenella sighed. "Can you do it while I'm out today? I'd rather not be here, if you don't mind."

"I'll make sure you don't see anyone," Mona told her, which didn't reassure Fenella in the slightest.

She headed for her bedroom to run a comb through her hair before she needed to pick up Jack. The phone startled her as she reached for her lipstick.

"Hello?"

"Ms. Woods? I'm Donna Cannon," the voice on the phone said. "I was meant to ring you last week, but I ended up in hospital and I couldn't manage it."

"I'm sorry to hear that," Fenella said when the woman paused. Fenella had no idea who she was or why she was calling.

"Yes, well, it's getting older, you see. I'm seventy-one, no, seventy-two, well, it's one of those. I've never been brilliant at maths, you see."

"I see," Fenella replied after another lengthy pause. "I hope you're feeling better."

"I had a nasty fall in ShopFast. I was wandering through the bakery and I tripped over my trolley's wheel. Fell right into the bread display and ended up on the ground covered in baguettes."

"My goodness, are you okay?"

"I'm fine. They checked me over and then kept me overnight in case I had a concussion from one of the day-old loaves."

"I'm glad you're okay."

"Oh, thank you. Anyway, I hope we'll see you on Monday."

Fenella frowned at the receiver. "Monday?" she echoed.

"Yes, oh, dear. I hope you haven't forgotten. We've only just enough people to run the class, you see. If you aren't coming we may have to cancel."

"Class?" Fenella said slowly. She glanced at the calendar on the wall and then realized. "The class in reading old records starts on Monday," she exclaimed. "I'd nearly forgotten about that, actually. I signed up months ago and put it on my calendar, but then it was Thanksgiving and Christmas and it sort of slipped my mind."

"Yes, dear, that's why I'm ringing, you see. Marjorie asked me to ring everyone in the class for her. She's rather busy with other things, but she gave me a discount on the class if I agreed to be her helper."

"That's nice," Fenella said during yet another gap in the conversation.

"It is nice, yes. Marjorie is lovely. She's a very good teacher, too. You should take her class in Manx."

"Manx? I'm not very good at languages," Fenella replied. As part of her PhD program, she'd had to demonstrate a level of proficiency in a foreign language, a requirement that had very nearly prevented her from finishing the degree. As she understood it, she'd received the lowest possible passing score in French, and now, many years later, she could remember nothing she'd been taught except for the French word for umbrella.

"You are coming to the class on Monday, though, aren't you? I'm so looking forward to meeting Mona's niece."

Fenella swallowed a sigh. It seemed as if everyone on the island wanted to meet her and she couldn't help but feel as if she were a disappointment to them all. Fenella felt rather bland and colorless when she heard stories about her glamorous and somewhat wild aunt. "I'll be at class on Monday," she confirmed.

"Excellent. I'll just put a little tick next to your name so I don't accidentally ring you again. I've already rung one man three times, you see, because I forgot to put a tick next to his name."

"It's an easy mistake to make," Fenella assured her. "I hope you don't have many more people to call."

"There are only six on the list and you're actually the last one. The list was alphabetical, you see. I'm first on the list, but I don't have to ring myself, do I?"

"No, I suppose not."

The other woman laughed. "So I'm done now, and everyone has promised to be at class on Monday. Marjorie will be pleased. She always worries that no one will turn up, you see. She's had to cancel a number of classes in the past due to poor attendance."

"That's a shame."

"It's a small island. There just aren't that many people interested in learning more about its past."

"That's also a shame."

"Marjorie said you're a historian. I hope you're going to do some research while you're here. Maybe you could even write a book about the island."

"Maybe, one day. For now I'm still getting settled. I haven't even been here for a year yet."

"No, of course not. You only arrived in March, didn't you? And then you found that dead body, which must have been unpleasant for you. I'm glad it didn't send you right back to New York."

"It was unpleasant, but it didn't stop me from falling in love with the island."

"That's just as well, since you haven't stopped finding bodies ever since," Donna cackled. "Still, that's one way to keep that handsome young police inspector at your door, isn't it?"

Fenella flushed and then bit her tongue. This time she wasn't going to reply. She'd just wait it out until the other woman spoke again, she decided. The silence seemed to stretch on and on until Donna finally cleared her throat.

"We'll see you on Monday, then," she said brightly. "I've enjoying chatting with you, but I really must go."

Fenella didn't get a chance to reply before the phone went dead. "Yeah, nice chatting with you, too," she said as she put the phone back in its cradle.

"You should have let the machine answer that call," Mona told her as Fenella topped up Katie's food and water bowls. "Donna Cannon will talk your ear off if you let her."

"You should have warned me," Fenella suggested. "She was just calling to check that I hadn't forgotten about the class on Monday."

"Which you had."

"Well, yes, but it's on the calendar, so I would have remembered eventually. Things have been rather busy with Jack here."

"And you very rarely bother to look at the calendar."

"I must try harder, actually, now that I'm starting to take classes."

"You need to start working on your social life. When I was alive I was never home in the evening, at least not home alone."

"I have Katie."

"Wouldn't you enjoy having a strong, handsome man for company, too?"

"I'm not sure Katie would like that."

"Katie won't mind for the right man," Mona insisted. "You should be more involved in other things, too, like charity events."

"I went to loads of them with Donald. They were all boring."

"Now that you're settled here, you're going to start getting invited to things yourself. I'm surprised it's taken this long for the invitations to start coming in, actually."

"I've had a few, but I've made excuses and not gone to any of them. I don't like the idea of being invited places because people think I'll give them money."

"But that's how charity fundraisers work. Oh, never mind. You go and entertain Jack for his last day on the island. I have a party to get ready for, anyway." Mona faded away.

"I'm going now," Fenella told Katie as she slid on her shoes and grabbed her handbag. "You be a good girl. I'll be bringing Jack by later so you can say goodbye to him before he goes back to Buffalo."

Katie stared at her for a minute and then shrugged before heading off to the kitchen. Fenella let herself out and then locked the door behind herself. Today was all about letting Jack see the island for the last time. That would best be done in Mona's little red sports car rather than in the far more sensible four-door car that Fenella had bought for herself.

The drive from Fenella's apartment to the house on Poppy Drive where Jack was staying seemed to take only seconds in the fast car. Jack must have been watching for her, as he was out of the house and into the car almost as soon as she'd stopped.

"I want to see everything again," he told her as they headed south. "Both castles, every museum, anything and everything historical or interesting, all of it."

"I'll do my best, but we won't be able to stop everywhere," Fenella replied.

"I'll settle for just driving past some things, but let's stop as much as we can. I'm really going to miss this little island."

Fenella drove to Cregneash Village in the south of the island where she and Jack had a slow walk around. Then they headed north, stopping in Castletown as they went. They had lunch in Douglas before continuing on their way north, visiting Laxey and Ramsey before heading to the Point of Ayre. Fenella drove back down through Peel and then across the island past Tynwald Hill on their way back to Douglas. It was starting to get dark when they reached the house on Poppy Drive again.

"That was just about perfect," Jack told her as they got out of the car. "I can't believe how beautiful everything is here."

"It is pretty wonderful."

Jack opened the door to the house and then stepped back to let Fenella in first.

"Do you want to get a pizza?" Fenella asked as she dropped onto a couch in the living room.

"We could. I don't care what we eat."

"Are you okay?"

"I'm sad," Jack admitted with a sigh. "I'm sad to be leaving the island, and I'm sad to be leaving you. I still love you, you know."

"I love you, too, but not in a romantic way."

Jack nodded. "I wish I could change that, but I know it would probably make things even more complicated than they already are. I won't promise to stop calling you once in a while, but I am going to try to move on with my life."

"I hope you do, and I hope you find a wonderful woman with whom to share it."

"Pizza," Jack announced, getting to his feet. "Let's get pizza from the place around the corner."

They ate in the kitchen, carefully chatting about the snowy weather back in Buffalo and other innocuous subjects.

"Thank your friend for letting me stay in his house, please," Jack said at the end of the meal.

"I will," Fenella agreed, feeling slightly guilty for not telling Jack the truth. The house on Poppy Drive was just one of the many properties that Fenella had inherited from Mona. She'd previously let her brother, James, stay in the house, but she hadn't told him it was actually her property, either. As uncomfortable as the mild deception made her feel, she felt even worse about discussing the extent of her inheritance.

"I can do that," Jack told her as Fenella began washing the few dishes they'd used.

When Jack had first arrived, he'd piled nearly all of the plates, glasses, and other crockery on a table in front of the house's main entrance as a makeshift burglar alarm. When Fenella had arrived the next morning and been unable to rouse Jack, she'd had Daniel force the door open, breaking nearly all of the tableware. Mona had boxes and boxes of such things in her storage unit at the apartment complex, so Fenella had replaced everything with somewhat sturdier alternatives. While Jack had only broken a few plates while washing them since, it seemed safer for Fenella to handle the simple task.

"It's your last night. Washing the dishes is the least I can do," she told him.

"I can't believe I'll be back in Buffalo tomorrow. It seems like I just arrived here."

"It's been over a month."

"And I've changed a lot. I realize that. I'm not going home the same person that I was when I arrived. I don't know what's going to happen when I get back to Buffalo, though. I may fall right back into my old habits."

"Only you can stop that from happening."

"I know. I just hope I don't let inertia become the ruling force in my life again."

Fenella laughed. "That's a wonderful expression. I'm going to use that one myself."

They chatted for a while longer and Fenella found herself remembering everything that had attracted her to him in the first place, a decade earlier. He was witty and interesting and he could talk about just about anything. It was getting late when she finally got up to leave.

"I'll be back around nine to take you to the airport."

"I'll be ready," Jack promised.

He let Fenella out and then stood in the doorway and watched her walk to her car. She opened the door and then stopped when she heard someone call her name.

"Fenella?" Daniel's voice cut through the darkness.

Daniel lived in the house that was almost exactly across the street from the one where Jack was staying. Fenella watched as he crossed the road to her.

"I was just going up to bed when I saw you come out of the house," he explained. "I was going to ring you tomorrow."

"I hope nothing's wrong?" Fenella exclaimed.

"Not at all. Jack is leaving tomorrow, isn't he?" he asked.

That's the third time I've been asked that question today, Fenella thought as she nodded. "Yes, I'm taking him to the airport in the morning."

"I was wondering if you'd like to have dinner with me tomorrow night, then," Daniel said. "Maybe we could go to that little Italian place with the garlic bread."

Fenella didn't have to think twice about where he meant. That restaurant was one of her favorites. "Sure, that would be great," she said, wondering if Daniel was hoping to restart their relationship once Jack was gone.

"Terrific. I have another cold case I want to discuss with you,"

Daniel said. "If Shelly isn't busy, invite her along, too. You have great insights, but she might be helpful as well."

Fenella nodded. "I'll see if she's free," she said, trying to hide her disappointment. She enjoyed discussing cold cases with Daniel and was flattered that he valued her opinion, but cold cases were hardly very romantic.

"I'll meet you there around seven, if that's okay," Daniel continued.

"Sure, fine," Fenella muttered. "See you then."

She climbed into her car and drove back to her building.

"He just wants my help with another case," she told Katie as she climbed into bed a short while later. "He even told me to invite Shelly along."

"Meerooww," Katie said as she curled up in the exact center of the king-sized bed.

"I could pretend to forget to invite Shelly, but I think it might be better if Shelly did come along. Things are still, well, odd between Daniel and me."

Katie almost seemed to roll her eyes at Fenella before she put her head down and went to sleep. Fenella sighed and then shut her own eyes, certain she'd never be able to get to sleep herself.

2

The alarm startled both Fenella and Katie the next morning. Fenella switched it off and then looked at Katie. "I'm sorry, but I need to get up a little early if I'm going to get Jack to the airport on time."

Katie turned her back to Fenella and snuggled back down into the bedclothes. It was six-thirty, half an hour before the time Katie usually woke Fenella. Clearly, the kitten didn't appreciate being woken herself.

As Katie was still in bed, Fenella took a shower before she went into the kitchen to get breakfast for herself and the kitten. Katie strolled in at exactly seven o'clock and began to nibble daintily at her breakfast. Fenella was being far less delicate with her toast, which she'd liberally smothered in jam.

"I shouldn't feel this sad about Jack leaving," she told Katie.

"Maybe you're more upset about Daniel than Jack," Mona suggested as she appeared at the kitchen counter.

Fenella jumped, launching her toast into the air. It landed, jam side down, on the kitchen floor. Katie pounced on it as if it were a mouse and began to wrestle with it. Jam spread everywhere as Fenella tried to get the mangled piece of her breakfast away from her pet.

"You put a lot of jam on your toast," Mona said as she surveyed the huge smear of jam that seemed to cover nearly the entire kitchen floor.

Fenella threw the toast in the trash and then picked up Katie and cleaned off her jam-covered paws and face. The kitten complained loudly the entire time. When Fenella was done, she tucked the animal into the bathroom so that she could clean the kitchen floor.

"She's going to make a mess in there," Mona predicted.

Fenella grinned. "I put the toilet paper in a drawer and the tissues under the sink. There isn't too much for her to destroy, although I'm sure she'll find something."

It didn't take Fenella long to wipe up the jam, and when she opened the bathroom door to release Katie, she found the animal sitting in the middle of the floor calmly washing her paws. A quick glance around the room suggested that Katie had actually behaved herself during her short imprisonment.

"Is there any way you could signal your arrival so that I don't jump when you talk to me?" Fenella asked Mona as she slid a fresh piece of bread into the toaster.

Mona shrugged. "I could make the lights flicker," she suggested. She waved an arm and the kitchen lights began to turn on and off.

"How are you doing that?" Fenella demanded.

"I'm flipping the switch," Mona laughed. "I can't really control electricity."

"How are you flipping the switch, though? You aren't solid."

"I'm solid enough to flip a switch if I want to," Mona told her.

A dozen questions about the subject sprung into Fenella's mind, but she didn't bother to ask any of them. "What makes you think I'm upset about Daniel?" she asked instead.

"You told Katie that he'd invited you to dinner but told you to bring Shelly along as he wants to discuss a cold case with you."

Fenella tried to remember exactly what she'd said to Katie, but she couldn't. "Even if I did tell Katie that, when did you talk to Katie?"

"I didn't talk to Katie. I don't speak enough of her language to communicate all of that. I overheard you talking to Katie, but I didn't materialize, as I didn't want to disturb you."

Again, Fenella ignored the questions that rushed into her head.

"Right, okay, whatever. I'm not upset about Daniel, anyway. I'm upset about Jack."

"Of course you are. He was part of your life for ten long, boring, seemingly endless years, and now he's going away. While you're happy to see the back of him, you're going to miss feeling needed, aren't you?"

"Not at all," Fenella snapped. "Jack didn't need me, anyway, he just liked to pretend to be helpless."

"And you were happy to play along."

"I was hoping you might try to make me feel better."

"I am trying to make you feel better," Mona countered. "I'm pointing out where you went wrong with Jack so that you don't make the same mistakes with Daniel."

"I'm not going to make any mistakes with Daniel. We're just friends. He just likes to go over cold cases with me, that's all."

"You need to give Daniel time. He's still working his way through everything that happened when he was away. As long as he's making excuses to see you, then I don't think you need to worry."

Fenella sighed. "I don't want to talk about this right now. I'm going for a long walk on the promenade before I have to get Jack to the airport."

She grabbed her handbag and was out the door before Mona could respond. The elevator wasn't on her floor, so she headed for the stairs, racing down them to the ground floor almost as if she were being chased. The physical exertion helped her forget about her problems. When she reached the promenade she started to walk at the fastest pace she could manage, determined to tire herself out before her emotions could get the best of her.

She'd only gone a few hundred yards when she heard excited barking. When she turned around, she was nearly knocked over by the huge dog that was straining at the end of his leash.

"Winston, my goodness, it's good to see you, too," she exclaimed as she hugged the giant animal. A few sharp barks reminded Fenella to say hello to Winston's companion, Fiona, as well.

"He nearly pulled me off my feet," Harvey Garus said as he caught up to his dogs. "He's always so excited to see you."

"I'm always excited to see him, too," Fenella admitted. She lavished as much attention on both animals as she could, basking in their affection.

Due to a series of unusual circumstances, Fenella had looked after both dogs for a short while some months earlier. Now they were back with their proper owner, Harvey, who lived in the building next door to hers. Fenella sometimes took one or both dogs on walks to give Harvey a break. When he'd recently taken a short trip, Fenella had been delighted to keep the animals again, just for a few nights.

"You were walking pretty fast," Harvey said. "If you want a good workout, you can take Winston for a run."

"I will, actually," Fenella told him. "I feel the need to wear myself out today."

Harvey nodded. "Off you go, and don't mind Fiona if she complains. She'll be fine with me."

Fenella grinned and then took Winston's leash. They set off at a brisk walk, but Winston was clearly eager to increase the pace with every step. They ended up jogging until Fenella didn't think she could manage any longer, before dropping back to a fast walk.

"You're hard work," she told Winston.

He gave her an impish grin and then began to pull on his leash, heading for the sea.

"Oh, no, you don't," she told him. "I'm sure Harvey has better things to do today than take you for a bath."

Winston gave a few more gentle tugs on his leash before he gave up and settled for running forward a few paces, stopping to wait for her catch up, and then repeating the game. They were nearly back to the bench where Harvey and Fiona were resting when Winston began to bark loudly.

Harvey walked over to join Fenella as she watched Winston barking at a large storage shed on the side of the road.

"What's he all worked up about?" Harvey asked.

Fenella shrugged. "He's barking at the shed."

"I hope he hasn't found a body," Harvey told her. He flushed. "I didn't mean to suggest that you keep finding bodies or anything," he said quickly. "I mean, I just meant, that is, I hope he hasn't found a dead mouse or something."

"Yes, of course," Fenella said dryly, well aware of what Harvey actually meant.

"Should we ring the police?" Harvey asked.

"Does Winston usually bark at sheds?"

"We walk past this one every day. He's never shown any interest in it at all."

Fenella felt a familiar sense of dread as she looked from the dog to the shed and back again. The last thing she wanted to do was find another dead body.

"Maybe you should ring that friend of yours, the police inspector one. Maybe he should come and see what's in the shed," Harvey suggested.

"Maybe I'll just take a peek. I'd hate to bother the police if it's just a dead mouse." She handed Winston's leash to Harvey and took a step forward, and then another. "What is this shed for, anyway?" she asked.

"They store the beach chairs in it during the summer," Harvey told her. "They may store them in there during the winter, too. I don't know. It should be locked up tight this time of year, anyway."

There was a padlock on the door, and from what Fenella could see, it was intact. Winston had stopped barking, but he was still staring at the shed with intense focus. Fenella sighed. "I'm going to have to call the police."

"That's probably wise. Ring that friend of yours."

Fenella debated with herself for a minute. She could call 999 and they would send the closest constable to investigate, or she could call Daniel. Which was likely to be quicker, she wondered as she glanced at the time. She still had to get Jack to the airport.

Daniel answered his mobile on the first ring. "Is everything okay?" he asked before she'd even spoken.

"I hope so. I'm on the promenade with Harvey and Winston. Winston is barking at the storage shed at the far end and he won't stop."

Fenella was sure she heard the man on the other end of the line sigh. "I'll send someone and I won't be far behind," he said. "Don't go inside the shed."

"It's padlocked."

"So I need to find someone with a key."

"I have to get Jack to the airport."

"I'll be as quick as I can."

Daniel disconnected. Fenella looked at Harvey and shrugged. "Someone is on their way."

Harvey nodded. "I supposed they'd be cross if I went home, wouldn't they?"

"Yes, they would. If there is any evidence of any sort of crime, they'll want to talk to you."

"Yeah, that's what I thought. I'm going to go and sit down, anyway."

Harvey walked back over to the bench, pulling the dogs' leashes so that they followed. Winston barked a few times before he gave up and joined Harvey. Fenella stayed where she was, wondering what the police were going to find inside the shed.

"Ms. Woods, what a surprise," a familiar voice said a few minutes later.

Fenella forced herself to smile at Constable Howard Corlett. She'd first met him when he'd responded to her 999 call after she'd found her first dead body. She was really hoping that whatever was in the shed wasn't going to add to her body count.

"How are you?" she asked, "and how is little Odin?"

The constable grinned. "He's getting big now. Jenny is going all out, planning a huge first birthday party for him. We've a few months to go, but it's going to take her that long to get everything sorted." He showed Fenella a few pictures from his phone while they waited.

"Inspector Robinson should be here soon," he said after they'd looked at dozens of nearly identical photos. "He's trying to track down the man with the key."

"And he managed it," Daniel added as he walked around the corner of the shed. "He'll be here in a few minutes."

Fenella glanced at her watch. "I hope so," she said softly.

"I appreciate your ringing me," Daniel told her. "A lot of people would have just kept walking, especially if they had somewhere else they needed to go."

"With my recent experiences, I couldn't just keep walking."

A van pulled up to the curb and parked. The man who climbed out looked as if he'd been dragged out of bed. "I'm Jake. Is there a problem?" he asked Daniel as he walked toward them.

"A neighbor was walking his dog past the shed and the dog got excited," Daniel told him. "We thought it was best to check that everything is okay."

"It's probably a dead rat or something," Jake shrugged. "Happens all the time."

"I hope you're right," Daniel told him. "I'd appreciate it if you could give me the key and let me open the door."

"Boss said I'm supposed to open the door."

"In that case, I'm going to ask you to wear gloves."

Jake frowned. "How about you open the door," he suggested.

Daniel put on a pair of gloves and then took the key from Jake. The constable snapped a few photos with his phone as Daniel approached the shed's door. The lock seemed to stick for a second, but then it snapped open. Daniel removed it, dropping it into a plastic bag before handing it to the constable.

As he slowly began to pull the door open, Fenella found that she was holding her breath. Behind her, she could hear Winston barking in spite of Harvey's efforts to calm him down.

"Are there lights inside?" Daniel asked Jake.

"There should be a switch right inside the door. Can't remember which side it's on, though."

As Daniel flipped the switch and the small building was filled with light, Fenella began creeping forward. Daniel took a step inside the shed and then began to chuckle.

"You're laughing," Fenella said. "That has to be a good sign."

He nodded. "Take a look," he invited.

Fenella joined him the doorway to the small building and then blew out a relieved sigh. In the back corner of the room, tucked between dozens of folded chairs, a cat stared back at them.

"It's just a cat," she called to Harvey.

He shook his head. "Winston never bothers cats. Make sure she's okay, please."

Daniel and Fenella exchanged glances. "Can I check on her?" she asked him.

"I think that's going to be up to her," Daniel replied. "She doesn't look very friendly, though."

Fenella nodded. The cat began hissing softly as Fenella approached her. "Hey, there, I just want to check that you're okay," she told the animal in a gentle tone. "I won't hurt you. I just want to help you."

The cat stopped hissing, but didn't look any happier when Fenella stopped. She held out a tentative hand. "I have a kitten at home. Her name is Katie. Maybe I should take you home so you can meet her," Fenella said. As the cat continued to stare, Fenella babbled away about Katie and her apartment and anything and everything in the friendliest voice she could manage. As she spoke, she crept closer and closer to the animal, with a hand outstretched.

"It's just a stray." Jake had joined Daniel in the shed's doorway. "We chase them away when we see them."

Fenella put her hand on the cat's head and scratched gently. For a moment she thought the animal was going to run, but instead she took a hesitant step toward Fenella. As she did so, Fenella noticed that she had a badly damaged front paw.

"She needs a vet," Fenella told Daniel. "I don't know what happened to her, but she's suffering."

"I'm surprised she hasn't bitten you yet," the other man said. "Strays like that one are usually pretty mean."

Fenella ignored him as she tried to get a better look at the cat without upsetting her. She pulled her hand back a bit and the animal stepped forward again. There appeared to be an ugly cut running across her body, and one of her back paws looked damaged as well.

"I'm going to try picking her up. She needs Mr. Stone," Fenella said. As she reached for the animal, she saw movement from further in the corner. "Kittens," she exclaimed.

"Kittens?" Daniel repeated.

The other man sighed. "I wasn't planning on taking kittens to the shelter today."

"I think they're too small to be away from their mother," Fenella said, eyeing the tiny bundles.

"How many?" Daniel asked.

"Three or four. I'm going to bring you the mother cat and then I'll come back for the kittens."

Fenella picked up the injured animal as gently as she could, talking softly to her as she did so. "Now you stay here with Daniel while I see to your babies," she told her.

Daniel looked slightly uncertain as she handed him the cat, but he didn't object.

"There are four kittens," Fenella announced. She picked them up carefully and then walked back to Daniel. "They're small and incredibly sweet. Let's get them to Mr. Stone's office."

The veterinarian's office was only a short distance away. While the constable helped Jake lock up the shed, Daniel and Fenella headed to the vet's office with the cat and her kittens.

"It's Sunday," Daniel said when they reached the office and found it dark. "He doesn't have Sunday hours."

"There's an emergency number," Fenella said, nodding toward a small sign on the door. "My hands are full. Can you call him?"

Daniel tried to shift the injured mother cat so that he could get to his phone, but the animal objected loudly.

"I've rung him," a voice said from behind Fenella. "I have his emergency number in my phone."

Fenella smiled at Harvey. She'd nearly forgotten about him. "What did he say?"

"He'll be on his way in a few minutes. I think I woke him, not that he admitted to that."

"What time is it?" Fenella asked, suddenly remembering Jack.

"Quarter to nine," Harvey told her.

"What time are you supposed to be collecting Jack?" Daniel asked.

"Nine."

"I suppose you can leave the kittens with me," he said, sounding uncertain.

One of the kittens opened its eyes and began to mew softly. The mother cat tried to jump out of Daniel's hands to get to her baby.

"I think it might be best if I stay here," Fenella said as Daniel tried to calm the mother. "I was allowing plenty of time. If I'm a few minutes late, it won't matter."

Mr. Stone arrived a short time later. "They're pretty tiny, aren't they?" he said conversationally as he unlocked the door to his office. He led them into one of the exam rooms and then checked over the mother.

"It looks as if she was in a fight with a larger animal. It may have been another cat, or a dog, maybe. She's a fighter, though, from the looks of it. I'm going to have to use a local anesthetic to stitch up her side. Some of her other injuries might need stitching as well."

"What about the kittens?" Fenella asked.

Mr. Stone called one of his assistants and asked her to come in to help with the mother cat before he turned his attention to the kittens. "They all appear to be in good health," he said. "They're young and will still need their mother, if possible, for at least a week yet."

"So what happens now?" Daniel asked.

"I'm going to sort out the mother and then do my best to feed the kittens with an eyedropper," he told them. "I'm hoping my assistant might be willing to take the whole family home tonight, as I'm nursing a sick collie at my flat and I don't think being around an angry dog will be good for the cat family."

"You haven't said anything about payment," Fenella said, "but I'm happy to pay for whatever treatment any of them need."

Mr. Stone smiled at her. "That's kind of you. I'll charge you at my cost for supplies, and donate my time. I wasn't doing anything today, anyway."

Fenella knew that the man loved animals, but she also knew she could afford to pay for the stray cat's care. Before she could argue, though, Daniel interrupted.

"If your assistant can't look after them, what will happen to them?" he asked.

"I'll have to start ringing around to try to find someone else," Mr. Stone sighed. "If you'd like to volunteer, I'd be delighted."

Daniel shook his head. "I don't have the time to look after them properly."

"I do," Fenella told the men. "If your assistant can't take them, I will."

Mr. Stone chuckled. "Are you quite sure? Once the mother is recovered, they can all go to a shelter, of course, but that isn't the best place for her and the kittens while she's unwell."

"I can take them for a short while, anyway," Fenella said, beginning to regret her impulsive offer.

"Let's see how things go," Mr. Stone said. "If you come back in an hour or so, I should be able to tell you more."

"I have to get to the airport," Fenella said, looking at the clock. It was already nine. "It will probably be closer to two hours before I get back."

"I'll still be here," Mr. Stone told her. "I want to take things slowly and easily with our little family here."

Daniel walked back outside with Fenella. "You're going to have to take them home, you know," he said.

"Yeah, I know," she sighed. "I just didn't want them stuck in a shelter, that's all."

"Knowing you, you're going to want to find good homes for all five of them as well, aren't you?"

Fenella shrugged. "I can't keep them all, that's for sure. Do you want a kitten?"

Daniel laughed. "I wasn't lying when I said I didn't have time to look after them properly."

While she thought about arguing, Fenella was painfully aware of how quickly time was passing. Daniel walked with her to her building.

"I'm just relieved we didn't find a body," she said at the door.

"That's a good point. Do you want to ring me when you find out what's happening with the cats? If you're going to be looking after them, you might need to reschedule our dinner tonight."

Fenella frowned. "I hadn't thought of that."

"Ring me when you've spoken to Mr. Stone again," Daniel suggested. "I can always come to your flat with Chinese food or something."

"Great, thanks." Fenella rushed up to her apartment to grab her car keys. She was on her way down to the parking garage under the building when she realized that she'd picked up the keys to Mona's car rather than the more sensible one she usually used for errands. While she loved driving Mona's convertible, she wasn't sure that Jack's bags would fit inside its tiny trunk.

Not wanting to waste any more time, she decided to take Mona's car anyway. They could always call a taxi to take the bags if necessary. The priority at the moment was getting to Jack before he got too upset.

"Are you okay?" he demanded as he opened the front door. Fenella was barely out of the car.

"I'm fine. I took my neighbor's dog for a walk on the promenade and the dog started barking at a storage shed."

"Do I even want to ask why that made you late?" Jack looked confused.

"I'll explain in the car." Fenella grabbed the largest of his suitcases and carried it to the car.

"That's never going to fit in there," Jack told her as she opened the small trunk.

Fenella picked up the bag and turned it sideways. It took a bit of wiggling, but once she'd slid it into the trunk it seemed to take up very little room.

Jack carried his other two bags down and then shook his head. "I can't believe that one fit. You'll never get two more in there."

The other two bags were easier to maneuver into place. Fenella shut the trunk and then smiled at Jack. "All set?" she asked.

He stared at her for a minute and then nodded. She did a quick walk through the house to make sure that he hadn't forgotten anything and then locked the door behind them. They were halfway to the airport before Jack spoke.

"How did you get the bags to fit in that tiny trunk?" he asked.

"This was Mona's car," Fenella explained. "Mona was magic."

"What about a barking dog held you up this morning?" was Jack's next question.

Fenella was surprised that he didn't question the magic, but then, he'd seen it with his own eyes. She spent the rest of the journey telling him about calling the police and finding the kittens.

"I never would have called the police for something like that," Jack said.

"I wouldn't have a year ago, but things have been different since I've been here."

"Yes, well, since I've been here, I've been caught up in a murder investigation myself, so I suppose I see your point. Are you entirely sure that the island is a safe place to live?"

"It's very safe. Bad things can happen anywhere."

By the time Fenella parked and helped Jack get his bags into the building, it was nearly time for him to board his flight.

"Please go straight through to security," the girl at the check-in desk told him. "We'll be boarding shortly."

Fenella walked with Jack to the security area. "I can't go any further," she told him.

"I had a lot of things I wanted to say to you before I left, and now I'm late and flustered and I can't remember any of them," Jack told her. "Always remember that I'll always love you."

"I'll always love you, too," she replied. "Call me and let me know that you got home safely."

He nodded. "I enjoyed seeing the island. I may come back one day."

"I'll be here if you do."

"I'm counting on that."

He pulled her into a hug and then kissed her with far more passion than she'd expected. It was a pleasant enough kiss, but it was missing the spark of chemistry that Fenella always felt whenever Donald or Daniel kissed her. When Jack let her go, she found that she was even more certain that she'd made the right choice in ending their relationship.

"Take care of yourself," he told her.

"You, too."

A single tear trickled down her cheek as she watched him walk away. While she knew she'd made the right decision, she was going to miss him and the feeling of security that being in a relationship had always given her. Dating, especially at her age, was not fun.

She drove back to Douglas with the top down, in spite of the cold

January weather. After parking the car back in its space, she made her way up to her apartment.

"We might be getting some temporary guests," she told Katie.

"What have you done now?" Mona asked. "I saw you with Daniel on the promenade. I was sure you'd found another body."

"Winston started barking at something in the storage shed. It turned out to be a mother cat and four kittens."

"And you've agreed to let them stay here?" Mona sounded appalled at the idea.

"Just for a short while. The mother had been in a fight and needed treatment. The kittens are too small to leave her. Mr. Stone didn't think a shelter would be good for them, all things considered."

"So you're going to be running a kitten nursery for the next month," Mona sighed. "They won't be litter-trained. They'll want to chew on everything. My beautiful furniture will be ruined."

Fenella frowned. "I hadn't thought of that. Katie is very good about everything, but I think I've been lucky with her."

"I've spent many hours talking with Katie about her behavior. She's a very well-mannered little creature, really. I'm not sure a stray cat will have the same manners."

"Mr. Stone was going to see if his assistant could keep them. I'll just have to cross my fingers that she will."

"She won't," Mona predicted, "not if Mr. Stone tells her you volunteered. I'm sure they both end up taking home far more animals than they should as it is. If they have someone else who is willing, why wouldn't they let you take them?"

"I need to get back to Mr. Stone's office and find out what's happening," Fenella said. "We'll worry about the rest later."

"She's a tough little thing," Mr. Stone told Fenella a short time later. "I've stitched up the ugly gash in her side and did my best with her paws. They may not look perfect once they've healed, but they should be reasonably serviceable."

Fenella looked at the cat who was lying on her side on a large bed. She looked tired and a bit anxious. The small cone around her head would prevent her from undoing Mr. Stone's hard work, but it did make the animal look slightly ridiculous.

"And the kittens?"

"They've all been given some milk and some extra vitamins. Their mother should be able to feed them herself by the time they get hungry again. They're ready to start on kitten food, as well, but they'll still want milk. I suggest you put them together for a short space of time when the kittens are hungry and then separate them again after they've eaten. I don't want the kittens playing with my stitches. They should be fine overnight together, but during the day, when the kittens are active, try to keep them separate if possible."

"I'm taking them, then?" Fenella asked.

Mr. Stone nodded. "My assistant is currently keeping her father's puppy while he's on holiday. A rambunctious puppy isn't the best companion for an injured cat."

"You'd better give me a full list of instructions, then," Fenella said, swallowing a sigh. She had volunteered, after all. This was her own fault.

Mr. Stone put the mother cat into one carrier and the kittens into another. He insisted that she take the cat bed that the mother had been using, and gave her a huge bag of food especially for mother cats and another for kittens. He supplied two new litter boxes and a huge bag of litter, too. Even with him carrying things, it took them two trips to get everything back to Fenella's apartment.

"You have my number," he reminded her after the final trip. "Ring me anytime, day or night, if you need me. Bring them all in on Tuesday so I can check on them."

Fenella nodded and then locked the door behind him. When she turned around, she found Katie curled up in the new cat bed.

"That isn't for you," she said sternly. "You have your own bed in the other room."

Katie ignored her, so Fenella opened the carrier and gently helped the mother cat climb out. Katie took one look at the new arrival and yowled angrily. The mother cat hissed, her fur standing on end.

"My goodness, what a noise," Mona said. "I don't think this is going to work."

Although Fenella did everything she could think of to try to help the two cats get along, an hour later she was forced to admit defeat.

"Okay, this isn't going to work," she sighed as she put the mother cat back into her carrier. "I need another plan."

"Put the new arrivals in the house on Poppy Drive," Mona suggested. "The furniture there isn't nearly as nice."

Fenella thought about it and then nodded. "I'll move there with them," she said. "Shelly can keep Katie for a few days."

"I think I'll let Max take me on that holiday he's been suggesting," Mona said. "Just don't get yourself involved in anything interesting while I'm away."

"Daniel wants to talk about a cold case," she reminded her aunt.

"Okay, well, then just don't solve it until I'm back. What am I saying? You'll need me to solve it, I'm sure." Mona laughed and then faded away, leaving Fenella with two angry cats and four hungry kittens.

3

Shelly was happy to agree to keep Katie for a few days. "Smokey and I will love having her," she said.

Katie had walked into Fenella's apartment right after Fenella had arrived on the island. The kitten had quickly made herself at home, and within days Fenella couldn't imagine life without her. Only a short time later, Shelly had decided to adopt a kitten of her own. When she'd visited the nearest shelter, however, she'd ended up falling in love with an older cat she'd named Smokey. Katie and Smokey had regular playtimes together. Katie's kittenish antics seemed to amuse the older animal, and Fenella could only hope that some of Smokey's maturity might wear off on Katie.

"I'll come by to visit every day," Fenella promised. "I don't want to leave the kittens alone at the house for very long, though, at least not before I've seen how they'll behave."

"Good luck," Shelly laughed. "Katie can be hard work. I can't imagine how much trouble four kittens will manage to cause."

She helped Fenella load the animals and all of their things into Fenella's sensible car and then rode with Fenella to the house on Poppy Drive.

"This is really nice," Shelly said as she helped carry everything inside. "This is exactly what John and I would have wanted if we'd ever had children."

When Shelly had been widowed, she'd sold the small house that she'd shared with her husband and bought the apartment next to Mona's. The two had quickly become close friends, as Mona had helped Shelly work through her grief. It was Mona who'd convinced Shelly to fully embrace life. For Shelly, that had meant wearing bright colors to celebrate every day. Today she was wearing a bright red skirt with a floral print sweater on top. On anyone else it might have been too much, but Shelly's exuberant personality seemed to go perfectly with the outfit.

"It's far too much house for just me," Fenella replied. "I suppose it's perfect for me and five cats, though."

"I never knew Mona owned a house like this. I can't see her ever living in it, of course," Shelly commented.

Mona and Max had started their relationship when Mona had been only eighteen. He'd moved her into a room in one of the hotels that he'd owned and Mona lived there for many years, spending much of her time hosting lavish parties in the hotel's grand ballroom. When Max decided to convert the hotel into luxury apartments, he'd had the largest one designed and decorated for Mona, gifting it to her when it was completed. That was the apartment where Fenella now lived, and Fenella couldn't imagine her aunt even visiting the rather ordinary family home that she'd owned on Poppy Drive. "It isn't really her style, is it?" Fenella laughed.

"I hope you don't start to think that it's yours," Shelly told her.

"I love my apartment on the promenade far too much to ever move here for good," Fenella assured her. "Once mommy cat is recovered and the kittens are a bit older, they can all go to a shelter. I'll be back in my apartment that same day, and I'll have Doncan get this house rented out straight away so I can't do anything as dumb as offer to keep a family of cats again."

Shelly laughed. "From the way you've told the story, you offered to keep them before you even thought of moving them here."

"Yeah, that's true, but I'm a lot smarter now."

Fenella drove Shelly back to their building. It only took her a few minutes to pack a small bag with everything she thought she would need for a few days and nights on Poppy Drive. After a short debate with herself, she decided to drive Mona's car to her temporary home. The house had a garage, but it wasn't very large. Mona's car would fit far more easily than her larger one.

"You be a good girl for Shelly," she told Katie, "You could have been more welcoming to our guests," she added.

Katie narrowed her eyes at her and then walked away to stand by the front door. Fenella grabbed her bag and then followed the animal.

"I know you've been very good about Winston and Fiona every time they've come to visit. I would have thought you'd be even more welcoming to another cat," she said to Katie as she knocked on Shelly's door.

"There's my new little lodger," Shelly laughed when she opened the door a moment later. "We're going to have so much fun while you're here."

Katie purred in Shelly's arm for a moment and then wiggled to get down. As soon as Shelly set her on the floor, she dashed off and started chasing Smokey around the room.

"Maybe she was just horrible to our guests so that I would let her stay with you for a while," Fenella said.

"I could keep her and you and the other cats could stay in your flat," Shelly suggested.

"I don't think I want five cats in my apartment," Fenella told her. "I offered to have them without thinking it through. They won't be litter trained and they might chew on the furniture. All of Mona's things are antiques. The stuff at the house on Poppy Drive is much less valuable."

"I'm going to miss having you next door. With whom will I go to the pub?"

"Tim?"

Shelly blushed. She and Tim Blake had been seeing one another for a few months now. He was an architect who played with a local band. Fenella thought they seemed very happy together. "He's going to London for a few weeks," Shelly said. "He has some sort of work conference to attend. He suggested I might want to come with him."

"Do you?"

"Maybe. No, but yes," Shelly said, shaking her head. "I simply don't know. He'd be working all day, which means I'd be on my own in London. I've never been on my own anywhere, really, not in a very long time, anyway."

"You might find that you like being on your own."

"Or I might be too terrified to leave the hotel room. That's another thing, though. I'm not sure about sharing a hotel room with him. Our relationship hasn't progressed to that point yet, and I'm just old-fashioned enough to think that if I'm going to sleep with a man I should have a ring on my finger."

Fenella nodded. "You should tell Tim what you just told me."

"I know, but it all feels awkward. I think I'm just going to tell him I can't go because I'm looking after Katie."

"Don't do that. I can make other arrangements for Katie. I don't want you to miss out because I was dumb enough to volunteer to babysit a family of cats."

"I'll think about it," Shelly said. "You should get going. The kittens could have caused a great deal of mischief while you've been gone."

Fenella frowned. "They were all asleep in their carrier when I left. I opened its door for them, but I was hoping they would all still be asleep when I get back."

"Good luck with that," Shelly laughed.

Fenella said a quick goodbye to Katie and then headed for the garage. She pulled into the driveway of the house on Poppy Drive a short time later. While there was a garage, there wasn't any automatic door opener like she'd been used to in the US. It seemed to take ages to park the car, climb out, unlock the garage, and then wrestle the door open. She pulled the convertible inside and then left the door open. She'd close it later, after she'd checked on the kittens, she decided.

The house felt ominously quiet as she let herself in through the door that connected to the garage. The mother cat was lying on her cat bed, seemingly fast asleep. Fenella peered into the other carrier. It was empty. She looked around the house's living room with a frown on her face. Where were the kittens?

Fenella walked through the house as quickly as she could, doing a quick scan for the animals. She finally spotted one in the largest of the bedrooms, hiding under one of the beds. She scooped the tiny animal up. "How did you even get up the stairs?" she demanded.

The kitten mewed softly. Fenella carried her back down to the living room and put her on the cat bed with her mother. "Now stay there while I look for your siblings," she said sternly.

After a few steps, she glanced back and was relieved to see the kitten settling in to eat. Maybe that would keep it busy while Fenella did some more searching.

She found another kitten chasing a spider under the dining room table. "Where were you five minutes ago?" she asked as she picked up the animal and squashed the spider.

Finding the first kitten still in the cat bed when she dropped off the second was a pleasant surprise. The house had an open plan, which meant there were no doors on the ground floor, only spacious door-ways between rooms. There was no way for Fenella to keep the animals in the living room while she looked for the others.

"Maybe you could just call them," she suggested to the mother cat as the second kitten snuggled in for a drink.

The cat looked at her and seemed to shrug. Fenella sighed and then tried to think like a kitten. Where would I want to explore, she asked herself. The tiny bathroom next to the front door caught her eye. The door was half shut. Fenella had glanced inside on her first trip around the house. Now she switched the light on and took a better look. A kitten was behind the wastebasket, fast asleep.

"You'll be more comfortable with the others," Fenella told it as she picked it up and carried it back into the living room.

That left only one lost kitten. Perhaps if she left it long enough the missing animal would simply wander back on its own.

A knock on the door startled her. She smiled at Daniel when she found him on the doorstep.

"I saw your car," he explained, nodding toward the still open garage.

"I forgot to close the garage," Fenella replied. "I may have to go back out anyway. I think I need some sort of fencing or something to keep the kittens in one place."

"Should I ask why the kittens are here?"

"It seemed a better place to bring them than my apartment," Fenella explained. "Everything here will be easier to replace if the little family goes on a rampage."

"Is that likely?"

"I certainly hope not, but I've already lost the kittens once."

"They seemed too little to wander too far from their mum."

"You'd think so, wouldn't you," Fenella sighed. "I found one upstairs."

"How did he or she get up the stairs?"

"I've no idea. Anyway, as of now, I'm still missing one kitten."

Daniel laughed. "Do you want me to come in and help you find it?"

"I'm sure you have better things to do."

"It's Sunday," he reminded her. "It's my day off, unless I get called in to deal with dogs barking at random sheds."

Fenella flushed. "Sorry about that."

"It's fine. I'd rather you rang me and it turned out to be nothing than ignore it and later found out that there's a real problem."

"I've completely lost track of time, and I don't remember having any lunch," Fenella said. "We were going to have dinner together."

"We still can. I'll go and get something later. It's only two o'clock now."

"In that case, I'm going to have a snack. I'm sure Jack left something in the kitchen."

Daniel followed her into the kitchen. She found a loaf of bread and some jam and made herself a sandwich. "Are you sure you don't want anything?" she asked between bites.

"I'm fine. I had lunch," he told her. "Would you like me to go and search for kittens?"

Fenella carried the rest of her sandwich with her as they walked back into the living room. The mother cat was napping, her four kittens curled up around her. "Now I just need to find a way to keep them all there," she said.

"I'm sure they do gates and other, similar things for babies," Daniel said.

"Shopping means leaving them alone again," Fenella said doubtfully. "I only just found them all."

"I thought you said you only found three."

"Yes, well, the last one must have wandered back on its own."

"Which suggests that they'll all come back to their mother when they get hungry enough."

"I suppose so. I just don't like the idea of them wandering all over the house."

"Tell me what you want me to buy and I'll go shopping," Daniel offered.

Fenella thought about it and then shook her head. "I've no idea what's available. Let's go and see what we can find. I'm sure they'll be okay for an hour or so. Maybe they'll just sleep."

"We can hope," Daniel muttered.

Daniel offered to drive, as his car was larger. Not wanting to embarrass herself by trying to explain the magic trunk in Mona's car, Fenella agreed. She'd never been inside the shop in Douglas that specialized in baby items. For a moment she stood on the threshold, staring at all of the things she'd never needed. The familiar pang of sadness surged through her. It had been many years since her miscarriage, after which the doctors had told her that she'd never be able to have children of her own. The pain had been almost unbearable at first, but she'd learned to live with it. When she was reminded of her loss though, it felt almost as fresh as it had been all those years earlier.

"Are you okay?" Daniel asked.

"Sorry, I've just never seen so much baby stuff in one place," Fenella told him. "Do you have any idea where we need to go to find gates and things?"

"Upstairs," he told her.

Fenella followed him through the shop. "Why do you know that?" she asked.

"Work," he replied. "I can't say more than that."

The second floor was full of cribs, highchairs, and strollers. Along the back wall there were a variety of different gates that could be attached to stairs to keep children from climbing them.

"The kittens could get through the bars on these," Fenella said.

"This one is better," Daniel said, pointing to a gate that had several crossbars that were close together.

"We sell a lot of those for pets," the salesclerk said. "They work for babies, too, but they're more expensive than the others and the others are perfectly adequate for babies."

"I have kittens," Fenella told her.

"If you want to keep them confined to one level, that's probably the gate you want, then," the girl replied. "The wide bar on the bottom makes it difficult for animals to climb up the crossbars."

"I'll take one of those," Fenella agreed. "I'd really like something to keep them all in one room, too."

"We have cots and playpens," the girl offered, waving a hand toward another display.

Fenella looked at what was on offer. "It seems cruel to put them in something like this," she said, looking at Daniel.

"It would keep them from getting themselves into trouble around the house, though," he pointed out. "Maybe you could only use it when you're out and at night."

Fenella nodded. "That's a good idea. I'm supposed to be keeping the kittens away from their mother whenever possible, too. Mr. Stone was worried that they might pull out her stitches. I forgot about that."

"So you'll need two playpens?" the girl asked.

After a moment's hesitation, Fenella nodded. "Two playpens and a gate," she said. "That should be enough for today." She settled on a playpen that had bars rather than mesh, reasoning that the kittens could probably climb the mesh. The bars were very close together on the model she ended up choosing. Daniel loaded everything into his car and then drove them back to her house.

"Are you planning on staying here with the cats, then?" he asked as he helped her put the playpens together.

"For a few days, anyway. Katie is staying with Shelly. She didn't like our guests."

"That's odd. She's so good with Winston and Fiona."

"Maybe she didn't think the dogs were potential rivals," Fenella shrugged. "Whatever the reason, she was upset, and the mother cat wasn't happy, either."

"You should give her a name."

"I don't want to get attached. Even if I wanted to keep her, I can't, not after Katie's reaction to her."

"Then you'd better not name the kittens either."

Fenella nodded. They had both playpens built. The mother cat was still resting in her bed, but the kittens were nowhere to be seen.

"Do you want to find them?" Daniel asked.

"Let's see if they turn up," Fenella replied. "We can put the gate on the stairs anyway. If one of them is up there, it will get a surprise when it comes down."

The stair gate didn't take long to fit, and it only took Fenella a few tries before she worked out how to open and close it. "What now?" she asked Daniel.

"It's just gone four," he replied. "Do you want to talk about my cold case for a short while before dinner?"

"That's a good idea."

"I'll go and get the files."

"I'm going to make coffee. I got up early today and it's catching up with me."

Daniel was back before the coffee had finished brewing. Fenella poured them each a cup and then sat down at the kitchen table with him.

"The chief constable told me to go through the old files and select any case I wanted to look at," he told Fenella. "I don't think he was expecting me to start with one of the oldest files, though."

"It's an old case?"

"About fifty years old."

Fenella stared at him. "How can you possibly solve a fifty-year-old case?"

Daniel shrugged. "I chose the last two cases we discussed because I just had an odd feeling about them. I have the same feeling about this case." He shook his head. "I know that sounds crazy, but I feel certain we can find the answer."

"It doesn't sound crazy," Fenella told him. "It sounds like intuition. After all your years of doing this job, it's only natural that you should have developed some. You're probably subconsciously picking up on something in the notes that's a clue that was missed the first time. We just have to work out what you've found."

Daniel didn't look as if he agreed, but after a minute he nodded and then opened the file in front of him. "I can't share more than what was in the newspapers at the time, but it appears from the records that nearly everything in the case file was leaked to the papers as the case was being investigated."

"Oh, dear."

"It was one of a very few murder cases on the island in those days. I'm not sure that the investigating inspector had ever dealt with murder before. He may have been leaking information to the papers himself to try to break the case."

"That seems an unusual approach."

Daniel shrugged. "I'm sure he did what he thought was best. They didn't have the same investigative techniques all those years ago."

Fenella nodded. "I'm sure things were very different. It was murder, then?"

"The coroner was quite sure about that, even if he wasn't sure about much else."

"Oh?"

"I'm not being fair. It's just frustrating, reading his report now in light of how differently things are done today. Let me tell you what I do know."

"That sounds good." Fenella got up and refilled both cups. She found a packet of cookies in the cupboard and put it on the table between them.

Daniel helped himself to a cookie before he spoke again. "It was June, 1967. The police were called to an address a few streets up from the promenade around eight o'clock in the evening. A young woman had gone to collect a friend. They were meant to be going to a party together, but the friend hadn't answered the door. When the young woman tried the door, she found it unlocked, so she let herself in and found her friend on the floor in the house's kitchen."

"Poor girl," Fenella said sympathetically.

Daniel nodded. "The victim was twenty-five years old. Her name was Mabel Gross. She had been living in the house for about six months, renting it from a family friend. The woman who found the body was Jeanne Richardson. She and Mabel worked together and had known one another since primary school."

"Primary school," Fenella repeated. "That's little kids, right?"

"Yes, from reception to year six, generally."

"Those words don't really help," Fenella laughed. "What ages would children be in those grades?"

"I believe children start reception at four or five. That would make year six children around eleven, I believe. It's been a few years since I was at school. I don't really remember how old I was when I left primary school."

"Jeanne had known the victim for a long time, anyway," Fenella concluded. "Possibly for twenty-odd years."

"That sounds about right. Obviously, the constable who responded to the call found young Jeanne in hysterics. According to what she told the papers, Mabel's head had been bashed in from behind."

Fenella winced. "What an awful thing to discover."

"As I said, she was reportedly hysterical at the scene. She ended up being taken to Noble's for a few days."

Fenella suddenly felt better about how she'd dealt with all of the dead bodies she'd discovered since she'd been on the island. None of them had been friends of hers, but still, she'd never needed hospital treatment after finding any of them. "What else?" she asked.

"The party the pair had been planning to attend was an engagement party for another friend, a Marilyn Marshall. There was another girl in their immediate circle, a woman called Donna Cannon."

"Donna Cannon?" Fenella echoed. "Do you know if she's still alive?"

Daniel frowned. "Don't tell me you know her? I know it's a small island, but that would be a coincidence."

"I don't know her, but she called me yesterday."

"Go on."

"She's another student in the class I'm taking starting Monday," Fenella explained. "She was helping Marjorie Stevens. Marjorie is the instructor who's teaching the class. Donna was calling all of the students to remind them that the class starts on Monday."

"Did she sound elderly?"

"She did, actually. Elderly and maybe slightly confused."

"I haven't spoken to any of the witnesses from the investigation yet, but I have confirmed which ones are still alive and on the island. Ms. Cannon still lives here. As far as I can determine, she never married. She's in her mid-seventies now."

"The woman I spoke to said she was around that age."

"I'm almost afraid to tell you any more," Daniel sighed. "You probably live next door to one of the other witnesses or something."

"I live next door to Shelly on one side and Peter Cannell on the other. You know them both. I assume they aren't witnesses in this case. They're both too young, surely."

"They are," Daniel agreed. "It's just uncanny how often you seem to stumble into the middle of these things."

"I haven't stumbled into anything. You brought up the case. It's just an odd coincidence that one of the witnesses is in the class I'm taking. It is a small island, after all. Maybe all three of Mabel's friends will be in the class. Donna said there were only five or six of us taking it."

Daniel didn't speak for several minutes. He ate another cookie and then drained his coffee cup. "I think it's time for some dinner," he announced. "I'll leave the newspaper clippings here in case you want to read through them while I'm gone. If you find anyone else mentioned that you know, I may have to reconsider discussing the case with you."

"That doesn't make any sense," Fenella argued. "You aren't sharing anything confidential with me. Surely there's no harm in discussing the public aspects of the case with anyone you like."

"I'm going to think about it while I go and get us some dinner. Chinese, Indian, or pizza?"

"Pizza," Fenella replied. "We were going to go for Italian, after all."

Daniel nodded and got to his feet. "I'll be back soon," he said, walking out of the room before Fenella had even stood up. She trailed behind him into the living room and watched as he let himself out.

"It isn't my fault," she said loudly to the back of the closed door.

"Meeroow," the mother cat replied.

"I'm going to put you into your pen," Fenella told her. "You'll be safe there from the kittens' antics. You need rest so you can recover."

She picked up the animal and her bed. It only took a moment to arrange the bed in the bottom of one of the playpens. The cat settled back into place and shut her eyes. Fenella looked around the room but didn't spot the kittens anywhere. They'd turn up when they were hungry, she decided as she headed back into the kitchen. Getting through the newspaper clippings before Daniel got back was her priority.

The headlines on the earliest papers screamed about murder, but the articles seemed to have very few facts. Fenella read about how Jeanne had been excitedly planning for a fun night out with her friends when she'd stumbled across the most gruesome find the island had ever seen. A paragraph detailed how Mabel had been living on her own for six months, working for a local advocate. She'd been involved in her local church and had been devoted to her younger brother, Clyde.

A few days later, the papers seemed to have run out of new revelations about the case. Instead, they printed interviews with Mabel's three closest friends, Jeanne, Marilyn, and Donna. They all said nearly the same things about how sad they were to have lost their friend, what a lovely girl Mabel had been, and how their lives would never be the same again.

A later paper had an interview with the man who'd owned the property where the body had been found. Howard Quinn was around thirty and worked with Mabel's father. His wife, Patricia, had inherited the property and they'd decided to keep it and rent it out rather than sell it outright. From what the paper said, they were now regretting that decision.

As the weeks went by, the papers began to hint that Mabel hadn't been quite as sweet and wonderful as their initial articles had suggested. Fenella felt herself getting angry at the reporter who'd suggested that any young woman living on her own might be suspected of having loose morals. The article pointed out that all three of Mabel's friends still lived with their parents, subtly suggesting that Mabel would still be alive and well if she'd stayed at home as women were meant to do.

Fenella shut the folder and paced back and forth in the kitchen, wanting to shout at someone. It was fifty years ago, she reminded herself. Things had been different in those days. That didn't make it right, but there was nothing she could do about it now. Feeling oddly sorry for Mabel, Fenella looked back through the folder, reading the last few articles. They were nothing much more than speculation about why Mabel might have been killed. One suggested that a serial killer might have made Mabel his first target, but presumably the idea was dropped when there were no further murders.

After reading all of the articles a second time except for the one that had angered her so much, Fenella felt ready to discuss the case with Daniel when he got back. She walked into the living room and found two kittens trying to reach their mother. A third was complaining loudly from the stairs behind the safety gate. Fenella put them all into the playpen with their mother for a meal. A knock on the front door interrupted her search for the fourth.

4

"Sorry that took so long," Daniel said as Fenella let him in. "I thought, since I'd promised you Italian, that I should keep my promise."

Fenella's mouth began to water as she recognized the name of the restaurant on the lid of the box that Daniel was carrying. "They do carry out?" she asked in surprise.

"Usually only pizzas, but I asked really nicely," he told her. In the kitchen, he put everything he was carrying down and smiled at her. "I got garlic bread, spaghetti Bolognese, gnocchi with tomato sauce, fettuccine Alfredo, and a huge salad."

"You could have skipped the salad," Fenella laughed. She pulled down plates and bowls.

"I also brought a bottle of wine," Daniel added. "You're staying here and I only have to walk back across the street to get home. I didn't think a few drinks would hurt us."

Fenella got down wine glasses that she hadn't realized the house even had and smiled at him. "Wine sounds good."

Daniel opened the bottle and poured them each a glass while Fenella opened the containers of food and found serving spoons. They each filled a plate and then sat down at the kitchen table.

"Delicious," she said as she munched her way through a piece of garlic bread. "I hope it wasn't too much trouble."

"It wasn't. Anyway, I had to apologize somehow."

"Apologize?"

"I was an idiot earlier, getting upset because you know one of the witnesses in the case. As you said, it's a small island. It's hardly your fault."

"You'll feel better knowing that Donna's name is the only one I recognized."

"It shouldn't matter, but I do feel better," Daniel said with a chuckle.

They talked about the kittens and the weather while they enjoyed the delicious food and sipped their wine. It wasn't until Fenella had found another packet of cookies for dessert that Daniel mentioned the case again.

"Any initial thoughts on what you read?" he asked Fenella as they settled onto one of the living room couches with their cookies and the rest of the bottle of wine. One kitten was still missing, but the other three were tucked up in the playpen with their mother and all four of them seemed to be fast asleep.

"The papers seem to hint that Mabel was killed because she was a woman living on her own. That doesn't strike me as much of a motive."

Daniel nodded. "From everything I've read, no one was ever able to find any real motive for the killing. She was hard working and had a few thousand pounds in savings, but as far as anyone knew, she didn't keep cash around the house. There was no sign of a break-in, anyway, and nothing had been taken from the house. She was wearing a simple gold chain and a gold ring when she was found. If someone was planning on stealing from her or the house, they were interrupted before they managed to get anything."

"Were break-ins of that type common in those days?"

"Not at all. If anything, they're more common now, and compared to the rest of the world, the island's crime rate is very low."

Fenella nodded. "What about boyfriends? The article doesn't mention any."

"She'd been seeing someone before she moved into the house. He didn't approve of her living on her own and ended things."

After counting to ten in her head very slowly, Fenella spoke. "That's ridiculous."

"Yes, well, it was a long time ago. He moved to Liverpool and then London right after he and Mabel split up. The police did everything they could to break his alibi, but he'd been at work until six the day the body was found. He didn't have time to come over and kill Mabel and then get back to his flat before the police knocked on his door around nine that night."

"I didn't see any of that in the local paper," Fenella commented.

"It may not have made the papers as it wasn't interesting or helpful to the case. The man passed away over twenty years ago, and as far as I can tell, led a blameless life in London until his death."

"You said she'd been in the house for six months. Surely she'd have found a new boyfriend in that time?"

"Jeanne and Donna were adamant that she hadn't. Marilyn told the police and the papers that she thought Mabel was seeing someone, but that she'd been very secretive about it."

"That's suspicious," Fenella said.

"If it's true," Daniel agreed. "Marilyn couldn't pin it down any further than that and no one else agreed with her."

"You said she was close to her brother. What did he say about boyfriends?"

"If Jeanne was devastated, Clyde was something beyond that. I'm sure one of the papers reported that he needed to be hospitalized for some time after the murder."

Fenella nodded. "I do remember reading something like that. Does that mean the police never actually spoke to him about the case?"

"No, he was questioned eventually, but he didn't say much."

"Was he a suspect?"

"You know better than that. Everyone is a suspect. He didn't have an alibi, but that isn't unusual. I'm trying to remember how the papers put it. They said something about him being a typical young man, out on the town for the evening."

Fenella flipped through the newspaper clippings until she found the relevant article. "'Mabel's younger brother, Clyde, was enjoying an evening with friends at a pub near his sister's house. Only twenty-one, the young man has been under his doctor's care since the murder. We wish him well and hope to interview him when he's recovered from his loss,'" she read out.

"They did interview him, too. I may not have included that clipping. It didn't add any useful information to the investigation. He denied knowing much of anything about his sister's social life."

"What about the man from whom she was renting the house? Did he know anything?"

"I'm sure I included the interview he and his wife gave the papers in the file," Daniel replied.

Fenella flipped through the sheets and then shrugged. "Sorry, I missed that one. I read the larger article at the top of the page. That one was an interview with Jeanne. I didn't notice the smaller one at the bottom." She quickly skimmed through the brief interview with Howard and Patricia Quinn.

"They make Mabel sound too good to be true," she commented when she was done.

"I'm not sure they would have rented their house to her if they didn't think that she was going to behave impeccably."

"According to the article, they'd told Mabel she wasn't allowed to have overnight guests without their approval, and that she'd never once asked. I wonder if any of her three friends ever spent the night. I was also curious about her brother."

"They all denied doing so when they were originally questioned, but I did wonder the same thing. Just after the murder, they would have lied to protect Mabel's reputation, but maybe they'll be willing to tell me more now that so many years have passed."

"I can't imagine Mabel having a whole house to herself and not letting a friend stay over once in a while. How many bedrooms were there in the house?"

"Three, and all three were furnished. For what it's worth, none of the beds in the spare bedrooms were made up for guests on the night that Mabel died."

"Where was the party they were supposed to attend?"

"At a restaurant a short walk from Mabel's house. Jeanne was planning to leave her car at Mabel's while they walked to the party."

"Where did Jeanne live?"

"Over in Onchan. It wasn't far away, but it wasn't walking distance to the party, either."

"I don't suppose anyone checked to see if Jeanne had an overnight bag in her car that night?"

Daniel shook his head. "No one asked and there was no reason for anyone to search her car."

"If I were going to a party that was walking distance from a friend's house, I'd probably arrange to stay with that friend afterward. I assume they were all going to be drinking."

"Remember that drink driving laws weren't the same in those days, and people weren't as concerned about it, either. She didn't have all that far to go to get home. She might have simply planned to drive herself home after the party."

Fenella nodded. "Things were very different fifty years ago, I suppose. Even so, I still would have rather stayed with my friend than drive home. Jeanne lived with her parents, right? Mine wouldn't have approved if I came home drunk, whether I'd been driving or not."

"I'll be discussing all of this with Jeanne and with the other women," Daniel told her. "I need to try to build a picture of Mabel in my head. Everything I've read suggests she was, as you said, almost too good to be true. Marilyn was the only one who ever hinted that she might have kept secrets from time to time. I'm going to talk to her first."

"And you won't be able to tell me anything she says," Fenella sighed.

He shook his head. "There's going to be an article in the local paper about the case tomorrow. They're starting a series on unsolved murders on the island. I'm hoping to get this one solved before they run the next article next month."

Fenella frowned. "Have there been that many unsolved murders on the island?"

"Not really, but if they run one a month, they'll start making people think there have been. Actually, I believe they're going to include other unsolved cases, like disappearances, as well. That should give them a story a month for the year."

"I wonder how Mabel's family and friends will feel about the case being back in the news."

"They should welcome a new investigation. At least, everyone but the killer should welcome a new investigation."

"Which of the people we've discussed were actual suspects, then?" Fenella asked.

"Mabel's three friends are on the list. Mabel was small enough physically that another woman could have killed her. None of them had alibis that covered them for the entire window in which the murder could have taken place. Mabel's brother also has to be on the list, as do her parents. Sadly, they've both passed away now."

"I read their interview with the paper. It didn't sound as if they knew anything about Mabel's life once she'd moved out."

"No, I don't think they approved of her going and I suspect they more or less cut their ties with her once she was gone. No one ever said that in so many words, but it was hinted at, anyway."

"Could they have been mad enough about her going to kill her?"

"Anything is possible, of course, but of everyone interviewed, they had the best alibi. There were enough small gaps to make it just possible that one or the other of them could have killed Mabel, but the investigating inspector had them at the bottom of his list of suspects."

"What about Mabel's job? What did she do, and were there any suspects associated with that?"

"She was a secretary to one of the island's more influential advocates, a man called Andrew Neil. Jeanne worked in the same office, along with a third woman, Helen Hendricks."

"Was Helen a suspect? Or the advocate?" Fenella asked, feeling odd about using the Manx term for a lawyer.

Daniel chuckled. "This bit didn't make it into the papers, but it was the talk of the island at the time. When the police went to question Mr. Neil about his whereabouts on the night of the murder, he was evasive and eventually outright refused to answer any questions. It didn't take the police long to discover that he'd spent the night in a hotel room in Port St. Mary with the aforementioned Helen Hendricks."

Fenella gasped. "I'm going to guess that Mr. Neil was married."

"He was. His wife was in Edinburgh visiting her mother at the time. Both Helen and Mr. Neil were able to provide unbreakable alibis once they'd admitted where they were. They had dinner together in the hotel's dining room and then spent some time in the bar, drinking, before retiring to their room. Mabel's body was found while they were still at the bar."

"Poor Mrs. Neil."

"As I understand it, she never returned to the island. Mr. Neil didn't remain here for long, either, after everyone found out about his affair."

"What happened to him?"

"I talked to one of the reporters at the local paper today about that. He kept track of Mr. Neil, mostly just out of personal interest. Mr. Neil moved to Poland with Helen, actually."

"Poland? That seems an odd choice."

"Apparently Helen's mother was Polish. It was 1967. The affair was something of a scandal. Poland was far enough away to let them escape their past."

"What about Mrs. Neil?"

"As far as anyone knows, she stayed in Scotland. There's no record of the couple ever divorcing. It seems that Mr. Neil and Helen told everyone in Poland that they were married, and no one ever questioned it. They had two children together and, eventually, six grandchildren. Mr. Neil passed away in the late eighties, but Helen is still alive. Whether she and Mr. Neil were ever legally married or not, I don't know."

"I'd love to fly over to Poland and talk to Helen," Fenella said. "I don't suppose you can find an excuse to question her and then let me tag along?"

"I may try interviewing her by telephone at some point, just for background information, but I can't see the department paying for me to fly to Poland to speak to her in person. As I said, she's been eliminated as a suspect."

Fenella nodded. She had more than enough money to pay for the flights herself, but simply being nosy and wanting to meet the woman wasn't enough of a reason to try to find her. "Who else is on the list, then?" she asked.

"Howard and Patricia Quinn, either separately or together."

"Maybe Mabel was involved with Howard," Fenella suggested.

"From all accounts, he and Patricia were devoted to one another. Perhaps I should say that they are devoted to one another, as they're still together. They're both in their eighties now, of course."

"What about children?"

"They never had any."

Fenella nodded. The interview with them in the paper had mentioned something about that. Patricia had said something about God not yet granting them the blessing of children when she'd been talking about how sorry she felt for Mabel's parents. Apparently, God didn't bless them after the murder either. "Maybe Patricia was involved with Mabel," Fenella suggested as the idea popped into her head. "Maybe that's why the couple never had children."

"It's possible, of course, but it seems unlikely. Such things were never discussed or even hinted at fifty years ago, of course, but I find it hard to believe that Patricia and Howard would have stayed together for all these years if Patricia preferred women."

"It's possible, though," Fenella said. "It might have given either of them a motive, too."

"If she were having an affair with either of the Quinns, we can assume they both had motives for wanting her dead. What we don't have is any evidence that Mabel was doing any such thing."

"Is that everyone on the suspect list?"

"Aside from a person or persons unknown, it is. As I said, Mabel had had other boyfriends, but the inspector who conducted the original investigation talked to all of them and didn't feel any of them were viable suspects."

"What about the men who were involved with her three friends? Marilyn was getting married, right? What about her fiancé?"

"Being that he was a police constable, he was never considered a serious suspect," Daniel told her. "I would have investigated him more closely if I'd been in charge of the case, but the inspector knew the young man personally and eliminated him from the list of suspects immediately."

✦ "Did Jeanne have a boyfriend?"

"Not on the day of the murder," Daniel said with a grin. "I gather she went through boyfriends very quickly. She was between men when Mabel died, otherwise she might well have been going to the party with a man rather than with Mabel."

"And the body might not have been found for several more hours," Fenella speculated. "I wonder if that's relevant."

"I'm not sure why it would be, but it's an interesting thought."

Fenella yawned. "What else?" she asked.

"I think that's probably enough for tonight. I'll leave the clippings for you, in case you want to go through them again. I have another set at the office. I'm really just looking for your thoughts on the case, nothing more. You've already given me a great many things to think about that I hadn't considered before. That's exactly the sort of help that I need."

"I'm really looking forward to meeting Donna Cannon tomorrow."

"Please be discreet if you start asking her questions. I'd rather people didn't think you were helping with a police investigation."

"Maybe I'll just casually mention that I've found a few dead bodies since I've been here. That might be enough to get her talking about the murder case in her past."

Daniel looked as if he wanted to object, but after a minute he yawned and then got to his feet. "I should go home and get some sleep," he said. "Tomorrow I have to start tracking down all of the witnesses from my fifty-year-old case."

"Good luck with that."

"It's a lot easier here than it is across. If people have stayed on the island, they're pretty easy to find. I'd like to talk to as many as I can before everyone on the island starts talking about the case."

"Good luck with that, too," Fenella laughed.

"Should we find the missing kitten, then?" Daniel asked.

Fenella sighed. The other three kittens and their mother were all still fast asleep in a cuddly ball in the middle of one of the playpens.

Where was the fourth kitten? "I suppose we'd better. I don't want it wandering around the house all night. It might get hungry, too. Actually, it must be hungry now."

"I'll start down here if you want to try upstairs."

Fenella nodded and then wrestled the baby gate open. She shut it carefully behind herself and then climbed the stairs. She started with the smallest bedroom, checking every corner, looking under the bed, even moving the curtains that reached the floor to make sure the kitten wasn't hiding behind them. As she emerged back onto the landing, she shut the bedroom door, hoping that would keep the kitten out of the room she'd already searched. Half an hour later, she'd shut every door and hadn't found the kitten.

When she got back downstairs, Daniel was standing in the middle of the living room with a frown on his face. "I thought for sure you'd have found it," he said.

Fenella shook her head. "I was very thorough, too. The kitten isn't upstairs."

"I don't think it's down here, either, but maybe we need to try harder."

"I'll do down here. You try upstairs," Fenella offered.

Another half hour of searching proved fruitless.

"I'm starting to get worried now," Fenella admitted as they met back in the living room. "How long can kittens go between meals?"

"I've no idea, but surely if the kitten were hungry it would come back here to its mother."

"Unless it's lost or hurt or something. What if it accidentally got out somehow?"

"I can't imagine how it could have done that, but we can take a walk around the house if you'd like."

Fenella looked out the window. A light rain was falling, it was dark, and it looked cold. "I hope the poor thing isn't out in that weather," she said as she went to the closet for her coat.

Daniel put his coat and shoes on and then stopped her at the door. "Wait here a minute and I'll go and get a torch."

"A torch?" she echoed. "We call them flashlights in America, although I'm not sure why, as they don't flash."

Daniel grinned at her. "One day we should make a list of all the words we don't have in common."

"There are hundreds or maybe even thousands," she replied.

She watched as Daniel dashed across the road into his house. He was back only a moment later, carrying two large flashlights. Daniel handed her a light and then they split up to walk slowly around the house.

"Here, kitty, kitty, kitty," Fenella called softly as she went. A large black cat raced toward her as she turned the corner around the garage. Fenella gave the animal a pat, relieved to find that it was wearing a collar. "You should get yourself off home," she said. "It's raining."

The cat purred for a moment and then dashed away, while Fenella continued on her quest. She and Daniel met in the middle of the backyard.

"Nothing?" he asked.

"I met a lovely black cat who needed a bit of love, but that was all."

"If your kitten did get out, we might have to wait until morning to try to find it," Daniel told her. They walked together back around to the front of the house. Fenella heard a noise from under a bush near the door.

"What was that?"

"I didn't hear anything," Daniel said.

Fenella crouched down with her flashlight, searching the bush for signs of life. Daniel did his best to help, but neither of them could see anything. The rain was getting harder and Fenella was starting to shiver when the police car pulled up in front of the house.

"We're in trouble now," Daniel chuckled as a young constable climbed out of the car.

"Good evening," he called to the constable who was approaching them with his own flashlight in hand.

"Good evening," the constable replied. "Is everything okay?"

"We're searching for a lost kitten," Daniel replied. "I'm Inspector Daniel Robinson, Douglas CID. I don't know that we've met."

The young man looked surprised and then suspicious. "Inspector Robinson?" he repeated. "Do you have any identification on you?"

Daniel patted his pockets and then shook his head. "It's all at home. I just live across the street," he explained, nodding toward his house.

"Who's your friend?" the constable asked.

"This is Fenella Woods. She owns this house and it's her kitten that's lost."

"It's a stray, actually." Fenella felt the need to disclaim ownership of the animal. "I found the mother cat and four kittens this morning, and now one of them has disappeared."

"You were the one who found the animals on the promenade this morning," the constable said. "I heard about that."

"I suspect everyone on the island has heard about it," Daniel laughed. "It caused quite a bit of excitement this morning."

"Yes, sir," the constable agreed.

"I assume one of the neighbors rang in about people walking around one of the houses with torches," Daniel said. "It's good to know that our neighbors are keeping an eye on things."

"Yes, well, I'm really supposed to see identification," the constable said hesitantly.

"Mine is in the house," Fenella replied. "I don't have anything with this address on it, though. I'm only staying here temporarily while I'm looking after the cats."

The constable frowned. "You can't prove you have the right to be in the house?" he asked.

"You can call Doncan Quayle and talk to him," Fenella suggested. "He's my advocate and he keeps track of all of my properties."

"All of your properties?" the man echoed.

"I inherited a lot from my Aunt Mona," Fenella explained.

The constable nodded. "You're Mona's niece. I should have recognized the name. I didn't realize that Mona owned any houses in this neighborhood."

"Come inside with us and check Fenella's identification," Daniel told him. "I'll pop home and get mine as well. We need to do everything by the book."

The young man nodded and looked relieved. Fenella led him into the house. She peeled off her coat, which was soaked through and then hung it on a convenient hook. The constable did the same with his.

Hoping that the floors would be okay with the amount of water now dripping onto them, Fenella showed the constable into the living room. Her handbag was sitting on the end of one of the couches.

"I'm sure I have my driver's license in here somewhere," she said, digging through the bag. She found her wallet and then her license. The constable took a good long look at it and then pulled out a notebook.

"I'm just going to make a note of this, if you don't mind," he said.

"Not at all."

He handed her the card back and she returned it to her wallet. Daniel returned as she dropped the wallet back into her bag.

"Here you are," he said, handing the constable his own driver's license as well as his police identification card. The constable made notes about both of them and then gave them back.

"As you're a police inspector, I'm not going to worry about anyone proving that they have the right to be here," he said. "I'm satisfied with your story about the missing kitten. How many did you say you're meant to have?"

"One mother cat and four kittens," Fenella replied.

"Maybe I should ring Mr. Quayle," the constable said. "There appear to be four kittens safely tucked up in that playpen."

Fenella and Daniel both crossed to the playpen. "Where did the fourth kitten come from?" Fenella demanded. "He or she couldn't possibly have climbed into the playpen without help."

"Maybe you miscounted them when you put them in," Daniel suggested.

"We'd had some wine, but not enough to make me forget how to count to four," Fenella retorted. "Maybe one of them slipped through the bars."

Daniel looked at the kittens and then at the playpen's bars. To Fenella's eyes it seemed very unlikely that any of the kittens were small enough to squeeze through, but that seemed to be the only possible answer.

"I'll find you Doncan's number," Fenella said as she turned back to the constable.

He shook his head. "The look of shock on both of your faces was enough to convince me that you really did think you'd lost one of the kittens. I'll ring your concerned neighbor back and assure her that everything is fine."

"Thank you," Daniel said. He walked the constable to the door while Fenella took another look at the sleeping animals. Even all squashed together in a big pile, they were easy to count, and there were clearly four kittens in the pile.

"Maybe I'm losing my mind," she muttered to herself.

"If you are, I'm in trouble, too," Daniel told her. "I would have sworn on my mother's life that there were only three kittens in that playpen when we went outside."

"We wouldn't have been stomping around in the rain otherwise."

"Exactly."

An awkward silence descended as Fenella shifted her weight back and forth and tried to think of something to say.

"I'm going to get home, then," Daniel said eventually. "Maybe we could talk again on Tuesday. I'll be interested to hear what you think of Donna."

Fenella nodded and then followed him to the door. "I'm sure I'll still be here on Tuesday, trying to keep track of kittens. Why don't you come to dinner? I'll even cook."

"That sounds great. Don't go to too much trouble, though."

"I'll make something simple and get a bottle of wine. That was nice tonight."

"It was," Daniel agreed. He stared at her for a minute and then sighed. "Whichever way I go, I'm going to regret it," he told her.

"What do you mean?"

"I want to kiss you, but I'm not sure that's wise."

Fenella frowned and then took a step closer to him. "Maybe just a quick, friendly kiss," she suggested.

Daniel's smile sent a warm rush to the pit of her stomach. He pulled her close and then lowered his lips to hers. The kiss was definitely not quick, but it felt very, very friendly indeed.

After what felt like a long, wonderful time, Daniel lifted his head. "Maybe I won't regret that after all," he said softly before he released her and walked away.

5

After checking on the kittens one more time, Fenella opened the baby gate and headed up the stairs. She wasn't sure whether she should shut it behind herself or not, but in the end she decided she'd rather shut it than leave it open and find a kitten in her bedroom in the morning. If one of them could fit through the bars, they probably all could, whether they'd realized it or not.

The bedroom felt odd and the master bathroom was small. Fenella was missing her apartment by the time she climbed into bed. It only took her a minute to realize that she was missing Katie, too. While she often grumbled to herself about the kitten sleeping in the middle of her bed, this bed felt empty and lonely as she tried to get comfortable. The pillowcase smelled like Jack, which didn't help. Fenella hadn't thought to change the bedding before her impromptu stay.

She tossed and turned for several minutes and then got up and tore the bed apart. There was a second set of bedding in the small linen closet on the landing. It took a bit of time to remake the bed, but she felt better snuggling under sheets that smelled of laundry detergent and fabric softener. It was odd to think that Jack had been sleeping in the bed only twenty-four hours earlier. She had to hope that he'd arrived back in Buffalo safely, as she hadn't been at her apartment if he'd remembered to call to let her know he was home. Now that the idea had crossed her mind, she found herself worrying about him.

"He got himself to the island on his own. He's quite capable of getting home again," she told herself firmly. Trying to push Jack out of her head, she started thinking about Daniel's cold case. The papers had run a grainy black-and-white photograph of poor Mabel Gross. From the picture, it looked as if she'd had light brown hair and dark eyes. She'd been laughing when the picture had been taken, and Fenella felt a stab of sympathy for the young woman who'd been brutally murdered at such a young age.

With worries about Jack and thoughts about murder chasing one another through her head as she fell asleep, it was hardly surprising that Fenella had nightmares. None of them were bad enough to wake her, but they all kept her from sleeping well. When she woke up the next morning, she was disoriented and felt more tired than she had when she'd gone to bed. The clock on the nightstand told her that it was eight, an hour later than the time Katie usually woke her. Wishing that she felt as if she'd had an extra hour of sleep, she stumbled into the bathroom and took a long, hot shower.

Feeling only slightly more awake, Fenella headed for the stairs. She hadn't felt up to trying to manage the baby gate when she'd first woken up, but now she needed coffee so badly that she was prepared to climb over it if that was the only way she could get to the kitchen. Once the coffee was brewing, Fenella checked the living room. All four kittens were still tucked up with their mother, seemingly fast asleep. The litter tray needed attention, so Fenella swapped it for the one from the other playpen, which hadn't been touched and then quickly cleaned it out. Dropping it back into the empty playpen, she checked on the kittens again. One of them opened its eyes and then squeezed them shut again.

"Coffee," Fenella said as the smell hit her nose. "That will help."

After drinking half of the pot, she felt better. The kittens were awake and stretching when she walked back into the living room after breakfast.

"Good morning, everyone," she said. "I've put some lovely breakfast for you in the other playpen."

She gave the mother cat an affectionate scratch and then started picking up kittens. With all four of them safely moved to the second playpen, Fenella gave the mother food and water and then grabbed her handbag.

"I won't be gone long," she told the animals. "Behave yourselves and I'll let you all out for a run as soon as I get back."

As she started her car she began to feel guilty about leaving the kittens stuck in the playpen. They would have a lot more fun if they could explore the house while she was away. Sighing deeply, she went back inside and let them out, putting their food and water dishes on the floor next to the playpen. "Now stay out of trouble," she told them.

The mother cat looked quite content to stay where she was, so Fenella left her alone. She checked that she'd shut the gate to the stairs before she once more headed for the front door. The drive back to her apartment didn't take long at all.

"How's my baby?" she asked Shelly when Shelly answered her impatient knock.

"Katie is fine," Shelly laughed. "She and Smokey slept together in Smokey's bed last night, even though I told her she could sleep with me if she preferred."

"She has a perfectly good cat bed at home, and she never sleeps in it," Fenella sighed. "Maybe I should have Smokey stay over once in a while."

She played with Katie and Smokey for a short while before heading back to her own apartment. "I'll visit her again tomorrow morning, if you don't mind," she told Shelly on her way out.

"Of course I don't mind. You know you're always welcome."

"I really appreciate your keeping her for me. I'll see you tomorrow."

"How was your evening?" Mona asked as Fenella let herself into the apartment.

"It was fine. Daniel came over and we talked about his cold case. Then we hunted everywhere for one of the kittens until the police came. What could be more romantic than that?"

Mona laughed. "The police came? Why?"

"We were hunting outside with flashlights and one of the neighbors got suspicious."

"At least Daniel was able to reassure whoever arrived that everything was okay."

"Except he didn't have any identification with him. It was all okay in the end, but it wasn't fun."

"Tell me about the cold case, then," Mona said as Fenella headed for the bedroom.

"It's a murder case, a woman called Mabel Gross."

"Really? How fascinating."

"Why is that fascinating?" Fenella asked as she began to dig out more things to take to the house on Poppy Drive. She'd only packed enough for a few nights, and it now seemed likely that she was going to be staying there longer.

"I remember the case. It was quite the sensation at the time. There were plenty of people who seemed to think that she'd been foolish for living on her own the way that she was."

Fenella made a derisory noise. "No one would have said that if she'd been a man."

"No," Mona agreed. "Obviously, I never agreed with that opinion. I'd been living on my own for many years by that time, and I felt perfectly safe."

"You were living in a hotel, though, not in a house."

"And I had Max looking after me. Poor Mabel was entirely on her own, aside from her brother. Clyde thought the world of her."

"You knew him?"

"Yes, of course. He used to work at ShopFast. He's been retired for many years now, but he worked his way up to be one of the managers of the store that's right around the corner from here."

"What did you think of him?"

"He's a lovely man. Very quiet and almost shy, but he could be firm when he needed to be if customers or staff caused any trouble. He never married and I always felt as if he'd never quite recovered from losing his sister. As I said, he adored her. They were something like five years apart and he was the younger of the two. It wasn't just him, though, they both seemed to enjoy spending time together."

"I love all four of my brothers," Fenella said. "I'd be devastated if anything happened to any of them."

"And Clyde was devastated when Mabel died. I'd met her once or twice, actually. I didn't like her."

"Why not?"

"I'm not sure. I only met her in passing. She worked for Andrew Neil, and Max sometimes used him as his advocate for small things. He had a team of advocates and solicitors in the UK to handle most of his concerns, but sometimes, with minor issues, he'd have Mr. Neil deal with them."

"Tell me about Mabel."

"She was pretty, but she knew it very well. I don't think she was all that dedicated to her career, but she liked to pretend that she was, and her pretense seemed to fool Mr. Neil. I suspect, had she lived, she would have found herself a husband before too much longer and then settled down to have babies. That was what women did in those days."

"But she was between boyfriends when she died?"

"As far as I know, but as I said, I barely knew Mabel. She was a close friend to one of the other women in Mr. Neil's office. Neither of them liked the third woman who worked there, but as we found out later, the third woman was Mr. Neil's favorite, anyway."

Fenella nodded. "Daniel told me that story."

Mona frowned. "What a shame, I'd have enjoying telling you that one myself."

"What do you know about the other women, the ones that were Mabel's friends?"

"You're asking me to remember people I may have met only in passing fifty years ago," Mona said. "I'm not sure that I can help."

"I know you knew Donna Cannon, because you commented on her when she rang the other day."

Mona frowned. "I'd forgotten that Donna was one of Mabel's friends. You're right, of course. I remember it now. There were two or three women who gave interviews to the local papers at the time. I'm sure Donna loved all of the attention. Knowing her, she gave the papers a lot more information than they needed or wanted, without saying anything relevant. Donna can talk for hours and say very little."

"It sounds as if you don't like her."

"I don't dislike her, exactly, but she can be something of a bore. She never married and has always been a generous supporter of certain charities around the island. Whenever we were both invited to events, the organizers would almost always put us at the same table, often with recent widows or other unmarried women. We used to laugh about it, actually."

"What sort of charities does she support?"

"Anything to do with women's issues and women's rights. As I said, she never married. She lived with her parents until her mother passed away. A short while later, she moved her father into a care home. He had memory problems as well as mobility issues. As far as I know, Donna still lives in the same house where she grew up, but it's hers now, of course."

"I'm going to meet her tonight. It will be interesting to see what she has to say about Mabel's murder."

"She'll have plenty to say," Mona predicted. "I doubt any of it will be at all interesting or useful, but you'll get an earful."

"What about Jeanne Richardson?" Fenella asked.

"She was the other woman who worked for Mr. Neil. It was obvious that she was just holding down a job while she was waiting to get married. She went through men at an alarming rate, never seeming to find one who was willing to make any sort of commitment. I believe she was nearly thirty and still living at home when she finally got married."

"Are they still together?"

"As far as I know, yes. She's Jeanne Reese now. They had three or four children in fairly rapid succession. The first arrived about six months after the wedding. Anyway, I'm sure I heard that she's in a care home now. All of the women will be in their mid-seventies, if I'm doing the math correctly."

"That sounds about right," Fenella agreed. "What about Marilyn Marshall?"

"She's Marilyn Coleman now, and has been since not long after Mabel died. It's all coming back to me now. It was her engagement party that Mabel was meant to be attending on the night she died. They went ahead and had the wedding a month later anyway. Marilyn told everyone that they'd scaled it down out of respect for Mabel, but it was a lavish affair by island standards, whatever she said."

"Really?"

"Her fiancé was just a police constable, but Marilyn's mother had grand ideas. She'd been planning Marilyn's wedding since the day Marilyn was born and she wasn't going to give up on her dreams for anything. I believe she and Marilyn's father spent every penny of their savings to throw the most lavish wedding they could afford. They had the reception in the ballroom here."

"What was Marilyn like?"

"I've no idea, really. I was at the wedding. They'd invited Max and he took me along. From what I could see, she was completely dominated by her mother and more than a little afraid of her."

"Oh, dear."

"Marilyn's father passed away about two years after the wedding and her mother moved in with Marilyn and her new husband. Poor Constable Coleman ended up leaving the police and going to work at ShopFast. Clyde was working there and I'm sure he helped the young man advance in his career. The pair had three children, but all three had serious health issues and I don't believe any of them survived much longer than a year."

"How very sad."

"I used to see Marilyn's mother once in a while at events and she would talk endlessly about how tragic it was, which it was, of course, but she always seemed to think that it was more her tragedy than Marilyn's. I don't know. I didn't like the woman and I always felt as if Marilyn would have been better off if she could have escaped from her."

"Surely she isn't still alive?"

"No, she passed away about three years ago, but Marilyn has been in a care home since before her mother died. Her husband passed away about ten years back, and Marilyn was in a bad car accident not long after his death. She's never fully recovered and her mother eventually agreed to move her into a home so that she could get the sort of care she needs."

"Poor Marilyn. It sounds as if she's had a difficult life."

"I don't think it was a very happy one," Mona said.

"Can you think of any motive any of the three women might have had for killing Mabel?"

Mona shook her head. "They were all close friends. I didn't really know any of them, but because of my connections through Mr. Neil, I probably would have heard if there had been a serious fight between them. Young women tend to fight over men. I'm fairly certain Mabel wouldn't have been interested in Constable Coleman. She may have gone out with some of Jeanne's former boyfriends, but as I said, Jeanne went through them very quickly. I don't believe Donna was interested in men."

"What if one of the three started a relationship with Clyde? Would that have upset Mabel?"

"What an interesting thought," Mona said. "Marilyn wouldn't have done any such thing, not when she was getting married soon. If anyone had a fling with Clyde, it would have been Jeanne. I can imagine it happening, too, now that you've said it. I'm just not sure how Mabel would have reacted."

"I can't see why anyone would kill Mabel over it, anyway," Fenella sighed.

"Maybe Mabel was angry and Clyde was so in love with Jeanne that he killed his sister so that he could be with Jeanne," Mona said dramatically.

"I thought you said he adored Mabel."

"He did, but maybe he was crazy in love with Jeanne."

"Since you knew them both, does that seem likely?"

Mona thought for a minute. "Not even the least little bit," she admitted. "Jeanne wasn't the type to inspire that sort of passion, and I can't see Clyde killing Mabel over anyone or anything."

"Maybe Jeanne wanted to get involved with Clyde, but Mabel didn't like the idea, so Jeanne killed her," Fenella suggested.

"More likely, but still farfetched," was Mona's opinion.

"What about Howard and Patricia Quinn?"

"I'd be more than happy to see Patricia Quinn arrested for murder."

"Really? Why?"

"She's one of the most annoying women I've ever met. She never approved of my lifestyle and she made sure to tell me and everyone else that at every opportunity."

"Gee, I can't wait to meet her."

"Don't tell her we're related and you should be fine," Mona told her. "Also, don't tell her that you live alone, and don't mention having men in your life. Patricia doesn't approve of women who aren't married unless they live with their parents."

"My parents are both dead."

"Yes, well, then you should live with one of your older brothers so that he can look after you."

"This is the twenty-first century. Ideas like that went out of fashion years ago."

"Not for Patricia. She is in her eighties now, so one must make allowances, I suppose."

Fenella sighed. "Do you think she might have killed Mabel?"

"If she happened to walk in on Mabel with a man, she might have. I'm sure she had very strict rules about what Mabel could and couldn't do in that house. If she thought Mabel was using her house for immoral activities, she'd have kicked the girl out."

"That's a rather different thing from killing her, though."

"Yes, but maybe she walked in on an intimate moment and lost her temper."

"What do you think happened to the man involved, then?"

Mona frowned. "I hadn't thought of that. Maybe she killed both of them and took the man's body away to get rid of it. While she was gone, Jeanne found Mabel's body."

"What about her husband?"

"Howard? He was, and probably still is, completely under her thumb. I met him once or twice at charity events. Patricia liked to support a few children's charities. They never had children of their own, but she used to volunteer in the children's ward at Noble's."

"If she's so opposed to women living on their own, why did she rent out the house to Mabel in the first place?"

"I suspect Mabel found a way to get Howard to agree when Patricia wasn't around. Once Howard said yes, Patricia would have gone along, even though she didn't like the idea. Husbands get to make the important decisions in a marriage, of course."

Fenella snorted indignantly. "Mabel would have had a chance to get Howard alone? Maybe the pair were having an affair, then."

Mona shook her head. "I can't see it. As I said, Patricia dominated the relationship, even though she always insisted that he made all of the decisions. He and Mabel's father were good friends, though. I'm sure Mabel would have had opportunities to talk to Howard on his own. For that matter, her father may have been the one to talk to Howard. I'm sure Howard would have been happy to do his friend a favor, like letting his friend's daughter rent out his house."

"But it was really Patricia's house, wasn't it? I'm sure I read in the paper that she'd inherited it from someone."

"She'd inherited it from her father, so yes, technically it was hers. I believe she was the one who wanted to keep it and rent it out, actually. She'd grown up in the house, and I don't think she wanted to sell it, at least not straight away. If I'm remembering correctly, Mabel was their first tenant."

"What happened to the house after Mabel's death? Do they still own it?"

"They sold it almost immediately. The new owners tore it down and built a new, much larger house on the property."

"Maybe I'll take a walk past the site later," Fenella mused. "I know there won't be anything to see, but it might be interesting anyway."

"It isn't far from here." Mona gave her directions. "Maybe you should settle for driving past. Don't you need to get back to the kittens?"

Fenella frowned. "I suppose I do. Do you have any other thoughts on the case?"

"Nothing specific. I'm going to think about it while you're gone, though. I hadn't given Mabel Gross a single thought in years. Maybe I'll be able to remember more now that you've reminded me of her."

"Maybe you could ask Max what he remembers," Fenella suggested. Mona often talked about spending time with Max. According to Mona, Max spent most of his days in what had once been the hotel's ballroom. It had now been divided into offices for the various employees of the apartment complex, but Mona always said she didn't think Max noticed.

"His memory isn't reliable, unfortunately. I may mention the case to him in passing, but I don't expect him to be able to help."

Fenella nodded, not sure how much to believe of what Mona said. "I'd better get going," she sighed. "I'll drive past where the house used to be and then get back to Poppy Drive before the kittens destroy all of the furniture."

"You'll be back tomorrow?"

"Yes, to see Katie, mostly."

"Thanks," Mona said dryly.

"Sorry, I didn't mean it that way."

"I look forward to hearing about your conversation with Donna Cannon tomorrow, then," Mona told her.

"I'll tell you all about my class, too."

"Oh, good," Mona said flatly.

Fenella made a face at her. "I'm really excited about the class. I've never been able to do research with original sixteenth- and seventeenth-century documents before. Learning how to read them is going to be fascinating."

Mona yawned and then shrugged. "And yet we're related in some way."

Ignoring the comment seemed the safest thing to do. Fenella picked up her handbag and headed for the door. "I'll see you tomorrow, then," she told her aunt. Mona nodded and then slowly faded away. That was a neat trick, Fenella thought to herself as she locked her door behind her. She thought about popping back over to Shelly's apartment, just for a minute, for one last snuggle with Katie, but she didn't want to become an annoyance to her friend. Shelly was being kind enough to look after Katie. She didn't need Fenella knocking on her door every five minutes for the duration of Katie's stay.

Following Mona's directions, Fenella quickly found the house that had replaced the one where Mabel had been murdered. She was surprised to find a small crowd gathered in front of it. Unable to resist being nosy, she parked at the curb and joined them. A quick look around didn't give her any clue as to why they were all standing on the sidewalk in front of the house.

"What's going on?" she asked eventually.

A tall woman in a long black trench coat turned and looked at her. "It's the murder house, isn't it?" she replied. "A girl was murdered in there." She nodded at the house in front of them and then went back to staring at it.

Fenella looked at the house and then shook her head. "It's not the same house," she told the woman, hoping that Mona was right about what the new owners had done to the property. "That house was torn down."

"It's the same thing," the woman retorted, never taking her eyes off the house. "I can feel the girl's ghost. She can't get out because she was brutally murdered in her bed."

Except Jeanne had found the body in the kitchen, Fenella thought. She was sure she was remembering that fact correctly, but she didn't want to argue with the woman.

"The body was in the kitchen," someone else from the crowd said.

"That doesn't mean she wasn't murdered in her bed," the first woman countered. "The killer might have dragged the body to the kitchen. Maybe he was going to take the body away and hide it, but then he was interrupted."

"Or maybe she got killed in the kitchen," someone replied.

"The ghost told me she was murdered in her bed," the first woman said emphatically. "She should know."

"Ask her who did it," a man urged. "Then you can tell the police and they can solve the case."

"She said it was a stranger," the woman told him. "A man she didn't know came to the door, and she was foolish enough to let him in."

"I think you're crazy," the man said. "You aren't talking to a ghost. You're just imagining things. Ghosts aren't even real, are they?" he demanded, looking around the group.

A few people muttered noes. Fenella kept her mouth shut. She took another look at the house and then headed back to her car. The house looked different enough from its neighbors to suggest that it had been built at a different time than the others. Mona was probably right. This was probably a completely different house. As for the ghost that may or may not have been in residence, she'd ask Mona about that. As she slid behind the steering wheel, another car stopped at the curb. Fenella recognized the driver of the police vehicle, and she quickly put her window down to eavesdrop.

Constable Corlett stepped out of his car and approached the group on the sidewalk. "Good morning," he said brightly to the small group.

"Good morning, Constable," one of the women replied. "We aren't doing anything wrong. We're just standing here."

"You're worrying the neighbors," the constable replied. "I'd appreciate it if you'd move along."

"But this was the murder house," the woman in the trench coat told him. "It was in the paper today."

"That house was torn down years ago," he told her. "This is a completely different house. No one has ever been murdered in this house."

"The ghost told me who did it," she replied. "It was a stranger, someone from across, maybe."

Constable Corlett nodded. "I'll pass that along to the inspector. If I could get your name, he may want to talk further with you."

The woman gave him a suspicious look and then began backing away from him. "I don't need to give you my name. You need to talk to the ghost, not me. Anyway, I should be going." She spun around and fled up the sidewalk, turning at the first corner and disappearing.

Constable Corlett shook his head and then smiled at the others. "I really would appreciate it if you'd disperse."

"That was Annie Logan," one of the men said. "She lives at the end of the road."

"Yes, I know Ms. Logan," the constable replied. "I didn't get your name, though."

The man nodded. "Let's keep it that way, shall we?" He nodded at the group and then walked over to a newer model luxury car. As he drove away, Fenella saw the constable making a note of the car's plate number. That seemed to be all the other people needed to see. By the time the man's car reached the end of the road, all of the others had scattered. The constable smiled and then walked over to Fenella's car.

"Hello, Ms. Woods. I wasn't expecting to see you here today," he said.

"I was driving past and I wondered why the crowd had gathered. They were all just staring at the house."

"Yes, a lot of people have a macabre interest in murder."

The constable's tone suggested that he would include Fenella on that list. She flushed. "I should be going," she said. "I have kittens to look after."

He nodded. "I heard they're hard work. Good luck."

As Fenella drove away, she wondered who'd been talking about the kittens with the constable. It wasn't hard to imagine that the young constable who'd visited the house the previous evening had been telling everyone about it, of course. The fact that a police inspector had been involved would probably have made it an even more interesting story for the man to repeat over and over again.

Back at the house, the kittens had managed to spill what looked like the entire contents of both food and water bowls all over the living room. Fenella corralled all four animals in with their mother before she cleaned up the mess. Once that was done, she let all five of them out and made herself some lunch.

The rest of the day was mostly about cleaning up after kittens. The mother cat took a short walk around the house and then went and stood next to her playpen, mewing softly. Fenella put her back inside and the animal curled up and went to sleep. Wondering how long it had been since the cat had felt safe and secure, Fenella rubbed her head gently and then made sure she had plenty of food and water. The kittens chased one another everywhere around the house as Fenella sorted out what she needed for her class.

"A notebook, three pencils, three pens. What else might I want?" she asked the kittens. They didn't pay her any attention.

She'd brought a small tote bag with her from her apartment, specifically for her class. After a light dinner, she rounded up the kittens and put them into the playpen with their mother. "Get some rest," she told them sternly. "I'm going out now."

For a minute it seemed as if the kittens were going to object, but after a short while, they all settled down. Fenella switched the lights off in the living room as she left the house, leaving only the light in the foyer on for her return.

❧ 6 ❧

The class was being held in a meeting room at the Manx Museum. Fenella hadn't realized that the museum would be closed when she arrived. She pulled on the large glass door, but it didn't open. Frowning, she tried each of the doors in turn, but they were all locked.

"Now what?" she said loudly.

"Are you here for the class?" a voice asked from behind her.

Fenella spun around as her heart skipped a beat. "I didn't know anyone was behind me," she said as she stared at the elderly woman standing there.

"So I gathered. When there are classes after the museum is closed for the night, they leave the door at the back open for us," the woman told her. "Come along."

Fenella followed the other woman as she slowly made her way to a second set of doors about halfway along the building. The doors looked heavy, so Fenella quickly climbed up the steps to open the door for the other woman. She pulled on the handle and was relieved when the door swung open.

"After you," she told the older woman.

"Thank you."

A man in a black uniform was sitting at a small desk just inside the door. "Names, please," he barked in a loud voice.

"Don't be ridiculous, Walter," the other woman scolded. "You've known me since you were a child." She glanced over at Fenella. "I taught him to read and write and now he thinks he's important because he's wearing a fancy uniform." She turned back to the man. "You can put a little tick next to my name without me saying a word."

The guard looked very much like he wanted to argue, but the woman gave him a stern look and he quickly nodded. "Yes, of course, Miss Clague. I didn't mean you, anyway. I remember you."

"I'm sure you do," she laughed.

"I'm Fenella Woods," Fenella said, feeling awkward.

He checked the sheet of paper in front of him and then nodded. "You're on the list. You can go in. The class is in the small conference room on the third floor. The lifts are in the lobby, right next to the main entrance."

"You should let us in through the main entrance, then," Miss Clague told him. "All this walking back and forth at my age isn't easy." She shook her head. "I'm going to have a word with Marjorie about this."

The guard shrugged. "I'm just doing what I was told," he said defensively.

Miss Clague opened her mouth to reply, but the door behind Fenella suddenly opened.

"Good evening," a tall, distinguished-looking man said as he swept into the room. He appeared to be around seventy, with a full head of silver hair. Fenella was surprised to see him wearing a suit. Surely the class wasn't anything formal, she thought as she took another look at Miss Clague. She was reassured to see that the other woman was wearing pants and a sweater, an outfit quite similar to Fenella's.

"Good evening, Robert," Miss Clague greeted him. "So lovely of you to join us."

He smiled at her. "Ah, my dear Annabelle, I'm delighted to be here."

"I'm sorry, sir, but I need your name," the young guard said.

"I'm Robert Platter," the man announced. Fenella felt as if Robert was waiting for a gasp of recognition or even applause after he'd announced his name. He looked slightly disappointed when the guard simply ticked his name off the list in front of him.

"The class is on the third floor," Annabelle said. "We have to walk back to the front to get to the lifts."

"Do you still walk five miles every day?" Robert asked her.

Annabelle shrugged. "Yes, of course, for my health, but once that's done, I do rather feel as if I've walked quite enough for the day."

"You'll have to turn around a few paces early on Monday nights for the next six weeks," Robert suggested.

Annabelle took a deep breath and then sighed. "Let's go, shall we?" she asked. Robert offered his arm and the pair walked away, down the corridor into the museum.

Fenella thought about following, as she had no idea where she was going, but she felt rather unwelcome. The guard grinned at her.

"There are two others coming. You might as well wait for one of them. They're bound to be nicer than Miss Clague and Mr. Platter."

"She was a teacher?" Fenella asked.

"She taught reception for around a hundred years. She was my mother's teacher when my mother started school and Mum was really happy when she found out I was going to have her as well. I'm not sure what happened to Miss Clague in the years between my mother and me, but she definitely wasn't the same person my mother remembered so fondly."

"Oh, dear."

He shrugged. "It was a long time ago, anyway, but I still remember hating school for that entire year. Miss Clague didn't like messes, and what four-year-old boy doesn't love making them? She never took to me, and the feeling was mutual."

"Who was the man? I got the impression that he felt as if you should know his name."

"Robert Platter? He's an actor, or what passes for one on the island. He always has a part in the Christmas pantomime and he does other shows with different theatre companies around the island. He has a radio show on the local station, too. He plays movie soundtracks and West End show tunes for hours on a Sunday afternoon."

"I'll have to try to listen some Sunday."

The guard made a face. "If that's what you enjoy."

The door opened again, before Fenella could reply.

"Good evening," a pleasant voice said as a plump woman of around sixty walked into the space.

"Good evening," the guard replied. "I just need your name, please."

"I'm Margaret Vestal," the woman replied.

He nodded and made a mark on his paper. "The class is in the third-floor conference room," he told her.

"Same as last time, then," she replied cheerfully.

"Last time?" Fenella echoed. "You've taken the class before."

Margaret smiled at her. "I've taken it three times. I retired two years ago and I'm still rather overwhelmed by how much free time I have. I take classes every night of the week when I can. This one is one of my favorites, though. Marjorie is a brilliant teacher."

"That's good to hear. I'm Fenella Woods, by the way."

"Nice to meet you. I'm Margaret, but you already knew that."

Fenella nodded. "From what did you retire?"

"I was a nurse. I spent my entire career at Noble's, working in the children's ward. It was sometimes heartbreaking, seeing the children and their parents suffer, but I loved it, and I still miss it."

The door swung open again and a large man in a bright red over-coat seemed to burst through it. "I'm late," he exclaimed.

"Not at all, George," Margaret said, patting his arm. "You know Marjorie won't start without you, anyway."

George nodded. "I know, but I do hate to make everyone wait. Annabelle will be tutting under her breath, and Robert will make some remark that's funny but also a touch unkind."

Margaret grinned. "You're right, of course, so let's get up there and see what he comes up with tonight."

She grabbed George's arm and then smiled at Fenella. "Come along, I'll introduce you to George along the way."

"It's George O'Malley, then?" the guard asked.

"Yes, exactly," George replied as they began to walk down the corridor.

"Thanks," the guard called behind them.

"George, this is Fenella Woods. Fenella, this is George. He teaches mathematics at one of the Douglas high schools, a tiring and thankless job. He's only twenty-five, you know."

Fenella tried not to look shocked as she glanced at the man. She'd assumed he was somewhere around forty, with his greying hair.

George laughed. "I'm going to be forty-three this year," he told Fenella. "I love my job, and I even get thanked once in a while."

"It's nice to meet you," Fenella told him.

"I know you're wondering why I'm taking this class, when I teach maths," he added.

The question hadn't occurred to Fenella, but she didn't mind hearing the answer. "I hope there isn't any math in this class," she replied quickly.

He laughed again. "No, at least, not much. We sometimes get caught up with working out old money, but that's the extent of it. No, I always tell the teenagers I teach that their entire lives should be about learning. So many of them are focused on finishing school and getting a job, and I want them to realize that they should keep learning new things no matter what their age. I take at least one class every year, and I try to fit in more when I can. I think it keeps my brain active."

They'd made their way down the dimly lit corridor to the foyer at the main entrance. The elevators were only a few steps away. On the third floor, it was a short walk to the conference room.

"Ah, there you are," Robert said loudly. "So right on time as to make the rest of us feel as if we'd arrived rather too early."

Everyone chuckled at the man's words except Annabelle, who muttered something under her breath.

Fenella smiled at Marjorie Stevens, the woman teaching the class. Marjorie was the librarian and archivist for the museum, and she taught a number of different classes all around the island. Fenella had met with her a few times to discuss various research projects that Marjorie was hoping someone might pursue. As Fenella had a doctorate in history, Marjorie seemed eager to persuade her to start some research on the island. Taking this class was an important first step for Fenella, as very few of the old records had been transcribed.

"You are right on time," Marjorie told the new arrivals as they settled into seats around the long rectangular table. "Before we start working, I think we should all introduce ourselves. I'll start. I'm Marjorie Stevens. I've been teaching this class for something like fifteen years and I'm still always excited to find new documents for us to discuss." She nodded toward Annabelle who was sitting on her right.

"I'm Annabelle Clague," she said, frowning. "I'm a retired teacher and I've taken this class six times. I've been tracing my family tree for many years, but that isn't easy on this island when your surname is Clague."

Everyone around the table nodded.

"I'm Robert Platter. I'm retired as well, although I keep myself busy with bits and pieces. This is the fourth time I've taken this class, and I teach a few community education classes myself, in drama and theater."

"I took one of Robert's classes last year," Marjorie interjected. "It was tremendous fun."

"Thank you," Robert replied with a smile.

"I suppose I'm next," George said. "I'm George O'Malley. I'm not retired, and I'm quite jealous of those of you who are. I've taken this class half a dozen times or more and it's always one of my favorites."

"I'm Margaret Vestal and this is my fourth time taking this class," Margaret said. "I'm a retired nurse."

Fenella smiled nervously at the others. "I'm Fenella Woods. I only just moved to the island last year and this is the first time I'm taking this class. I took early retirement from my job as a university professor in Buffalo, New York."

"I'm Donna Cannon," the last woman said.

Fenella tried to study her without staring. She knew Donna was in her seventies, and she looked like someone's grandmother. Her hair was white and it curled gently around her face. She was curvy, but not fat, and her clothes were neat and tidy, but clearly not new.

"I'm retired, too. I worked in banking for many years. I was the first female vice president in the bank's history, and I had to work twice as hard as any of the men who had the same job. I never married, never had much use for men, really. I left school at sixteen, without many qualifications. Luckily, I was a hard worker and a quick study. I moved up at the bank even though I hadn't been to university. Once I retired, though, I realized that I'd missed out on a lot in terms of my education, so I started taking classes whenever I could. This is the tenth time I've taken this class."

She paused for a breath and Marjorie quickly began to speak. "That's everyone, then," she said brightly. "Let's start with our first document."

Marjorie passed around photocopies of a document from the museum's archives.

"Fenella, this will all be new to you, but the others can probably manage a lot of it. We'll go through it slowly, word by word, or even letter by letter. Once you get your eye in, you'll find that you can read a lot more than you'll initially think you can understand."

Fenella looked at the scrawled mess on the page in front of her and could only hope that Marjorie was correct. At the moment, she felt as if she'd struggle to identify much more than a few random letters.

An hour later, Fenella shut her eyes and then looked at the document again. While it hadn't been easy to work though, she now had a neat transcription of the entire page.

"I think we need to take a break," Marjorie said. "That was a tricky one to start with, and I have another tricky one for after the break. Right now, I think we could all do with some biscuits and tea."

Everyone sat back from the table and put their pens or pencils down. Fenella rubbed a hand over her eyes.

"You need one of these," Donna said, waving her magnifying glass.

"I think you're right," Fenella agreed.

"I should have lent you one," Marjorie said apologetically as she got to her feet. "I usually bring a few up from the archives, but I forgot tonight."

"It's fine. I managed," Fenella told her. "I'll buy one before next week."

Marjorie nodded and then headed for the corner where there was a small sink and a table with a kettle on it. While she began to make tea, Fenella stretched.

"What did you think of that, then?" Donna asked her.

"It was fascinating, but hard work," Fenella replied.

"It was a more difficult one than what Marjorie usually starts us with," Donna said. "We usually start with something easier and in a more standard form, like a will. Those all start the same and have a lot of the same wording throughout, so you can more easily get your eye in to deciphering the writing. This letter was something else altogether."

"It does get easier," George interjected. "The more you look at these things, the easier it gets. If we started after the break with another letter from the same person, you'd find you could read it with ease."

"I'm not sure about that," Fenella laughed, "but I could probably work out a few words here and there, anyway."

The others began to get out of their chairs, and after a few minutes they began to congregate near the table in the back.

"Custard creams and digestives," Marjorie announced as she opened packages. "Help yourself."

Fenella grabbed a custard cream and took a bite. They weren't as sweet as an American cookie would have been, but they were definitely better than digestives, which were more like an unsweetened graham cracker than a cookie.

"I saw your name in the paper today," Annabelle said to Donna.

Donna frowned and then shrugged. "I don't want to talk about it."

Annabelle looked surprised. "You don't want to talk about it?" she repeated. "I've never known you to not want to talk."

"One of my dearest friends was murdered," Donna told her, "and, what's worse, the killer got away with it. Whoever killed Mabel is still walking around, living his or her life quite happily. Mabel didn't live to see twenty-six. The killer has had fifty years of life since to enjoy."

"Unless he or she died, too," Margaret suggested.

Donna shrugged. "It seems as if the most likely suspects are all still alive."

"What's all this?" George asked.

"Don't you read the local paper?" Annabelle demanded, sounding horrified by the thought.

"I do, of course," the man replied quickly. "I haven't had time to read today's, though. I'll probably read it with my breakfast tomorrow morning."

An awkward silence followed George's words. Marjorie finally inter-rupted it. "The tea is ready," she announced as she began to fill cups.

Fenella took a cup and sipped it slowly. She wanted to hear more from Donna about the case, but she didn't want to be the one to ask.

"As no one else is talking, I'll tell you what Annabelle was talking about," Donna said after she'd finished a digestive. "Fifty years ago one of my closest friends was brutally murdered in her home. Mabel was a good friend and a good person and it breaks my heart that the police have never found the man or woman responsible for her death."

George nodded. "I'm sorry," he said. "If this happened fifty years ago, why was it in the paper today?"

"The new police inspector from across, Inspector Robinson, is reopening the investigation," Annabelle explained. "He's the one who solved Christopher Manderly's murder some time back."

"I do remember reading about that," George said happily.

"He's meant to be very good," Donna said. "Fenella can tell us more."

All eyes turned to Fenella, who nearly choked on her tea. "He is very good," she said after a short coughing spell. "He was the inspector in charge of the case when I found a body the day after I'd arrived on the island."

"And they've become good friends since then," Donna added.

Fenella felt herself blushing as she took another custard cream.

"It seems as if the police should have enough to do with current crime rates the way they are," Robert remarked. "Reopening old cases seems to be a waste of resources."

"Mabel was murdered. Her case deserves to be solved and someone deserves to go to prison for a long time," Donna said tightly.

Robert shrugged. "It was probably someone from across. This Inspector Robinson fellow will never track them down, not after all these years."

"I'm afraid Robert may be correct," Annabelle said. "It does seem likely that the killer was someone from across. Maybe it was a serial killer who came over and killed your friend and then went back to the UK to do the rest of his or her crimes."

"I'm sure we can find more pleasant things to discuss," Marjorie said firmly. "Fenella, what did you think of your first transcription?"

"The subject matter was fascinating, but it was hard work teasing out each word one at a time. It reminded me of the significance of each and every word in a sentence, too. That last line, where it said something about looking forward to seeing them again, took on a whole different meaning when I realized that the word 'not' was at the beginning of it."

Everyone chuckled. "I don't think the letter writer was very pleased with her older brother," George said. "Imagine fighting over an inheritance by post."

"I have the brother's reply for after the break," Marjorie said. "His handwriting is worse than his sister's, and his language is more direct. The first thing we'll do, though, is look at the envelopes from both letters."

"The envelopes?" Margaret asked.

Marjorie grinned at her. "You'll see."

A few minutes later, she passed out a sheet with copies of the two envelopes on the page. Fenella studied them for a second and then gasped.

"They lived in the same house?" she asked.

"They did, indeed," Marjorie replied. "The archives actually hold about fifty letters between the pair, and I believe nearly all of them are arguing about money. From what I've been able to work out, they lived together in the house that their parents had left to them in equal shares. From the sound of things in the letters, the atmosphere in the house must have been quite frosty."

The group spent the next hour reading through the second letter. While the handwriting was more difficult to read, Fenella found the transcription somehow easier. Some of the names and places mentioned in the letter had also been discussed in the first one, which helped. While the brother's handwriting was sloppy, it was consistent, so that the same word looked the same every time it was written. His sister often changed the way she'd made certain letters throughout the document, and her spelling was incredibly erratic.

"That was fun," George said at the end of the second hour. "Are we going to do more with this pair next time?"

Marjorie shook her head. "That's all from these two for this class. If anyone is interested in learning more about them, feel free to come down to the archives whenever it's open. I'd be happy to dig the letters out for you to go through. If you'd like to provide a formal transcription of the lot, I'd be grateful."

Fenella was tempted to try just that, but she didn't want to get caught up with the very first documents they'd studied. Knowing Marjorie, there would be a great deal of interesting material to come.

"Thank you for another wonderful class," Margaret said as she got to her feet. "As always, it was interesting, informative, and entertaining."

"Thank you," Marjorie replied.

"I loved it," George said. "I may just have to visit you one Saturday to read more of those letters. I'd really like to know what happened next."

"You'll have to share what you find with everyone," Marjorie said. "I don't know what happened next, either. One of my research assistants found the letters and suggested them to me for this class, but I haven't read any past those two. My assistant glanced through some later ones and told me that the pair were still arguing, but that's all I know."

"What a shame," Annabelle sighed. "I was an only child and I always wanted an older brother or sister. It's too bad they didn't get along."

"I have four older brothers," Fenella told her. "Happily, we don't fight about money." James, the youngest of her brothers, had been upset when Fenella had inherited Mona's estate and he'd received nothing, but after muttering for a while about suing for a share, he'd stopped talking about it after a recent visit to the island. Her other brothers were all reasonably well off financially.

"I have a younger brother," Robert said. "He's never forgiven me for the way I settled our father's estate. We haven't spoken in twenty years. After tonight, though, I am tempted to reach out to him. Perhaps I'll send him a letter."

"What a good idea," Annabelle said.

"My sister lives in America," George told the group. "She moved there when she was eighteen and hasn't been back here since."

"Have you ever been over to visit her?" Fenella asked.

George shrugged. "No, although visiting America is on my bucket list. We always send one another Christmas and birthday cards. Maybe I should suggest a visit when I send her next birthday card. I'll have to start saving my pennies, though. I'm sure flights won't be cheap."

"Where in America does she live? If she's near a big city, it might not be too bad. If you have to get multiple flights to get to her, those will add up," Fenella said.

"Somewhere in South Carolina," he replied. "She moved last year and I can't remember the name of the city or town where she is now. It wasn't anywhere I'd ever heard of before, but that isn't saying much. I'm sure the US is full of cities and towns about which I know nothing."

"I only know a handful of US cities," Margaret said. "New York, Washington, Los Angeles, Hollywood. I'm sure I know more, but those are the ones that spring to mind, anyway."

Fenella sat back and listened as the others named several other US cities. While they were talking, she thought about the number of UK cities she could name. As a historian, she'd probably known more than the typical American even before she'd moved to the island.

"As fascinating as this is, I really must go," Margaret said when the conversation lagged. "I'll see you all next week."

That seemed to be everyone's cue to start gathering up their things. Marjorie slid her binder into a large bag before she stood up. Fenella tucked her notes and photocopies into the tote she'd brought for the class. Now she just had to work out a way to strike up a conversation with Donna.

"It was a fascinating evening," Robert announced as he tucked his folded sheets into his jacket pocket. He sounded very much as if he were doing a radio promotion for the class or something similar, at least to Fenella's ears.

"I'm glad you enjoyed it," Marjorie said.

He nodded. "But I must get home and rest my voice. I'm doing the morning show tomorrow, filling in for a friend. Am I a terrible person for hoping for some exciting news to announce tomorrow? Reading out the news every hour can be incredibly dull, you know, when all I have to report is a new pub opening in Ramsey and the football scores."

"There's a new pub opening in Ramsey?" George asked.

Robert laughed. "I suspect so, as there always is, but really, that was just an example of the sort of news I have to report around here. Nothing much happens most days, anyway. Things get much more exciting when Fenella starts finding dead bodies."

Fenella flushed. "I don't find that exciting in any way."

"I've just had a brilliant idea," Robert said. "We could do a series of interviews about the various bodies you've found. I'm sure I could sell the series to the station, and maybe even find a place for it across. I'm sure people would be interested in hearing what it's like to find a murder victim."

"Sorry, I'm not interested," Fenella said flatly.

Robert frowned. "I can't offer you much, as I've no idea if I'll sell the idea across or not, but I'm sure we could work out some sort of financial arrangement."

Donna laughed. "Don't you know who she is?" she demanded.

"What do you mean?" Robert asked, looking confused.

"She's Mona Kelly's niece," Donna told him.

Robert nodded. "I do remember hearing that, now that you mention it."

"She inherited Mona's fortune," Donna continued. "She could buy half the island or more with what she has sitting in the bank. She's not going to be interested in making a series with you, no matter how much money you offer."

"If you don't want to do it for the money, you should want to do it for the good of the country," Robert told Fenella. "You can help people understand what they should do if they ever stumble across a dead body."

"I don't think you'll get a whole series out of 'ring 999,'" Fenella told him dryly. "I'm truly not interested in talking about all of the sad things I've seen since I've been on the island. I can't imagine people would be interested, anyway. The papers have covered everything a million times already."

"The papers can't let people hear your voice as you describe your horror," Robert said. "I'm sure I could teach you how to sound strong yet slightly frightened. It could be very lucrative for both of us, really."

"I'm sorry, but no," Fenella said firmly.

"Donna, what about you?" Robert asked.

"What about me?" Donna replied.

"Would you be interested in talking about your friend's murder? I can envision a whole series where I talk to the various loved ones of murder victims. I'm sure Sophia Manderly would talk to me. She's an attention seeker, that woman."

Fenella couldn't argue with him about that. Sophia would probably jump at the chance to tell everyone how devastated she'd been when her husband had died all those years ago.

"I'm sorry, but no. As I said, I don't want to talk about it," Donna said in a low voice.

"Fenella, you know Harvey Garus, don't you? Could you talk to him about the series for me? I'd like to know how he feels, knowing that he survived being held prisoner by a crazy serial killer," Robert continued.

"Harvey and I don't talk about his ordeal. As far as I know, he doesn't remember much about what happened to him, anyway. If you want to talk to him, you'll have to find a way to do that yourself," Fenella replied.

"What about anyone connected to the Hop-tu-Naa murder in Cregneash?" Robert pushed. "Karla's parents might not want to speak to me, but maybe Paul Baldwin would like some extra publicity. I can't believe I never thought about this before."

"I believe Paul is across," Fenella told him, wishing Robert had never had what she thought was a terrible idea.

Robert shrugged. "I'm going to go home and start making a list. Perhaps you'll both change your minds once the series gets started and begins getting noticed." He nodded at everyone and then rushed out of the room. Annabelle was on her feet after him within seconds.

"She's been chasing him for years," Donna remarked, nodding toward Annabelle's back.

"She never seems to get anywhere, though," George remarked. "Maybe she needs to start finding dead bodies."

Fenella winced, earning an apologetic smile from the man.

"I am sorry," he said quickly. "I didn't mean to imply, that is, I'm sorry."

"It's fine," Fenella told him. "Now I'd better get going. I'm looking after a bunch of kittens and I'm sure they've made a huge mess of my house while I've been out."

Everyone walked out of the museum together, back past the guard. When they reached the parking lot, Donna touched Fenella's arm.

"Are you truly in a hurry to get home?" she asked tentatively. "I'd really like a few minutes of your time if you can spare it."

7

"The kittens will be fine for a short while longer," Fenella assured her, hoping she was right. "Should we find a pub nearby?"

"I'm driving," Donna replied. "I never drink when I drive."

"I don't, either, but we could have soft drinks or tea," Fenella suggested.

Donna shrugged. "I don't often go to pubs. There's a nice café nearby that does cakes and several different types of coffee and tea. They have late hours and aren't usually all that busy."

"Cake sounds wonderful," Fenella laughed.

Donna gave her directions to the café, which was only a few streets away. "I'll see you there in five minutes," she told Fenella as they reached their cars in the parking lot.

Fenella waited until the other woman had pulled away before starting her engine. While she drove, she wondered what Donna wanted to discuss with her. It seemed most likely that it had something to do with the investigation into Mabel's death, but that was by no means certain.

The café was easy to find. Fenella parked next to Donna's car. There were only two other cars in the lot.

Inside, Donna was sitting at a table for two in the corner. A man in his forties was sitting by himself at a table for four on the other side of the room. He had papers piled all over the table and was busily typing on a laptop. As Fenella crossed the room, he took a long drink from his coffee cup and then frowned at it. The waitress was already on her way to his table with a fresh pot.

"I'll be over in a second," she called to Fenella as she went.

"This is charming," Fenella said as she took the chair opposite Donna.

"It's one of my favorite places," Donna told her. "My house is just down the road from here. I often walk here, rather than drive. They make their own cakes every morning, and they're all excellent."

"The problem is," the waitress said as she reached the table, "we're sold out of just about everything by this time of night. I have one slice of chocolate gateau left, some Victoria sponge, and lots of jam roly-poly. No one seemed to want that today."

Fenella frowned. She really wanted the chocolate gateau but didn't want to look rude. "What are you having?" she asked Donna.

"Victoria sponge for me," Donna replied. "It's my favorite, and if there's plenty, they'll give me an extra-large piece."

The waitress laughed. "For you, my dear, I always do."

"I'll have the chocolate, then," Fenella said happily, "and a coffee."

"Tea for you, dear?" the waitress asked Donna.

"Yes, please."

The two women chatted about the weather and some of the other restaurants and cafés on the island while they waited for the waitress to return. Once the cakes and drinks had been delivered, Fenella changed the subject.

"What did you want to talk about with me, then?" she asked before taking a sip of her drink.

Donna frowned at her. "I don't really know," she replied. "I mean, I do know, but I'm not sure about it, or anything, really. The thing is, I know who you are and I know you've been involved in a number of murder investigations. I thought maybe you'd understand how I feel."

"I've been caught up in murder investigations, yes, but none of those cases have actually involved any of my family members or friends."

Donna nodded. "That's a fair point, but I, well, I just need to talk to someone, and you seemed ideal, at least during class. If you don't mind my saying so, you're something of an outsider. You probably don't know anything about the case, aside from what you may have read in the paper. Everyone else has their own ideas about what happened based on who they know and what rumors they've heard over the years."

Fenella wasn't sure how best to reply to that. "I did read all about the case in the paper today," she said slowly, hoping she could remember what she'd read today as opposed to what she'd read in Daniel's file.

"They were very careful today to simply report the facts," Donna sighed. "That won't stop people from restarting the old rumors, though."

"What old rumors?"

"Mabel was a great friend. I loved her like a sister. She was always closer to Jeanne, but that was because they worked together. There were four of us, and to some extent we were like a family. Marilyn was breaking the family up, of course, by getting married, but she was never my favorite, anyway."

Fenella chuckled. "What did you think of her fiancé?"

"Ewan was okay. I almost felt sorry for him, really. He was a police constable, and not at all the sort of man that Marilyn's mother expected her to marry. Marilyn was very pretty and her mother wanted her to marry well, but once Marilyn met Ewan she never looked at another man again."

"That's very sweet, really."

"Yes, I suppose so, at least the way I've told it. I could tell it another way and make you think something else altogether, of course."

Fenella nodded. "Do you think they were in love? Was the marriage a happy one?"

"Marilyn loved the idea of being married and getting away from her mother. She also loved the idea of marrying a man that her mother didn't approve of but who was beyond reproach. I mean, what mother can actually complain about her daughter marrying a respected police constable? Ewan was an inspired choice, really. Marilyn's previous boyfriend had been a bartender at the local. She knew better than to introduce him to her parents."

"Did her father approve of the marriage?"

"I don't know that he cared, really. Men didn't get involved in such things in those days. His job was to pay for everything and he did that in a big way. It was far and away the most lavish wedding I've ever attended, and I've been to quite a few weddings in my day."

"Were they happy together?" Fenella asked again.

"Marilyn's parents or Marilyn and Ewan?" Donna asked. She laughed and held up a hand before Fenella could reply. "I know you meant Marilyn and Ewan, but for the record, I don't think Marilyn's parents were particularly happy. Her father had a bad habit of drinking too much and then, well, making rude suggestions to Marilyn's friends. It was incredibly uncomfortable for everyone involved, really."

"Rude suggestions? How awful."

Donna shrugged. "Times were different. Men often said inappropriate things to women, and we were meant to just shrug them off or even, heaven forbid, feel flattered by the attention."

Fenella nodded. Things hadn't changed that much by the time she'd started working. She'd had a few bosses in her younger days who had suggested that she could get ahead faster if she'd be a bit friendlier. Fortunately for her, those were temporary jobs that she'd only done while working on her degrees.

"As for Marilyn and Ewan, well, I never thought they were either happy or unhappy. They both seemed rather resigned to the life that they'd chosen for themselves and they both just seemed to be doing what they needed to do to get through it."

"That sounds horrible," Fenella exclaimed.

Donna chuckled. "I didn't mean to make it sound quite that bleak. Let me try again. Marilyn seemed quite excited to set up her own little household and get away from her mother's influence. Sadly, that didn't last long. She fell pregnant almost immediately and had a very difficult pregnancy. It wasn't long before her mother had moved into the spare bedroom in the newlyweds' little house. I don't really think she ever moved back out again."

"How awful."

"Marilyn did need someone to look after her, but I never felt as if her mother had Marilyn's best interests at heart. She was the sort of woman who's only happy when someone needs her, and she did everything in her power to make sure that Marilyn needed her. I think things may have worked out, but sadly, the baby was born early and suffered from some sort of genetic abnormalities. I never found out exactly what was wrong with him, but he was incredibly sickly and looking after him became something of a full-time job for both Marilyn and her mother. When they finally lost him just before his first birthday, Marilyn was already six months pregnant with her second, and having just as difficult a time with this pregnancy as she'd had with the first."

"How was Ewan coping with everything?"

"As far as I know, he was putting in as many hours as he could at work and trying his best to stay out of the way."

"And yet Marilyn got pregnant again," Fenella pointed out.

Donna laughed. "Yes, well, I don't think I want to comment on that particular aspect of their marriage. I'll just point out that they were both still in their mid-twenties. Marilyn was beautiful and Ewan was quite handsome, especially if you're attracted to men in uniforms."

"Are you?" Fenella asked.

"Not in the slightest."

Fenella nodded. "I'm fascinated by the story. What happened next?"

"As I said, they lost the first baby, and then Ewan nearly lost Marilyn, too. She had some sort of hemorrhage and nearly bled to death just a few days after the baby died. She spent the rest of the pregnancy on bed rest, with her mother dancing attendance on her, of course."

Mona had told her that none of Marilyn's babies had survived for long, but Fenella still found herself hoping that things were going to get better for Marilyn. "I hope the baby was okay," she said softly.

"Sadly, he wasn't," Donna told her. "The doctors told Marilyn that the blood loss had been too much for him. He was born alive, but he was incredibly weak and sickly. Marilyn and her mother did everything they could for him, but he passed away when he was six months old. Marilyn was devastated and had something of a breakdown, really, although no one would have called it that in those days. She went across for six months, to a specialist facility somewhere. Her mother went with her, of course."

"Why do I feel as if this story isn't going to have a happy ending?"

Donna shrugged. "When she came back, she got pregnant again almost immediately, even though her doctors had told her not to try for any more children after her hemorrhage. All things considered, her third pregnancy was her easiest, but something happened in the delivery room. They ended up having to do an emergency cesarean and that left her unable to have any more children."

"And the baby?" Fenella asked, blinking back tears.

"Had the same issues as their first. He lived for about three months before succumbing to the condition."

Fenella wiped her eyes. The miscarriage and infertility in her past made her feel terribly sympathetic toward Marilyn. While she'd carried on with her life and really couldn't imagine what life would have been like with children, there was still a part of her that grieved deeply for the children she'd never know.

"Did she and Ewan stay together after all of that?"

"Oh, yes. I can't imagine any reason why Marilyn would have ever divorced Ewan. Maybe she'd have considered it if he'd done something horrible, such as taking up with another woman, but he would never have done that. He wasn't the type."

"Wasn't? He's not still alive?"

"No, he passed away about ten years ago. He never got to live with Marilyn without her mother again. Marilyn's mother just died around three years ago, but Marilyn's been in a home for quite a while now. She was in a bad car accident not long after her husband passed. She's in a wheelchair, which means she needs quite a lot of care."

"Are you still friends?"

Donna shrugged. "I used to visit her once in a while, maybe twice a year, but I haven't seen her since her accident. We drifted apart after she married, really. I felt sorry for her when she lost her babies, but she had Ewan and her mother to help her through that grief. I found that I usually felt as if I was in the way when I tried to visit her in those years. I probably should make more of an effort to see her now, but I don't really feel as if we have anything in common any longer."

Fenella nodded. "Your lives went in very different directions."

"But we were going to talk about Mabel," Donna said as the waitress crossed to them.

"Refills?" she asked brightly.

After their drinks had been refilled and the waitress had gone, Fenella smiled at the other woman. "Tell me about Mabel, then," she suggested.

"I don't even know where to start," Donna sighed. "As I said, we were very close. We all went to primary school together, all four of us, and we'd been friends since the first week of reception. In those days, women were meant to finish school, get married, and have children. That didn't appeal to me. Jeanne, Mabel, and I all started jobs right out of school. Marilyn got a job, too, but she wasn't really interested in having a career. She made it clear she was simply working until she found herself a husband."

"Tell me about Jeanne," Fenella suggested.

Donna smiled. "She was smart and funny, but a bit obsessed with men, really. She talked with Mabel and me about having a career and not needing a man, but I always felt as if she didn't really mean what she was saying. Her problem was she could never find a man who was ready to commit to her."

"Did she ever find a husband, then?"

"Oh, yes, she got married just before she hit thirty. They had four children in five years. That's when Jeanne and I drifted apart, although it was somewhat more abrupt than that, really. I visited once in a while after the first one arrived, a scant six months after the wedding, I must add, but as she kept having more, I lost interest in seeing her. She could talk of nothing but her children, and I'm sorry to say I wasn't particularly interested in their rather mediocre accomplishments."

Fenella hid a smile behind her teacup. "Is she still alive?"

"Oh, yes, and so is her husband. They share a room in a care home near here. All of my contemporaries are in care homes, aside from the ones who are dead, of course. It's quite depressing, really."

"Annabelle and Robert both seemed close to your age," Fenella suggested.

"Robert is a few years older and Annabelle is a few years younger. They both have enough money to take proper care of themselves, I suppose. Anyway, I haven't seen Jeanne in ten years or more, and I'm not particularly interested in seeing her now, or I wouldn't be if it weren't for the police reopening Mabel's case. It's brought up all manner of memories, some of which I was hoping were buried forever."

"I'm sorry," Fenella said softly. "Do you want to talk about it?"

"Yes and no in equal measure. I've an appointment with the police tomorrow. No doubt your friend, Inspector Robinson, will have a great many questions for me. I thought maybe if I talked through some of it with you, I might feel better about having to see him tomorrow, but now I'm not so sure."

"Who do you think killed her?" Fenella asked.

"I wish I knew. I've had fifty years to think about that question and I don't think I'm any closer to an answer now than I was fifty years ago. It's almost impossible for me to believe that someone murdered her, really. Murders happen in cheap novels and on bad television programs, not in real life."

"Didn't I read that Mabel had a brother?"

Something flashed over Donna's face. "Yes, Clyde," she said.

"Do you not want to talk about him?"

"I don't care either way," Donna replied tightly. "He was four years younger than Mabel. We all thought of him as a younger brother, really. He was quite upset about the murder, but then we all were."

"When did you last see him?"

"At Mabel's funeral."

Fenella was surprised. If they'd all thought of the man as a younger brother, it seemed odd that she hadn't seen him in fifty years. It was a small island, too. Was it possible that Donna had spent fifty years deliberately avoiding Clyde? She took a sip of her drink and tried to decide what to say next.

Donna sighed. "We had something of a disagreement at the funeral," she said before Fenella had found the right words. "I assumed, at the time, that we'd work it through the next time we saw each other, but then, as time went on, we simply never seemed to see one another. After a while I began to believe that Clyde was avoiding me. When that continued, I found that I wanted to avoid him as well. He's in a home, too, now. I seem to be the only one left who is capable of looking after myself."

"What did you and Clyde argue about?"

"I won't discuss that, not with you, and not with the police, either."

Fenella didn't push the woman any further. Daniel could probably get the story from someone else, but even if he couldn't, there was little doubt in her mind that Mona would know what had happened.

"Who were the main suspects in the murder, then?" she asked, changing the subject.

"Jeanne, Marilyn, and me, for a start. I believe Marilyn had the best alibi, but I don't think it was completely watertight or airtight or whatever alibis are meant to be. I had nothing even close to an alibi. I'd been home alone, getting ready for the engagement party. Jeanne was in an even worse position, as she'd been alone at home, and then she'd gone to Mabel's house and found the body. She always felt that finding the body made her the main suspect."

"Do you think that Jeanne or Marilyn killed her?"

Donna hesitated and then shook her head. "Thank you for not including me in the question," she smiled. "I haven't spoken to either of them in years, but no, I don't think either of them killed Mabel. We were still like sisters in those days. I can't imagine why any of them would have wanted Mabel dead."

"Maybe she was having an affair with Ewan."

Donna looked surprised and then shrugged. "If she was, they were both incredibly discreet. As I said earlier, though, Ewan wasn't the type. He was crazy in love with Marilyn. At the time, I thought he couldn't really believe his luck. She was stunning in those days, much prettier than any of the rest of us. Besides, even if Ewan was interested, I can't see Mabel doing that to Marilyn. We were all happy for her, expecting her to finally get away from her mother."

Fenella nodded. "What about Jeanne, then? If Jeanne didn't have a steady boyfriend at the time, might she have been interested in Clyde?"

Donna stiffened and then frowned. "Impossible," she said flatly.

Fenella swallowed the dozens of questions that popped into her head. "What about a motive for Clyde?" she asked after a moment.

"He thought Mabel was the perfect woman. She was the one by whom he judged all other women," Donna said with a hint of bitterness. "He would never have done anything to hurt her, not in a million years."

"Whom does that leave?" Fenella asked.

"The house Mabel was renting was owned by Howard and Patricia Quinn. I always thought they should have been investigated more thoroughly."

"Why?"

"I don't know. There was something creepy about him and something terrifying about her."

"Really?"

"She was one of those people who always wants to talk about religion and how everything is God's will, that sort of thing. She didn't approve of Mabel living on her own and she used to make unannounced visits to the house just to check up on her. The four of us would be there, sharing a few bottles of wine and complaining about men, when the door would suddenly open and Patricia would storm in shouting about cars on the drive and overnight visitors."

"That sounds like fun," Fenella said sarcastically.

"After a while, it almost became funny, really. We were never doing anything wrong and we always left before midnight, which was reasonable enough for single women on a weekend night. I think that annoyed Patricia more than anything. I'm sure she was just looking for an excuse to throw Mabel out of the house."

"None of you ever stayed overnight? Not even when you were drinking?"

Donna flushed. "We didn't give drink driving much thought in those days, not that we drank all that much, really. Mabel's house was the one place we could go and just relax and talk about anything and everything. The rest of us lived with our parents, you see. But we always left by midnight. We didn't want to risk getting Mabel thrown out, you see. We loved having an escape, even if it wasn't really ours."

"You said Howard was creepy. What do you mean?"

"I only met him once or twice. He was at the little party that Mabel threw when she first moved into the house, but he mostly just sat in the corner and stared at everyone all night. Patricia kept stomping around, glaring at everyone who was drinking and remarking loudly on the time every ten minutes. Howard just sat and stared. It was uncomfortable."

"Do you think one of them killed her?"

"I think Patricia might have, if she'd walked in on Mabel doing something she shouldn't have been doing."

"Like what?"

"The obvious answer is having a man in the house, but knowing Patricia, it could have been something like not vacuuming often enough or leaving dirty dishes in the sink."

"You think she would have killed Mabel over dirty dishes?"

"That was just an example. Patricia was, probably still is, incredibly uptight. They never had children, which meant she had plenty of time to devote to her church and to do whatever she could to make Mabel's life miserable, too."

"Did she do other things besides visiting at all hours?"

"She would show up a week early and demand the rent money before it was due. Then she'd come back the following week and demand it again. Mabel learned to always have enough money in the house to pay the next month's rent. She also learned to get a receipt from Patricia."

"Did Mabel worry about having money lying around the house?"

"She kept it hidden under the mattress in one of the spare bedrooms. There was five hundred pounds there when the police searched the house after the murder."

"That sounds like a lot of money, especially in those days."

"It was a lot of money, but Mabel was incredibly thrifty. She hated to spend money. Actually, she was really good at getting people to buy things for her. Clyde spent most of his income on little treats for his older sister, and Mabel never had a boyfriend who didn't buy her at least one expensive trinket before he ended things with her."

"Was she seeing anyone when she died?"

"She'd recently ended a relationship and had decided to focus on her career, actually. I think she'd have done really well with that, too, if she'd lived."

"She didn't have any angry former boyfriends?"

"No, not at all. None of her relationships had been serious. She would have liked the last one to be, but he wasn't ready to settle down. She dropped a few hints about marriage. When he didn't take the hints, she decided to get her own house, and he used that as an excuse to end things with her. He moved away right after the relationship ended."

"I'm sure the police checked his alibi," Fenella said, knowing that they had.

Donna nodded. "He was in London by that time."

"Are those all the suspects, then?"

"I always wondered about her neighbor, Stanley Middleburgh."

Fenella was surprised. She'd never heard the name before. "I don't remember seeing his name in the paper."

"No, I don't think he was ever officially a suspect, but I didn't like him."

"Why not?"

"He was creepy, too, like Howard Quinn. He lived in the house right next door to Mabel's and he used to sit outside a lot. I always felt as if he was watching me whenever I was there."

"Tell me more. How old was he? What did he do for a living? Did Mabel find him creepy, too?" Fenella blurted out some of the questions that had sprung to mind.

"He was probably forty, which seemed old to me back then, when I was only twenty-five. As for what he did, nothing much is the answer. He'd been born into a wealthy family and I think he was meant to work for the family business, but I doubt he ever did anything. I believe he owned several properties on the island, but he chose to live in the house next door to Mabel's for some reason. He had a house-keeper who did all of his cooking and cleaning and a driver who took him everywhere he needed to go. From what I could see, he never wanted to go anywhere, though. He seemed to always be home, at least when I was at Mabel's house."

"I wonder why his name was never mentioned in the local paper."

"Because of his family's wealth, of course. The local paper has to be very careful about what it prints. If they anger the wrong person, they could find themselves getting boycotted, being bought out, or even find a new competitor suddenly arriving on the island. They were always scrupulously polite about Mona, for instance, because of her relationship with Maxwell Martin."

Fenella nodded. That wasn't something she wanted to discuss with the other woman. "Why would Stanley have killed Mabel?" she asked.

"I always thought he was interested in her. Mabel used to laugh it off, but I could see the way he stared at her. Maybe he finally told her how he felt and she laughed at him."

"Where is he now?"

"He moved out within days after Mabel's murder. I think he was running away before he could be charged. He went on an extended holiday to Canada and he never came back."

"Did he choose to remain there, or did something happen to him while he was in Canada?"

Donna frowned. "I'm not entirely sure, actually. There were all sorts of rumors and speculation, but I'm not sure I ever heard anything definite. All I know for sure is that he never returned to the island."

Fenella made a mental note to talk to Daniel about the man. Even if the local paper hadn't wanted to mention him, the police should have questioned him.

"Any other suspects, then?" she asked Donna.

"If it was indeed someone who knew her that killed her, then no. Her parents were at a party that afternoon and evening. She had other friends, but she wasn't particularly close to anyone else. I can't imagine a motive for anyone other than the people we've discussed, although it's always possible that the killer was simply a random stranger, isn't it?"

"Of course it is, which would make solving the case very difficult."

"I don't expect them to solve the case, not after all this time. I'm glad they're reopening it, though. As much as I don't like talking about Mabel, there's something almost cathartic about doing just that. She was one of my dearest friends and I miss her every day. As Jeanne and Marilyn and I have all drifted apart, I often wonder if Mabel and I would have done the same. I truly don't think we would have, though. We had a special bond."

"I'm sorry for your loss," Fenella told her.

Donna blinked back tears and then nodded. "Thank you. And with that, I'd better go. It's getting late and I have an early appointment tomorrow morning. I'll see you next Monday."

Fenella agreed and then insisted on paying for everything. Donna slipped out while Fenella was settling the bill. With her mind whirling from everything Donna had told her, Fenella headed for home. She was nearly at her apartment building when she remembered that she was staying at the house on Poppy Drive at the moment. Sighing deeply, she turned the car around at the next roundabout and drove back to her temporary home.

"Fenella?" a voice said as she climbed out of the car. "That was a long class."

She turned and smiled at Daniel, who was crossing the street behind her. "Donna wanted a chat after class," she explained. "We went to this wonderful little café that does fabulous cakes."

Daniel grinned and then named the café. "I love it there."

"And you've never mentioned it to me," she sighed, shaking her head.

"I'd like to hear what Donna said, if you aren't too tired to talk tonight."

Fenella swallowed a sigh. She was tired, but it would be better to talk to Daniel tonight, while everything was still fresh in her mind. She was eager to ask him about Stanley Middleburgh, too. "Come on in," she said.

8

The first thing Fenella did was check on the kittens. They were all happily curled up with their mother, seemingly fast asleep. She sent Daniel into the kitchen while she took care of a few little jobs for the animals and then joined him.

"How are you finding your house guests?" he asked as she got them each a cold drink.

"They're not too bad. I don't want to keep them forever, though. I must ring Mr. Stone and see if he's managed to find homes for any of them yet. I'm afraid finding a home for the mother cat will be the most difficult, although she's been no trouble at all, really."

"You can't keep her?"

"Katie didn't like her one bit."

Daniel nodded. "Tell me about your class tonight, then."

Fenella quickly ran through the class and then spent considerably longer telling him about her conversation with Donna at the café. Daniel took notes throughout.

"I'm going to have to look into this Stanley Middleburgh," he said when she'd finished. "I don't remember seeing the name in the files, although it might have been mentioned. There were several pages of interviews with the neighbors, none of which were deemed relevant at the time."

"Is it possible his family's money kept him out of the investigation?"

"I'd like to think not, but I'm not sure. I've no idea what money or social position could or could not buy on the island fifty years ago. I would hope that no amount of influence or money could protect someone from a murder investigation, but I'll have to dig a bit to make sure of that."

"I'm sure you can't tell me, but is there anything in the files about the fight between Donna and Clyde at Mabel's funeral?"

"Again, nothing that I remember. I'm going to have to read back through everything tonight, though, before I talk to Donna."

"Donna said she was seeing you tomorrow."

"Yes, I'm interviewing all three of Mabel's friends tomorrow. On Wednesday I'll be talking to Clyde, and Howard and Patricia Quinn. If I can track down Stanley Middleburgh, I'm going to try to find time to speak with him as well."

"If he was forty when Mabel died, I suspect you aren't going to be able to interview him."

Daniel nodded. "That's one of the biggest problems with this case. Nearly all of the witnesses are in care homes. I've had to talk to doctors and medical staff to get permission to interview each of them, and I've had warnings about the mental state of more than one of them."

"At least you're trying. Donna will be grateful for that, even if no one else is," Fenella told him.

"I hope everyone involved is grateful, aside from the killer, of course."

They chatted for a while longer before Fenella began yawning after every sentence.

"I should go and let you get some sleep," Daniel said, getting to his feet. "I assume you aren't planning anything for tomorrow that might see you meeting any of the other witnesses in the case."

"I'm going to sleep late and then go home for a bit to see Katie. I have some shopping to do, but beyond that I'll be busy looking after kittens," she told him.

Movement in the doorway made her frown. She'd stood up when Daniel had. Now she took two quick steps toward the door.

"Merroww," one of the kittens said, staring up at her with seemingly innocent eyes.

"How did a kitten get out of the playpen?" Daniel asked.

Fenella shrugged. "I've no idea. I just hope they didn't all get out." She scooped up the kitten and carried it back into the living room. The other four cats were all still safely in the playpen where they belonged. Fenella set the fourth kitten back inside the pen. "Now you stay there and get some sleep," she said sternly. "I'll let you back out in the morning."

The kitten nodded and then curled up against the mother cat, quickly closing its eyes.

"That one is trouble," Daniel said with a chuckle.

"I'm going to have to start keeping track of which one is which. If the same one keeps escaping, that won't be as bad as if they all manage it in turns."

"Ring me if you do happen to stumble over anyone else involved in the case. Otherwise, I'll ring you in a day or two. I hope to have some information about Stanley Middleburgh by then, anyway."

Fenella let Daniel out and then headed up the stairs, locking the gate behind her. Hopefully the little escape artist couldn't get through the gate, even if he or she could get out of the playpen. She was asleep within minutes and didn't wake until nearly nine o'clock.

The kittens were chasing one another around the playpen under their mother's watchful eye when Fenella reached the living room. She let the kittens out and then gave everyone fresh water and breakfast before she took her shower and then fed herself.

"Now you all be good," she told the animals as she headed for the door some time later. "I'll be back before it's time for lunch."

Shelly welcomed her with a hug and then left her alone with Katie and Smokey while she ran a few errands. Fenella fussed over Katie as much as Katie would allow and then settled into a chair with Smokey on her lap for a short while. Shelly returned before Fenella got tired of stroking the beautiful animal.

"You're spoiling her," Shelly laughed when she saw Smokey on Fenella's lap.

"Katie didn't want to snuggle, but Smokey was willing."

"Smokey is a great snuggler. Katie is too young to appreciate the joys of simply sitting still."

Fenella's apartment felt empty when she let herself in after a short chat with Shelly. She didn't really need anything from the apartment, but she'd wanted to ask Mona about the fight between Donna and Clyde at Mabel's funeral.

"Hello?" she called tentatively. Mona had sometimes complained that Fenella had disturbed her, which suggested that she could hear what was happening in the apartment, even when she wasn't there. "Mona?" Fenella called, feeling slightly ridiculous.

When she failed to get a reply, Fenella headed into the second bedroom to look over the bookshelf. Anticipating a quiet night in with the kittens, she chose a handful of books to try and then headed for the door.

"I do want to talk to you," Fenella said in the doorway. "It isn't like you to miss a chance to discuss a murder investigation."

After counting slowly to a hundred, Fenella sighed and then let herself out. She'd have to talk to her aunt another day. A quick trip around the grocery store was the last thing on her list before she could return to the house on Poppy Drive. As she let herself in, she counted kittens. Three of them were racing back and forth between the living room and the kitchen as she carried in the shopping. Where was the fourth, she wondered.

Rather than worry about hunting for the missing kitten, she simply filled up food bowls and waited. Within seconds four hungry kittens were gobbling up their lunch. Once Fenella had eaten her own lunch, she grabbed the phone and called Mr. Stone's office.

"Ah, yes, Ms. Woods," the reception said. "Mr. Stone was going to ring you later today. He wanted to discuss something with you with regard to the kittens. He's with a puppy right now, though. Would it be okay if he rang you back?"

"Of course," Fenella assured her. She put the phone down and then looked at the kittens. "I'm actually going to miss you, but you need proper homes where you'll be loved."

Tensions were rising in the third chapter of the thriller that Fenella had brought back from the apartment when the phone rang. Fenella jumped, startling the two kittens who'd curled up on her lap when she'd sat down to read. They both shouted at her as they jumped down and ran off.

"Sorry," she called after them as she reached for the phone.

"Ah, Fenella, I have a proposition for you," Mr. Stone told her.

"Really?"

He chuckled. "Some of the island's nursing homes are trialing a new program where they bring cats and dogs into the facilities to interact with the patients. Many of the older residents had pets when they lived on their own and they miss the unconditional love and affection that an animal provides."

"That sounds like a wonderful program."

"It's proving very popular and successful, especially with cats. Dogs are, as I know you know, quite a bit more work. Cats are proving quite adaptable to nursing home environments."

"I can see where dogs might be more trouble for the staff, certainly."

Mr. Stone chuckled. "Yes, exactly. Anyway, I was talking to one of the program coordinators about your kittens, and she wondered if you'd like to take them all for a visit to one of the nursing homes. She believes that the residents would love a chance to play with kittens, just for a short while, you understand."

"I could do that," Fenella agreed.

"I'm rather hoping that the home might actually be willing to adopt one or two of the kittens from you, as well," Mr. Stone told her.

"That would be good, too. Do you have an idea as to when she'd like me to visit?"

"How's tomorrow?"

Fenella thought about telling him she needed to check her calendar, but she knew there wasn't anything on it aside from her Monday evening class. "Tomorrow would be fine," she agreed.

"The company in question runs several of the island's homes. I'll have Crystal ring you later today to let you know which one she'd like you to visit."

"Crystal?"

"Yes, Crystal Hall is the woman who coordinates the program. She's really enthusiastic about it and about cats in general."

"I'll look forward to talking to her, then."

Fenella put the phone down. It seemed as if she and the kittens were going to have an adventure.

"I'm so excited to meet the kittens," Crystal said when she called a few hours later. "My boyfriend is allergic to animals, so I can't have anything at home. This program is as good for me as it is for the men and women in our care."

They settled on one of the Douglas area homes, agreeing to meet in the foyer the next morning at nine. "If it's okay with you, I'll bring the mother cat, too," Fenella tried to sound casual as she dropped that into the conversation.

"Of course, that's fine. I'm sure there will be several residents who will fuss over her as much as the kittens."

And maybe someone will adopt her, Fenella thought. The kittens were adorable and sweet. Finding homes for them would be a good deal easier than finding one for the mother cat, especially while she was still recovering from her injuries.

After dinner, Fenella drove back over to her apartment, hoping to find Mona at home.

"I wasn't expecting you," Mona said as Fenella let herself in.

Fenella looked around the room, wondering if Mona had guests visiting. She'd had a party at the apartment the other day, after all.

"Are we alone?" she asked after a moment.

Mona shrugged. "You can't see anyone else, can you?"

"That doesn't mean there isn't anyone else here."

"Let's not worry about that. What brings you here?"

"I live here."

"Yes, but you're staying at the house on Poppy Drive for the moment, aren't you? Or have you found a home for the kittens already?"

"No, I haven't found a home for the kittens yet, although I'm going to be working on that tomorrow. I'm taking them to a nursing home to meet the residents."

"Are the residents actually able to adopt animals?"

"I believe Mr. Stone is hoping that the home itself might adopt a few of the kittens. We'll see how tomorrow goes, though."

"Did you just drop in to admire the view, then?"

Fenella smiled. "I wanted to talk to you about some of the things that Donna told me last night."

"Oh, I nearly forgot about your murder investigation," Mona told her. "Things have been, well, let's just say busy, shall we? I do want to hear everything that Donna said, though. Just give me a minute."

Mona faded away, leaving Fenella to wonder what she needed to do and what she'd meant when she'd said things had been busy. Sometimes she really wished that the woman would stop being so mysterious all the time.

"Okay, tell me everything," Mona said a moment later as she reappeared on one of the couches.

Fenella sat down in the chair next to her and repeated as much as she could of the conversation she'd had with Donna the previous evening. When she was done, Mona sat back and stared out at the sea.

"I remember Stanley Middleburgh," she said thoughtfully. "I knew his father, of course. The family was very wealthy, especially by island standards. Stanley was around my age, actually, but he kept to himself mostly. While he would have been invited to just about every social event on the island due to who his parents were, he rarely attended any of them."

"Was he shy? Or was he creepy like Donna thought?"

"I never found him creepy, but he could be intense. I'm not sure that's the right word for it, but the few times I do remember him coming to events, I remember him sitting and staring at people all evening, rather than talking to anyone. As I was always busy with Max, I never tried to engage with him myself."

"Do you know what happened to him?"

"I remember him leaving, but I wouldn't necessarily have associated it with Mabel's murder. I suppose it was around the same time, though. I believe his father told me that he was going to the US to visit some distant relative who'd moved there years earlier."

"The US? Not Canada?"

Mona shrugged. "It might have been Canada, but I remember it as the US. To the best of my recollection, Stanley's father never mentioned him again."

"And you never asked?"

"I spoke to the man maybe once or twice a year. His wife was another of the women who didn't approve of me, you see. I only spoke to Stanley's father, whose name has gone from my memory, when she wasn't around, which wasn't often. When we did speak, it was to exchange pleasantries, mostly. I only recall him mentioning Stanley leaving because he and Max had a long conversation about the difficulty and expense of transatlantic travel."

"I hope Daniel can track Stanley down. I hate the idea that he might have killed Mabel and then run away to escape punishment."

"He was slightly odd, but he never seemed the type to hurt anyone. Mostly, he was just lacking in social skills, which is hardly a crime."

Fenella nodded. "What about the fight between Clyde and Donna? Do you know anything about that?"

Mona sighed. "I was there, at the funeral, and I don't recall any disagreements, certainly not any that were serious enough to end the friendship between the two. Clyde was devastated, of course. He sat with his parents during the actual service, but he spent much of the time before it with Mabel's three friends. They were inseparable at that point, of course. I think it's quite sad that they've grown apart over the years."

"The way Donna tells it, they simply no longer had anything in common."

"After the church service, everyone went back to Mabel's parents' house. I wonder if that's where the disagreement took place," Mona said thoughtfully. "I remember seeing Clyde with the three women at one point. Let me think." She stared out at the sea for several minutes while Fenella waited impatiently.

"I know you hate waiting, but tapping your foot like that isn't helping my memory," Mona said eventually.

Fenella hadn't realized she was tapping her foot. "I'll be back," she muttered, getting up and heading to the bedroom. She gazed longingly at the king-sized bed before she freshened up in the adjacent bathroom.

Mona smiled at her when she returned. "Something happened at the house after the service," she said. "I didn't really notice it at the time, but now that I think back, there was some tension between Clyde and the three women. It wasn't there when we first arrived at the house, but by the time we'd had a cup of tea and a few biscuits, it was obvious. It wasn't just Clyde and the women, though. Mabel's parents were clearly upset, not just about Mabel, but with the three women and maybe with Clyde, too. At the time, I believe I simply thought it was natural tension brought on by the extremely difficult circumstances."

"And maybe it was, at least most of it. It seems whatever happened between Clyde and Donna was more serious, though."

"Donna said she hasn't seen Clyde since the funeral, correct?"

"That's what she said."

"I wonder why he wasn't at Marilyn's wedding, then."

"Maybe he was but they managed to avoid one another for the day."

"He wasn't there," Mona told her. "I told you that I attended, didn't I? It was an incredibly lavish and unbelievably boring affair. I spent much of the afternoon studying my fellow guests, wondering how they'd been unlucky enough to have been dragged to such a dull occasion. Clyde wasn't there."

"Maybe he was sick or out of town."

"Maybe, or maybe he was trying to avoid Donna. It's possible he was trying to avoid all three women, of course. If I could turn back the clock, I'd make a point of watching him with the three women on the day of Mabel's funeral."

Fenella glanced at the clock. "I should go," she sighed. "I'm taking the kittens to the home early tomorrow morning. I need a good night's sleep if I'm going to spend my morning chasing them around a nursing home."

"I'm going to do my best to remember more about Mabel's funeral.

Maybe I'll see what Max can remember. He was with me, of course, but he probably wasn't paying attention. He might know more about what happened to Stanley, though. He did business with Stanley's father. I'm sure they spoke fairly regularly."

"Great. I'll stop back sometime tomorrow, but I'm not sure when. I believe my morning is going to be rather busy."

Fenella let herself out of her apartment. After debating with herself for a minute, she knocked on Shelly's door.

"I won't stay long," she told Shelly, "but I'm busy tomorrow morning, so I won't get to stop to visit Katie until the afternoon."

Shelly laughed. "I'm taking good care of her, truly I am."

"I know you are, that's why I keep visiting. I don't want her to forget about me or decide she'd rather just stay here with you."

"Tim's here," Shelly told her as she shut the door behind Fenella.

"Oh, goodness, I'm sorry," Fenella gasped. "I won't stay."

"Don't be silly. We were just talking. He leaves tomorrow for London."

Feeling as if she'd interrupted something, Fenella followed Shelly into the living room.

"Hello," Tim said brightly. "Come to visit your little darling?"

Katie was curled up on his lap. When Fenella walked in, she opened one eye and then squeezed it shut again.

Fenella laughed. "Clearly, she's missing me terribly. I won't stay, not if that's the reception I'm going to get."

"Go and say hello to Fenella," Tim told the kitten. He picked her up and put her on the floor.

She looked around and then strolled slowly over to let Fenella give her a quick pat. Almost as soon as Fenella had touched her, Katie rushed back over to climb back into Tim's lap.

"She's mad at me for leaving," Fenella said. "Never mind. I shouldn't have bothered you tonight."

Smokey had been sleeping near the windows. Now she jumped up and ran over to Fenella, winding her body between Fenella's legs. "At least you're happy to see me," Fenella said. She crouched down and began to pet the older cat, chatting quietly to her as she did so.

"Meeroowww," Katie said in an injured tone. She jumped back off Tim's lap and ran to Fenella.

"Are you jealous of Smokey?" Fenella laughed, petting Katie with one hand while still rubbing Smokey's tummy with the other. Eventually both cats seemed to get bored and they raced off together into Shelly's second bedroom.

"Thank you," Fenella told Shelly. "I'll get out of the way now."

"You weren't in the way," Shelly replied firmly. "You're welcome to stay for a drink or even come with us to the pub, if you'd like."

"I wish I could, but I'd better get back to the kittens," Fenella told her. "I'll see you tomorrow afternoon."

She'd left the kittens outside the playpen when she'd gone out. When she arrived home, three of them were curled up on the rug near the door. The fourth was tucked up inside the playpen with the mother cat.

"How are you doing that?" Fenella demanded as she put the other kittens into the pen. She wasn't even sure if it was the same kitten getting in and out each time. What she needed was colored collars, a different color for each animal. Then she'd know if she had one escape artist or more.

All four kittens were still where they belonged the next morning. After everyone had had breakfast, Fenella packed up everything she thought they might want or need for the morning and put it all in the car. Then she went back for the kittens and their mother. Everyone seemed happy enough to climb into the carriers for their trip to the nursing home.

"Ah, you must be Fenella," a pretty blonde woman who looked around twenty-five said as Fenella walked into the nursing home with the two carriers a short while later.

"I am, yes," she agreed.

"I'm Crystal Hall. Do you need a hand with anything?"

"I have their litter tray, bowls for food and water, and food, of course. If I can leave the cats with you, I think I can manage everything myself."

"I'm happy to keep the cats," Crystal told her.

Fenella put the carriers on the counter Crystal was standing behind and went back out for everything else. When she came back inside, Crystal was holding the mother cat.

"She's going to need some careful handling, isn't she?" she asked Fenella.

"Yes, she just had surgery over the weekend."

"I know just the resident to take her to," Crystal said. "We have a lovely older woman who would love to fuss over her, I'm sure."

"The kittens have a lot more energy," Fenella said, nodding toward the carrier where what looked like dozens of tiny paws were poking in and out of the mesh door.

Crystal laughed. "We'll take them to the residents' lounge. They'll have room to run around and lots of laps to snuggle on if they want a rest."

Crystal carried the mother cat while Fenella followed with the carrier full of kittens. Another member of the staff helpfully brought the supplies along for them. After checking that all of the doors and windows were shut, Crystal had Fenella release the kittens. The smiles that crossed the residents' faces as the tiny balls of fur began dashing around the room made Fenella glad they'd come.

"Now, if you'd like to come with me, we can introduce the mother cat to Marilyn. I'm sure she'll love her," Crystal said after a few minutes.

Crystal led Fenella down a short corridor. She stopped and knocked on a closed door.

"I don't want breakfast," a voice shouted from inside the room.

"I don't have breakfast. I have a visitor for you."

"I don't want visitors, either," the voice snapped. "My relationship with God is just fine and I don't need a doctor today."

Crystal laughed. "How about cats? Do you need a cat today?"

"A cat? What are you on about?"

Crystal winked at Fenella and then pushed the door open. "I'm sure I told you about the new program we're starting," she said to the woman in the wheelchair near the window. "We know you all miss your pets, so we thought we'd try bringing in a few cats or dogs for you all to cuddle."

"I never had any pets," the woman replied.

"So I should take this poor dear back to the lounge?" Crystal asked, holding up the mother cat.

"She's ugly," the older woman said.

"She's had a hard life," Crystal told her. "She was found in a storage shed on the promenade. Mr. Stone had to do emergency surgery to keep her alive. He believes she had to fight off other cats or maybe something else to protect her kittens."

"She has kittens?"

"Four of them. They're currently trying to destroy the residents' lounge, but I thought things were a bit too crazy in there for the mother cat."

The woman in the chair looked at the cat and then nodded slowly. "She's still recovering from her surgery."

"She is indeed. I thought maybe you could cuddle her for a short while. I think she needs some extra love."

The woman frowned and then nodded slowly. "Maybe. If she behaves."

"This is Fenella Woods," Crystal replied. "She's been looking after the cat and the kittens since they were found. I'll leave her here with you and the mother cat, if she doesn't mind. She can take the cat away if necessary. Fenella, this is Marilyn Coleman. Would you mind sitting with her and the cat for a few minutes?"

Fenella shook her head. "Not at all."

Crystal handed the cat to Marilyn, who took it eagerly. Within seconds, the cat had curled up and was purring softly as Marilyn gently petted her.

"I'll be back in half an hour," Crystal told Fenella in a low voice. "I hope you truly don't mind."

She was gone before Fenella could reply.

"Sit," Marilyn told her. "I'd rather stand, but that's something that's been denied me for the last ten years or more. You don't appreciate some things until you lose them."

There was a single chair opposite Marilyn. Fenella sat down and glanced around the room. It was simply furnished with the single chair, a hospital bed, and a small wheeled table. It looked like a hospital room rather than someone's home.

"I was in a car accident," Marilyn told her. "At the time, I was relieved that my miserable life was finally going to be over. That was ten years ago and my doctors keep telling me that I'm strong enough to carry on for another ten years or more."

Fenella wasn't sure how to respond. "I can't imagine how difficult your life must be," she said finally.

"Difficult? I'm not sure that's the word I would use." Marilyn sighed and then looked around the room. "I had dreams once. Things haven't gone at all the way I'd imagined they would. My mother ruined my life, of course, but I let her do it, so it's my own fault."

A single tear slid down Marilyn's cheek. Fenella held out the box of tissues from the table. The silence that followed seemed to go on for hours before Fenella couldn't stand it any longer.

"I believe I met someone you know last night," she said eventually.

"Did you?"

"I'm taking a class in reading old records. Donna Cannon is taking the class as well."

Marilyn froze for a moment, looking stunned. "Donna?" she repeated in a whisper. "You met Donna last night?"

"Yes. She mentioned your name, you see. That's why I recognized it when Crystal introduced us."

"Donna mentioned my name? Why? We haven't spoken in a great many years."

"Someone else in the class mentioned seeing Donna's name in the local paper. It was all to do with the police reopening the investigation into Mabel Gross's murder."

Marilyn seemed to lose what little color she had in her cheeks as she stared at Fenella. "The police, they were here yesterday. When Crystal knocked, I was afraid it was them again."

"Afraid? They're simply trying to work out what happened to Mabel."

"Someone killed her," Marilyn said flatly. "They investigated when it happened and never managed to solve the case. There's no way they'll be able to solve it now, not after all these years."

"Aren't you happy that they're trying?"

"All they're doing is stirring up a lot of bad memories for me and for everyone else involved. I'm sorry that Mabel is dead, but she did manage to escape from the many and varied horrors of adulthood. Perhaps she was lucky for getting away at twenty-five."

"I'm sorry you've had such an unhappy life."

Marilyn shook her head. "I'm just an old and bitter woman. I married the first man who asked me, mostly to annoy my parents, although my father couldn't have cared less. My mother simply spent the rest of her life making me pay for my transgression."

Feeling as if she didn't want to hear the whole sad story from Marilyn herself, Fenella tried to change the subject. "Who do you think killed Mabel, then?" she asked.

Marilyn looked surprised and then began to chuckle. "It would be very clever of the police to send you here with a cat to try to trick me into a confession," she said. "If I'd killed Mabel, I might even be willing to confess now, after all these years."

"I wasn't trying to get a confession, and I'm not from the police. I was just curious what you thought."

"I think the police should concentrate their efforts on Clyde."

"Clyde? Mabel's brother?"

"Mabel was seeing someone, but she wouldn't tell anyone about him. Clyde always knew more about her than anyone else did. He's been keeping Mabel's secrets for fifty years. If anyone is going to solve this case, they're going to need to get Clyde to talk."

"I hope you told the police that when they questioned you yesterday."

"I may have," Marilyn shrugged. "You should go and talk to Clyde with your cat. Maybe she'll convince him to talk."

Before Fenella could reply, there was a quick tap on the door and then it swung open.

"How are we doing?" Crystal asked brightly.

"I'm feeling much better," Marilyn told her. "In fact, I think I'd quite like a visit to the lounge to see the kittens, if that's allowed."

"Of course it's allowed," Crystal told her. "I'll just get someone to take you down there."

"I was telling Fenella that she should take the mother cat down to see Clyde," Marilyn continued. "I thought he might like to meet her."

"That's an excellent idea," Crystal exclaimed. "I'm sure Clyde would appreciate a visitor."

When a woman in uniform walked in a short while later, Crystal asked her to take Marilyn to the lounge.

Marilyn handed the cat back to Fenella before she went. "You might tell Donna that I don't get many visitors," she said in a low voice. "After all these years, it might be nice to see her again."

Fenella nodded. "I'll tell her," she promised.

"And now, let's go and see if Clyde is up to company," Crystal said brightly as Marilyn was wheeled out of the room.

9

"Clyde is usually in the sunroom," Crystal told Fenella as they headed back down the corridor. "It's his favorite place to sit, even on rainy days like today. Most of the other residents only sit in there when it's sunny, so he's probably on his own today."

Fenella nodded. Having seen the noisy and fairly crowded lounge, she didn't blame Clyde for wanting to be somewhere on his own. She could even understand why Marilyn preferred to stay in her room.

"Clyde, there you are," Crystal said as she and Fenella walked into the small sunroom at the back of the building. Glass walls all the way around gave everyone an excellent view of the large parking lot behind the building. Beyond the parking lot, Fenella could see a busy road. There were large fields beyond the road, although Fenella was sure she could see a "For Sale" sign in at least one of them.

"Yes, here I am," the man sitting on the couch replied. "Were you looking for me?"

"We have special visitors today," Crystal told him. "Ms. Woods has brought her cat and kittens to play."

Clyde looked over at Fenella and then smiled tentatively at the cat. "I used to have cats," he said softly.

"Do you want a cuddle?" Crystal asked in a syrupy voice.

Clyde seemed to swallow his first reply. "Sure," he said eventually.

Fenella handed the cat to Clyde. The animal quickly settled into his lap and went to sleep.

"What's she called?" he asked her.

"I found her in a shed and I'm only looking after her temporarily," Fenella explained. "I haven't named her or the kittens."

Clyde frowned. "She needs a name," he said firmly. "How about Crystal?"

The girl laughed. "I'm not sure you should name her after me."

Clyde looked at Fenella and winked. "Why not? It's a good name."

Fenella shrugged. "You can call her whatever you like," she offered.

"She'll be Crystal to me, then," he said happily.

Crystal's smile didn't reach her eyes as she turned to Fenella. "I'll just leave you with Clyde for a bit, if that's okay?"

"That's fine."

Crystal nodded and then turned and walked quickly away. Clyde chuckled as she went.

"She doesn't like me," he said, "because she knows I don't like her."

"She seems nice enough," Fenella countered.

"Oh, she's nice enough. That's part of the problem. She's always nice and she never raises her voice. When my neighbor turns his telly all the way up to jet engine volume, she taps on his door and asks him ever so nicely to turn it down a tiny bit, please. When Mrs. Christian changes the channel on the telly in the residents' lounge right in the middle of someone else's program, Crystal very politely listens to everyone's point of view until we've all missed whatever it was we were trying to watch, anyway." He shook his head. "I never should have let my doctor talk me into moving in here. A nice community full of like-minded people, he told me. Ha."

"I'm sorry," Fenella said as she sat down in the chair next to him.

He shrugged. "The food is good," he conceded. "I never did learn to cook very well, so it's nice not to have to worry about meals. Otherwise, I tend to keep to myself. It's cold and damp back here most of the time, so no one else uses this room. That suits me. I have my books," he added, nodding toward a small pile of books on the table in front of him. "They take me to faraway places and help me forget about all of this."

"Books are so much better than television," Fenella said.

"And they're more reliable. You read a book and then, ten years later, you read it again and everything is the same. I was in the lounge the other day and a program I used to watch came on. All of the actors I remembered were old people now and the new characters they'd added were dreadful."

"I know what you mean."

Clyde scratched the cat under her chin and then looked back up at Fenella. "Why are you here?"

"I brought the cat and her kittens."

"Yes, of course. I wondered if there was something more to it, that's all. Everyone seems to want to talk to me at the moment. I've been living here for four years without a single visitor. You're my second visitor in two days."

"I read in the paper about your sister. I assume the other visitor was with the police?"

"Yes, Inspector Daniel Robinson, CID. He was awfully young, too, like all those new characters on that show. Maybe it's just because I'm so dreadfully old, though."

"You aren't that old," Fenella countered.

He shrugged. "I feel old, but then I've felt old since the day my sister died. Tragedies age people."

"I'm sorry for your loss."

He looked surprised and then leaned over and patted her arm. "Thank you, my dear. No one has said that to me in a great many years, even though I feel the loss just as much now as I ever did. I don't believe I've ever recovered from losing Mabel."

"I don't want to pry, but if you want to talk about her, I'm happy to listen."

"I haven't spoken about her in more years than I want to remember, well, not until yesterday. It was, well, odd and distressing to talk about her with the police again after all these years."

"I certainly don't want to distress you."

"Crystal here is helping a lot," he replied. "The police should bring cats along when they interrogate witnesses."

"I visited with Marilyn earlier."

"Marilyn?"

"Marilyn Coleman."

"Marilyn Coleman," Clyde repeated slowly. "I've done everything in my power to block that name from my memory."

"I didn't realize."

He shook his head. "I see her once in a while, being pushed through the corridors. I don't know if she knows I'm here."

"She was the one who suggested you might like to meet, um, Crystal," Fenella said, nodding toward the cat.

Clyde frowned. "Did she? I shall have to think about that for a moment."

He sat back and shut his eyes, leaving Fenella to stare out at the rain. Cars were rushing along the road, windshield wipers sweeping back and forth at high speeds. She was just thinking about saying something when Clyde suddenly shifted in his seat.

"She suggested you visit with the cat?" he checked.

"Yes, she said she thought you might like to meet her."

"I see."

A long silence seemed to stretch between them. Fenella could think of a dozen different questions to ask, but none of them seemed appropriate or polite. She was relieved when Clyde spoke again.

"How is Marilyn?" he asked.

"I gathered from what she said that she spends most of her time in her room. She was going down to the residents' lounge to see the kittens, though."

He nodded. "She'll like that. She was always the motherly type. Jeanne and Donna were like sisters to me, but Marilyn was always more like another mother. I should say she tried to be more like another mother, always telling me what to do and how to do it and getting angry with me when I'd have a few drinks or whatever."

"That must have been annoying when you were younger."

"A little annoying, but also somewhat sweet," he countered. "She only did it because she cared. The four of them had met in primary school, when I was just a tiny baby. They'd all known me for my entire life. That made them all think they were entitled to opinions on everything I did."

"But you lost touch with them after Mabel's death?"

Clyde frowned. "I don't want to talk about it," he said tightly.

"Of course not," Fenella said quickly. "As I said before, I don't want to upset you."

Another awkward silence descended. "I used to work with Ewan. I know they had children. Why doesn't she live with one of their children?"

"None of their children survived for very long," Fenella told him.

He frowned. "Ewan moved to another store, and I'll admit that I did my best to avoid him. Things were so awkward between all of us by that point that it seemed easier. Poor Marilyn. All she ever wanted was a small house and a handful of children. She was desperate to get away from her mother and be on her own."

"As I understand it, her mother moved in with the newlyweds during Marilyn's first pregnancy and never left."

"I should go and talk to her," Clyde sighed. "All this talk about Mabel has reminded me of so many things."

He fell silent again. Fenella counted cars, first the ones going in one direction and then the other. Eventually Clyde spoke again.

"You seem to know a lot about Mabel's death."

"There was an article about it in the local paper on Monday," Fenella explained, "and I met Donna Cannon on Monday night."

An unreadable expression settled on Clyde's face. "Donna Cannon," he repeated slowly. "Tell me what she's been doing for the last fifty years, then. No doubt she married well and had a few children of her own."

"Actually, she never married. She said something about never finding much use for men. She became the first female vice president at one of the local banks, but she's retired now."

"Is she living here, too, somewhere?" he demanded.

"No, she still lives in the same house where she grew up."

"My goodness, I can't imagine," he exclaimed. "It would almost be worth going to visit her, just to see that old house again. I hope she

hasn't modernized it, although she probably has, after all this time."
He stared out the window, clearly not seeing the view in front of him.
"How many hours did I spend in that house, playing board games with
Mabel and her friends?" he asked.

"She told me she hasn't seen you in a great many years."

"We had a stupid argument at Mabel's funeral about something
insignificant," he told her. "I don't even properly remember what we
fought about, but it got heated. We were both upset about Mabel and
we took it out on each other, of course, but I didn't see it that way at
the time. Anyway, by the end of the day we weren't speaking to one
another, and over the years we were both too bloody stubborn to make
amends."

"You don't remember what you fought about?"

Clyde glanced at her and then looked down at the ground. "It was
fifty years ago. I'm seventy-two now. I don't remember much of
anything, really."

Fenella was certain he was lying, but she didn't argue. "Did you
fight with Jeanne and Marilyn then, too?"

"No, I never really fought with Jeanne or Marilyn. They knew that
Donna and I weren't speaking and, well, they both took her side,
which was to be expected, really. It was just easier to cut them all out
of my life than to try to resolve things, I suppose."

"How terribly sad."

Clyde looked at her and then nodded solemnly. "Looking back now,
it was terribly sad. At the time it felt temporary. I always assumed
Donna and I would cross paths at some point and everything would
simply resolve itself. It took me a while to realize that she was avoiding
me, but once I knew that, I did my best to avoid her, too. It's a small
island, but somehow we've managed to stay apart for fifty years."

"You live in the same building as Marilyn and you've managed to
avoid her," Fenella pointed out.

Clyde laughed. "I'm rather good at it now, I suppose. I've had many
years to practice."

"Maybe it's time to think about resolving things," Fenella
suggested.

Clyde shook his head. "I don't think so."

"You don't even remember what the fight was about."

"But it was important."

"It was important when you were twenty-one. Maybe it isn't so important now."

"I can't," he said softly. "I might be willing to talk to Marilyn, but I'm sure everything I said to her would get straight back to Donna."

"Donna told me she hasn't spoken to Marilyn in over ten years."

Clyde's jaw dropped. "I don't believe it," he said after a moment. "The three of them were like sisters. I can't believe they don't speak every day."

"According to Donna, they drifted apart. She doesn't talk to Jeanne anymore either. Jeanne got married and had several children in quick succession. I gather Donna didn't believe they still had anything in common after that."

He shook his head. "I can't quite get my head around all of this. Mabel would be so sad if she were still alive. I'm sure she expected them all to be friends forever."

"Perhaps they would have been if Mabel were still here."

"That's very true. Mabel was the one that they all revolved around, and I'm not just saying that because she was my sister. She was incredibly special and everyone who knew her loved her. She kept the little group together, and no doubt she would have continued to do so until now if she'd survived."

"As it is, I don't think any of the women still speak to one another regularly."

"Marilyn lost touch with Jeanne, too?"

"I believe so. She didn't actually say as much, but I got the impression that they haven't stayed in touch." As the words left her mouth, Fenella was sorry she hadn't specifically asked Marilyn about Jeanne.

"The police didn't tell me any of this."

"It isn't their job to tell people things."

Clyde nodded. "I suppose that's right. Inspector Robinson just asked questions, lots and lots of questions. I kept apologizing for not remembering things better. As I said, it was fifty years ago."

"Who do you think killed your sister?" Fenella asked.

If he was surprised by the question, he hid it well. "I think about that every single day. It's my first waking thought and the last thing to go through my head before I fall asleep. I wish I could help the police solve the case, but it's been such a long time..." he trailed off and then shrugged. "I'm not sure what the police hope to gain by reopening the case, really. We've all forgotten anything we might have known that could have helped."

"Sometimes people are more willing to talk many years later," Fenella suggested. "Maybe something they saw or heard has been nagging at them for years, but they've never felt as if they should mention it to the police before. I'm pretty sure the inspector is hoping for something like that, a tiny something that will break the case."

"A tiny something?" he repeated. "It seems a lot of fuss and bother for the man to go through just on the off chance that someone remembers something that seemed insignificant at the time."

"Maybe it didn't seem insignificant," Fenella replied. "Maybe someone will remember something that seemed important at the time, something that they felt they couldn't talk to the police about during the initial investigation. Maybe they heard something that implicated someone they loved or saw something that pointed to someone they had reason to fear. Fifty years later, maybe that person is dead or tucked away in a nursing home, leaving the witness free to talk."

Clyde chuckled. "So you think Donna is going to tell the police that I killed my sister?" he challenged. "It sounded like that, anyway."

"I didn't mean to suggest that at all. Inspector Robinson will be talking to everyone involved in the case. Goodness only knows what he might learn."

"I'm sure Donna will be happy to say horrible things about me. As I said, we had a disagreement. I'm sure she's spent fifty years blaming me for everything."

"Do you blame her?"

"I'm more inclined to blame the circumstances," he told her. "It was a very difficult time for all of us. I'm prepared to concede that I was too easy to anger and too slow to forgive. I doubt Donna would make the same concessions."

"If she's willing to do so, would you like to speak to her?"

Clyde blinked several times and then held up a hand. "Not so fast," he said. "I never said anything about speaking with her."

"It was just a suggestion. You, Marilyn, and Donna all seem sad about the situation. Maybe you should try to reconcile."

"I don't want to talk about this any longer," he told her. "I think you should go now."

"I didn't mean to upset you."

"Talking about Mabel is always difficult. I shouldn't have engaged with you at all."

"We can talk about something else," Fenella suggested. "Do you think the rain will stop soon?"

"It was raining that night, the night Mabel died. It was raining and far too cold for June."

Fenella patted Clyde's arm. "I think we should talk about something else," she said gently.

"I never talk about Mabel. I ended all of my friendships with all of her friends. I couldn't talk about her. I didn't want to think about her." Tears were streaming down his face, and Fenella felt horrible as she tried to find a tissue in her bag.

"I'm sorry," she said as she handed him a crumpled tissue.

He wiped his eyes and then sat back and patted the cat slowly. "What really brought you here today?" he asked in a low voice.

"I came with the cat and her kittens because Mr. Stone, the veterinarian, asked me to visit. I didn't know you were here, and I didn't know Marilyn was here, either."

He nodded slowly. "I hope you're telling the truth. I'd hate to think that the police are sending in cats to help with interrogations."

"I hope you don't think I interrogated you."

"Perhaps that was a poor choice of words. It was a difficult conversation, though, and not one that I enjoyed."

"I am sorry."

"I have enjoyed spending time with Crystal, though. Perhaps it was worth it."

Fenella smiled tentatively. "I hope, on balance, it hasn't been too awful. I truly never meant to upset you in any way."

"The police inspector yesterday, he was less kind. He asked all manner of questions and didn't seem to believe my answers. At least you've pretended to believe what I've told you."

"I'm just making conversation. It's Inspector Robinson's job to solve your sister's murder."

"He's wasting his time, and you can tell him I said so. No one is ever going to work out what actually happened to Mabel."

"I hope you're wrong. I think she deserves justice."

"You may think what you like."

"You don't agree?"

"When is Crystal coming back? I've had quite enough of you and your cat for today." He stood up abruptly with the cat in his arms. He handed her to Fenella and then grabbed a cane that had been leaning against the couch. She sat and watched as he slowly limped out of the room.

"I hope you didn't have any issues with Mr. Gross," Crystal said a moment later as she rushed into the room. "He can be difficult some-times, but he's usually a lovely man."

"I'm afraid I upset him. We started talking about his sister and the police investigation, and he got agitated."

"He was in a terrible state yesterday by the time the police left," Crystal told her. "I believe he and his sister were very close. I'm not certain that he's ever recovered from losing her."

Fenella followed Crystal back through the building to the large lounge where she'd left the kittens. It felt as if many hours had passed, but it had actually been less than ninety minutes since her arrival.

"The kittens have been a huge hit," Crystal told her. "We'd love to have them back again next week."

"Sure, I can do that," Fenella agreed.

"Are you, by any chance, free tomorrow?" Crystal asked. "We have another care home elsewhere in Douglas. I'm working there tomorrow and I think the kittens would be just as popular there as they have been here."

"Tomorrow? Why not?"

"It's less of a medical environment at that home, and the residents there are allowed to keep their own pets if they choose to do so. Maybe you'll find new owners for the kittens there."

"I'd like to find a new owner for the mother cat, too."

Crystal looked at the animal in Fenella's arms and shrugged. "She might be harder to, um, sell."

"She's a bit beat-up looking, but she's a lovely animal."

"Yes, well, I'll do what I can to help. The address is on my card. I'll see you there around nine, if that works for you."

"Nine will work for me."

The residents had great fun watching Fenella and Crystal trying to round up the kittens. More than one "accidentally" let a kitten hide under the blankets on their laps or inside their sweaters or shirts. After five minutes, Fenella had three kittens safely tucked up in their carrier. The mother cat was happy inside hers, which meant there was just one kitten left to find.

"Just leave the last one here," one of the residents suggested as Fenella dug out a box of kitty treats.

"He or she isn't old enough to leave the mother cat yet," Fenella said. "They haven't finished weaning yet."

One of the older women sighed deeply. "I'd better let him go, then," she said. She lifted up the blanket on her lap to reveal the missing kitten. The animal sat up and blinked and then snuggled back down on the woman's lap.

"Come on," Fenella said. "It's time to go home."

The kitten made a token protest as Fenella moved it into the crate with the others. Crystal thanked her again as she headed for the door, a carrier in each hand. Another member of the staff followed with the animals' supplies. Fenella put everything into her car and then slid behind the wheel.

"Thank you," the woman from the home said. "That's the brightest I've seen some of our patients in weeks. I hope you'll visit again."

"Crystal already asked me to come back next week. The animals are all available for adoption, too, if the facility would like to consider keeping a few of them permanently."

"I wish I could have one, but my son is allergic. Having them here would be the next best thing. I'm going to have a word with the managers. Maybe they would consider adopting one or two of the kittens."

Fenella drove off with her fingers metaphorically crossed. The kittens appeared to have enjoyed their time at the home, and it seemed the perfect place for them to go once they were ready to leave their mother. Back at Poppy Drive, she unloaded the animals and their things and then let the kittens loose.

"Do you want to come out and have a wander around?" she asked the mother cat.

The animal replied by going and standing next to her pen and shouting loudly. Fenella took the hint and put the cat inside the pen. She made sure everyone had food and water before she headed for the door.

"Good morning," Daniel called as she made her way toward her car. "Or is it afternoon already? I have a split shift today, so I came home for lunch."

"It's not quite afternoon," Fenella told him. "I was going to call you later, though. I bumped into two of your witnesses today."

Daniel's smile looked resigned. "Of course you did. Tell me more."

Fenella quickly explained about Mr. Stone's request and her trip to the nursing home. She did her best to repeat everything that Marilyn and Clyde had told her before mentioning that she was due to visit another home the next day. "I don't know if any of the other witnesses live there, but if they do, I'll probably see them. That's usually how my luck runs."

"It's uncanny," Daniel said with a sigh. "They both told you things that they didn't tell me, as well."

"Clyde was hiding things."

"He refused to answer some of my questions and was evasive on others. I'm planning to talk to him again after I've spoken to everyone else."

"I couldn't help but feel as if he holds the key to the whole thing."

"That would be nice, but it seems unlikely. His sister was murdered. If he knew who'd killed her, why would he have kept quiet for all these years?"

"Maybe he killed her," Fenella suggested.

"He's certainly on the short list."

"He didn't seem guilty to me, at least not guilty of murder," Fenella said, contradicting herself. "It just felt as if he had secrets."

"He wouldn't tell you why he fought with Donna?"

"At first he said he didn't really remember. Later in the conversation he said something about deliberately cutting his ties with all of Mabel's friends because it was too painful to remember her, or something like that."

Daniel nodded. "Thank you for telling me about the conversations. If you do meet anyone else tomorrow, you know I want to hear about it."

"Yes, I know."

Fenella climbed into her car and drove back to her apartment building. Shelly wasn't home when she knocked, so she let herself into her own apartment and then headed for the kitchen.

"How was your morning?" Mona asked as Fenella searched through the cupboards, trying to find something to make for her lunch.

"It was interesting," Fenella replied as she gave up and dug a frozen meal out of her freezer. Once it was cooking in the microwave, Fenella gave Mona a full accounting of her conversations with Marilyn and Clyde.

"It does sound as if Clyde knows something," Mona agreed when Fenella was finished. "I find it odd and sad that none of them are still speaking."

"I don't think it's as dramatic as that. Donna just said that they'd drifted apart."

"Except for her and Clyde," Mona reminded her. "I wish I knew what they'd fought about. It may have nothing to do with the case, but I still want to know."

"If I meet any of the others, I'll make getting an answer to that question a priority."

"I'd rather know who killed Mabel, of course. It's interesting that Marilyn told you to talk to Clyde. If she and the others all think that he killed Mabel, that would explain why they fought."

"Surely, if they really thought he'd done it, they would have gone to the police, not simply stopped speaking to him."

"And Marilyn is still insisting that Mabel was seeing someone."

"Yes, that may be what she thinks Clyde is hiding."

"If she's right, then the man in question must have been married or otherwise unacceptable," Mona said thoughtfully.

"That's an interesting thought. Maybe Daniel should take a closer look at Howard Quinn."

"Unless Mabel was involved with a woman," Mona added. "I'm sure Clyde would do everything in his power to hide that fact from the rest of the world."

"I can see that fifty years ago, but surely it doesn't matter as much now. If he was keeping that a secret and his doing so was letting someone get away with murder, surely he'd be willing to talk now."

Mona shrugged. "Whatever the rest of the world thinks, if Clyde still finds the idea unacceptable, he may be keeping his mouth shut."

"Do you really think Mabel was involved with another woman?"

"No, not really. That was just an example of something that I think that Clyde would hide from the police, that's all. I can see Mabel getting involved with a married man, though. Many women do, after all."

Fenella nodded, wondering how many married men her aunt had been involved with over the years. Mona's reputation suggested that she'd had an enormous number of relationships, but the more Fenella got to know the woman the more she came to realize that Mona's reputation was largely fabricated. Max had never married, and Fenella was starting to think that he was the only man with whom Mona had ever actually been involved.

"Did Max remember anything?" she asked.

Mona shrugged. "I haven't asked him yet. He gets confused and upset sometimes when we talk about the past. I may try to speak to him tonight. We'll see."

Fenella ate her lunch in front of mindless television and then spent a few minutes tidying up the apartment. She was just about to go back over to see if Shelly had returned yet when the phone rang.

✣ 10 ✣

"Fenella, darling, how are you?" Donald's voice came down the line.

"I'm fine. How are you?"

"I'm better, because I'm ringing from London. After much fuss and far too much bother, Phoebe and I are safely back on British soil."

"That's good news."

"There's a part of me that feels rather guilty about it all, because Phoebe loved her life in the US, but I needed to get back on the correct side of the pond, as it were."

"How is Phoebe?"

"She's, well, she's adjusting. The journey was very difficult for her, but she's always hated flying, even though she loved to travel. We flew over with a doctor, two nurses, and two aides, and between them all they were able to keep Phoebe calm on the flight, anyway. She's going to need a few days to adjust to the time difference and recover from her jet lag before we resume her therapies."

"How was the journey for you?"

"Long and incredibly tedious, but that's how flying should be. I don't want an exciting flight, I just want to arrive safely at my destination."

"Do you think you'll be able to move back to the island at some point?"

"It's far too soon to answer that question. I mean, I fully intend to come back one day, but I'm not sure whether Phoebe will be able to join me. In an ideal world, she'll recover completely, but then she won't want to join me. At the moment, we're taking one day at a time."

"I can't imagine how difficult this must be for you."

"I'm doing okay," he told her. "Tell me what you've been doing lately."

Fenella made him laugh as she told him about Winston's crazy barking and the totally unnecessary police presence at the storage shed. "And now I'm looking after an injured mother cat and four kittens," she said. "That's keeping me busy, I must say."

"It also suggests that this wouldn't be a good time for you to fly over to London for a few days," Donald sighed.

"It really isn't," Fenella said apologetically. "Shelly can look after Katie for me, but I can't saddle her with Katie and five other animals, not all at the same time."

"No, I don't suppose you can, unfortunately."

"You can't pop over here for a few days?"

"Not at the moment. I can't leave Phoebe until I'm sure she's stable and settled here. That won't be a quick or an easy process."

"At least we're back in the same time zone," Fenella said.

Donald chuckled. "I suppose that's something. You have my mobile number. Ring me once the kittens are sorted out and let me know. I'd really love to see you."

"I'd like to see you, too," Fenella replied, wondering if she was being totally honest with him. She'd enjoyed spending time with him, but while he'd been away, she hadn't really missed having him complicating her life. Maybe it would be better for both of them if she ended things now.

"I'll ring you again soon," Donald said, interrupting her thoughts. "Take care." He disconnected before she could reply.

Fenella put the phone down and frowned at it. "Maybe I should just let the machine pick up every call," she said. "I feel as if I'd rather avoid nearly everyone at the moment, anyway."

The words were hardly out of her mouth when the phone rang again. Frowning, Fenella answered it almost instinctively.

"Maggie, my darling, how are you?"

"I'm fine, Jack," Fenella replied, feeling the familiar touch of annoyance with the man that seemed to surface whenever he called. Now that he'd been to visit, though, surely conversations between them would go better.

"I just realized this morning that I never called you to let you know that I was home safely."

"That's right, you didn't," Fenella agreed, feeling slightly guilty that she hadn't really given the matter much thought.

"I did think that you could have rung me to check," Jack said, sounding hurt.

"I wanted to give you time to recover from your jet lag before I called. Anyway, I wasn't sure of your teaching schedule this semester. Calling and talking to your answering machine wouldn't have made me any less worried, would it?"

"So you were going to call me soon?"

"I would have called you over the weekend if you hadn't called," Fenella said. Maybe, she added to herself.

"My flight back to Buffalo was delayed twice."

"Yes, I know. I did watch the airport websites to make sure you were making good progress. From what I could see, it looked as if you landed in Buffalo about three hours late."

"Yes, that's about right. The whole experience was nearly enough to put me off the idea of traveling again."

"I'm sure it was unpleasant, but think of all the fun you had on the island."

"Yes, I keep reminding myself of what a wonderful adventure it all was, in spite of the murder and the delayed flight."

Fenella smiled at the way Jack lumped the two things together as if they were of similar importance. "At least you're home safe and sound."

"I am, and that's why I'm calling, actually. I did think that you might call to make sure that I was home safely one of these days. As I'm not going to be home for a short while, I thought I would let you know so that you wouldn't worry."

"What do you mean?"

"I'm taking another trip."

"You are? That's great," Fenella said, feeling surprised. "Where are you going?"

"Las Vegas."

"Las Vegas," Fenella echoed.

"It's in Nevada."

"Yes, I know where Las Vegas is. We even talked about it when you were here. You said there was a job there that you thought you might be interested in pursuing."

"Yes, well, do you remember the one night in your apartment when I borrowed your computer so that I could check my emails?"

"Yes."

"While I was checking them, I happened to look at the job website again and this little voice in my head told me that I should apply. I sent off my application without really thinking about what I was doing."

"A voice in your head," Fenella repeated, looking around for Mona.

"It's just a figure of speech," Jack said. "Anyway, when I arrived home I discovered that the university had replied and invited me for an interview. They're paying for me to fly to Las Vegas and stay for five days. At first, I wasn't sure I should go, but then I decided that it's really like a free vacation, isn't it? I'll have to spend some time at the university, meeting people and talking about the job, but they've promised me at least two free days to see Las Vegas."

"I'm sure that will be interesting," Fenella said.

"They've reserved me a room at one of the biggest hotels right in the middle of everything. It all sounds very exciting and not at all the sort of thing I do."

Fenella laughed. "Not the sort of thing you used to do, but your visit to the island changed you. You're much more adventurous now."

"I don't know about that, really. When I was there, I felt as if I should be traveling and seeing the world and now that I'm home, I'm not sure why I felt that way."

"Vegas will be a great adventure. I hope you don't stop there, either."

"Have you ever been to Las Vegas?"

"No. You'll have to tell me all about it."

"I was rather hoping you might like to join me."

"Join you? No," Fenella replied firmly.

Jack sighed. "I didn't think you'd actually agree, but I thought it was worth asking. We had fun seeing the sights on the island together. I think we'd have fun seeing Las Vegas together, too."

And if you would have asked me five years ago, when we were a couple and I was always begging you to take a trip somewhere, I would have gone in a heartbeat, Fenella thought. "I'm still looking after those kittens and their mother," she said. "I can't get away, even if I wanted to join you." Which I don't, she added silently.

"Right, well, okay then. I'll call you next week and tell you all about the trip. Maybe you'll want to come along on my next one."

"What else are you planning?"

"Nothing specific at the moment, but I did apply for more than a dozen different positions when I was on the island. I may have more interviews in the near future."

"Are you that unhappy in Buffalo?"

"Not unhappy, really, just willing to consider making a change. I don't think the position in Las Vegas is going to be for me, but I might be surprised."

"You might," Fenella muttered.

"Anyway, I'll call you when I get back and tell you all about everything. Do take care of yourself in the interim."

Jack hung up before Fenella could reply. She slowly put down the phone. What had Mona done to the man? No matter how hard she tried, she couldn't imagine Jack in Vegas. At least he seemed to have given up on wanting to get back together with her. Feeling weirdly sad, she headed for the door, hoping for a cuddle with Katie.

"He's going to Vegas," she told the kitten a few minutes later. "I can't imagine how he'll cope with the crowds and the casinos and everything."

"He'll be fine. He's very smart, after all. Maybe he'll fall in love with Vegas and decide to stay there forever," Shelly said.

"Maybe I'll stop answering the phone when he calls," Fenella replied.

Shelly chuckled. "That's what I've been doing with Gordon, so I can't even say anything."

"How is Gordon?"

"I have no idea. He was traveling nearly all the time before the holidays. He's rung me a few times now that he's back on the island, but I've genuinely missed every one of his calls."

Gordon Davison had been friends with Shelly and her husband for many years. He was a widower, and after Shelly's husband died, the pair had begun spending time with one another. While Shelly had enjoyed Gordon's company a great deal, she'd never felt as if she'd known where their relationship was going. Tim had come into her life while Gordon had been off the island for work and it had now been a few months since Shelly had seen Gordon.

"You should call him back and tell him about Tim," Fenella suggested.

"I can't do that," Shelly said, blushing. "Gordon and I were only ever friends. I can't ring him and tell him that I'm involved with someone else. It would be, well, odd."

"So you're just going to ignore him when he calls you?"

"He never asks me to ring him back. He always just says hello and that he's been thinking of me, and then says that he'll try to reach me again another time."

"How often did you call him when you were dating?"

"We weren't dating, we were just having meals together occasionally, and I never rang him, not once."

"In that case, I suppose I can understand you not wanting to call him now. Does Tim know about Gordon?"

"Yes, we had a long talk one day about all of our former relationships. His love life has been much more, um, colorful than mine, but we talked about everything, really. I told him all about Gordon and how I never really knew where I stood with him. Tim makes things a lot clearer for me."

"That's good. I just hope you're happy."

Shelly blushed and then nodded. "He makes me very happy, really. I can't quite believe how well things are going. I'm sure we're going to have a big fight about something one day soon."

"Did you and John fight a lot?"

Shelly looked surprised and then laughed. "John and I never fought. Oh, we had minor disagreements about things, but we never truly fought. We worked hard on communicating successfully, and I suppose it worked well for us. Tim and I seem to be doing okay on that front as well. Maybe I should stop expecting us to fight."

"I hope you keep getting along and stay happy," Fenella told her. "Now I need to get back to my other house and see how my kittens are doing."

"When does the mother cat go back to see Mr. Stone?"

"Actually, they all have an appointment this afternoon," Fenella exclaimed. "It's a good thing you mentioned it. I nearly forgot."

The kittens were less than excited about going back into their carrier when Fenella returned to the house.

"Come on," she coaxed one who was hiding behind the sofa. "We're going go see your friend, Mr. Stone. It will be fun."

The kitten seemed to consider her words and then wiggled backward into the corner. There was no way for Fenella to reach the animal without moving furniture. She sighed and then got up and headed to the kitchen. Waving the bag of kitten treats, she was soon surrounded by kittens.

"Here we go again," she muttered to herself as she loaded everything back into the car.

"Ah, Fenella, how are my favorite cats?" Mr. Stone asked when she was escorted into his office a short while later.

"You tell me," she suggested as she unlatched the door to the first container. The mother cat climbed out carefully and then stood quietly while Mr. Stone examined her.

"She's doing very well," he said happily. "Have you been keeping her and the kittens apart during the day?"

"She has her own playpen and she really seems to like it in there. The kittens run around the house while she stays tucked up in her pen."

"You can let her run around too now, if that's what she wants. Tucking them all up together at night isn't a bad idea, though." He put the mother cat back in her carrier and then opened the second one. Kittens suddenly seemed to be everywhere.

Fenella managed to grab two of them and Mr. Stone finally caught the other two. It only took him a few minutes to check each one over and then slip it back into the carrier.

"They all appear to be in excellent condition. They should be ready to leave their mother in another week. Crystal has already rung me to tell me that things went well at the care home today. They're seriously considering taking one or two of the kittens."

"That's great news. I'm visiting another home with her tomorrow. Maybe that one will take the other two. I'm afraid finding a home for the mother cat might be more difficult."

"I'm sure we'll find something, but if we haven't by this time next week, she can come and stay here once the kittens are all placed. I'm sure my office staff would love to have a temporary office cat."

"I wonder if they'd take her at the Tale and Tail," Fenella said.

"That's always a possibility. You said she didn't get along with Katie, though. Cats that go there need to get along with other cats."

Fenella nodded. The Tale and Tail was a pub that was only a few steps away from her apartment building. It had once been the library of a mansion, but the mansion had been sold and turned into a luxury hotel. The new owners had added a large bar to the middle of the library and opened it as a pub. Books still lined all of the walls and were available to be borrowed. A number of cats also called the pub home, and the room was dotted with cat beds. All of the feline residents had been rescued animals, and Fenella was pretty sure that the mother cat would fit right in, given the opportunity.

"Good luck tomorrow. I hope they'll take the kittens, anyway," Mr. Stone said as Fenella gathered up her charges.

"Thanks," she replied. She stopped to pay the receptionist.

"Oh, there's no charge for today," the girl told her. "Mr. Stone has a note here that the animals were rescued and all of their treatment is on him until they get a permanent home."

Fenella thought about objecting. She could certainly afford to pay for the animals' care, but there seemed little point in arguing with the receptionist. She would take it up with Mr. Stone another time.

Back at home, she let the cats out and then did some cleaning. There seemed to be cat hair everywhere in the house, even upstairs, where the cats weren't allowed. By the time she'd finished with the cleaning, it was time for dinner. She'd left the mother cat outside her pen when they'd come home, but now the animal was clearly ready for a rest. Three of the kittens were quick to demand to join their mother. That left one kitten racing around the house causing trouble while Fenella ate.

❀ After dinner, she spent several minutes trying to find the last kitten, but he or she seemed to have disappeared completely. It was too early for her to think about bed, anyway, so she curled up in front of the television. An hour later the kitten jumped into her arms and snuggled down on her lap. After a second hour spent watching something she didn't enjoy but couldn't change because she couldn't reach the remote without disturbing the kitten, Fenella had had enough. She scooped up the sleeping animal and placed it gently next to its mother. Upstairs, she washed her face and climbed into bed.

"Here we are," Mr. Stone said brightly. "One mother cat and six kittens. I knew you wouldn't mind." He handed her the carrier. "Have fun."

"But I don't want any more animals," Fenella protested as the man walked briskly away. She took the carrier into the house and slowly opened the door. Six kittens burst out and began to chase the original four around the living room. The mother cat leapt out and began to shout loudly at Fenella, the other mother cat, and the kittens. In the middle of the chaos, the doorbell rang.

"Just three kittens this time," Mr. Stone said happily, handing Fenella an open cardboard box. He was gone before she could reply.

When she put the box on the living room floor, the kittens were already scrambling out. The mother cat jumped out and hissed angrily at the other adult cats. When the doorbell rang again, Fenella didn't want to answer it.

"Three kittens, a mother cat, and the father," Mr. Stone told her as he passed her another box.

Fenella shook her head as she tried to balance the box. "I don't have room for any more cats."

"Oh, and this is just one cat," he added, pointing to the carrier by his feet. "But she's heavily pregnant. I reckon there must be at least five or six kittens in there, but we won't find out for another week or so, I expect."

"I can't, that is, I don't have room," Fenella began. Mr. Stone seemed to disappear in front of her eyes. One of the cats in the box she was holding began to lick her cheek.

"Oh, stop that," she said. "I love you all and I'd love to be able to keep you, but I simply can't. You're going to have to go to good homes."

The kitten made a noise and then began to lick her face again. Fenella shifted the box and then tried to push the kitten away. It grabbed onto her finger with its paws and then nipped at her.

"Ouch," she exclaimed, sitting up in bed. The kitten who was sitting on the second pillow gave her an innocent-sounding "mew" and then dashed away.

Fenella checked her finger, but the animal hadn't done any damage. "How did that kitten get up here?" she demanded loudly. The words seemed to echo around her in the empty house. She'd lived alone for many years and it had never bothered her, but now she felt unsettled. It was just after midnight and she suddenly missed her apartment, which was safely surrounded by other apartments. She also missed the security guards who monitored the building's entrances.

Knowing she'd never sleep until she'd checked, Fenella went down the stairs. Four kittens were huddled together in one corner of the playpen while their mother was sprawled across the middle of the pen. She counted the kittens three times and then shrugged. Maybe she'd only dreamt that one had been in her bedroom, she told herself.

Falling back to sleep proved almost impossible. The sun was starting to come up when Fenella finally dozed off. Her alarm woke her at eight.

You have to get up, she reminded herself as she fumbled for the clock. You're visiting another nursing home. Maybe you'll be able to offload a few kittens there.

After getting breakfast for everyone and drinking her first cup of coffee, she took a shower and got dressed. It wasn't long before it was time to round up all of the animals for the day's adventure.

"We're going to visit more lovely people," she explained as she tucked the kittens into their carrier. "Some of them may even want to keep some of you and that would be very good news indeed."

It didn't take her long to drive to the other home. Crystal was waiting for her in the building's foyer.

"We have a rather different mix of residents here," she told Fenella as she helped her carry the animals inside. "We have married couples as well as younger residents at this facility. Anyone over the age of fifty-five can apply to live in the community, which includes the terraced flats that you'll have driven past on your way here. The residents who live within the main building tend to be those who prefer to be part of the community more, but we have very few residents who spend all day every day in the residents' lounge here, unlike the facility you visited yesterday."

Fenella nodded. "I hope there are enough people here today to enjoy the kittens."

"Oh, there are always some people in there, and we did let everyone know about the visit, so there will probably be more than normal."

Crystal pushed open a door and led Fenella into a large, bright room. There were couches and chairs arranged in several different groupings throughout the room. About a dozen people looked up and Fenella tried to smile at everyone at the same time.

"This is Fenella," Crystal announced. "She's been looking after that stray cat and her kittens since they were found on the promenade."

A few people actually clapped, which made Fenella blush. She put the carrier she was holding on the nearest table and opened it. The mother cat walked out and then looked around the room. After a moment, she jumped off the table and headed straight for a couple in the corner. Fenella was temped to follow her, but Crystal chose that moment to open the other carrier. Kittens leapt out and scattered around the room.

"They're very energetic," Crystal said.

"They've been in the carrier for too long," Fenella told her. "They'll soon settle." She crossed her fingers and hoped that she was right. Ten minutes later, the kittens were climbing all over the residents and everyone seemed happy with that. Fenella suddenly remembered the mother cat.

"I hope she isn't bothering you," she said to the woman who was stroking the cat's back as the cat stretched out across her knees.

"Not at all," the woman assured her. "I'd love a cat."

"No," the man sitting next to her said gruffly.

The woman frowned. "We can talk about it later," she said.

"No," he told her.

Fenella didn't want to get in the middle of an argument. "I'll leave her with you for a while, then," she said, backing away slowly.

"I'm Patricia," the woman said brightly. "Sit down and chat with me for a minute."

Fenella glanced around the room and couldn't find an obvious excuse to use to make her escape. She sat on the edge of one of the chairs and then studied the woman across from her.

Patricia had to be eighty, judging by her appearance. Her hair was white and the hands that stroked the cat seemed to be crippled by arthritis. The man next to her on the couch appeared to be of a similar age. He was bald, with a grey moustache. It would be too much of a coincidence if they turned out to be Howard and Patricia Quinn, Fenella told herself.

"You didn't tell us your name," Patricia said.

"That loud woman who runs everything told us her name," the man interjected. "She's Fenella Woods."

Fenella frowned. As far as she could recall, Crystal had only given them her first name. "And you are?" she asked.

"Howard Quinn. Patricia and I have been married for fifty-four years."

"The best fifty-four years of my life," Patricia added, patting Howard's arm.

"How lovely for you both," Fenella said.

Howard shrugged. "In our day you didn't get divorced if things didn't work out. You stayed together and kept your mouth shut."

"Of course, we never had that problem," Patricia hastily interjected.

Howard shrugged and then fell silent.

"My only regret is that we never had children," Patricia told Fenella. "I prayed for them every single day from the day we were married until the day my doctor told me I'd grown too old to conceive. If I could change anything in my life, I would have liked a son for Howard and a daughter for me."

Fenella nodded. What she really wanted to do was ask the couple about Mabel Gross, but there didn't seem to be any way to bring her into the conversation.

"How many times have you been married?" Howard asked abruptly.

"Oh, I've never been married," Fenella blurted out.

Patricia frowned. "I hope you aren't living in sin with a man," she said sternly.

"I live alone," Fenella told her. "I always have."

Patricia's frown deepened. "What about your parents?"

"Sadly, they both passed away when I was in my forties," she explained. "I was a rather late surprise for them."

"Don't you have a brother or a married sister with whom you could live?" Patricia asked.

Fenella counted to ten before she replied. "I have four brothers, but none of them want me to live with them," she said. She knew that any of them, even James, would take her in in an emergency, but she couldn't imagine that any of them actually wanted her to move into their homes. She had no interest in living with any of them, anyway. She was quite happy on her own.

"You need to be careful, living on your own," Patricia told her. "Bad things happen to women when they live alone."

"I'm quite capable of looking after myself," Fenella said firmly.

Patricia glanced around the room and then leaned forward. "We once rented out our home to a young woman. She was murdered in her bed."

"I told you not to bring that up," Howard snapped. "It isn't something we should talk about."

"I was just trying to warn the nice woman," Patricia told him. "She doesn't seem to realize the danger of what she's doing. The island feels lovely and safe, but bad things happen here, too, perhaps rather more frequently than most people realize."

"I'm sure she'll be fine," Howard said.

"My dear, maybe you should look at finding someone with whom to share your house or flat. You'd be better off finding a husband, of course, but I suppose you've already tried that."

Fenella wasn't sure whether she wanted to laugh or slap the woman. "As I said, I'm quite happy on my own."

"That's what Mabel always said," Patricia told her. "I used to go and visit her, just to keep an eye on her. I was always so worried about her. She always told me that she was happy on her own, right up until the day she died."

"That's quite enough," Howard told her sharply.

Patricia nodded. "I can still remember the last time I saw her. I went to get the rent money, but she'd already paid Howard when he'd gone over to repair her kitchen sink. He'd forgotten to tell me, of course, so I made a completely unnecessary journey to the house."

"You were always at the house, anyway," Howard muttered.

"It was my house," she retorted. "It was my house," she repeated to Fenella. "My father left it to me when he died. Howard and I were going to sell it, but I'd grown up in that house. It meant a lot to me."

Fenella nodded. "When my parents died, my brothers insisted that we sell the house that had been their home for many years. It had been my childhood home, but they were all older when we'd moved into it and it didn't mean as much to them. It would have been foolish to keep it, really, but I still feel sad whenever I think about that house."

Patricia patted Fenella's arm. "See, you do understand," she said approvingly. "Howard doesn't understand at all. After the murder, he made me sell the house. I didn't get a lot for it, either, because someone had been murdered there. The new owners, they just tore the whole house down and built something new, which was horrible."

"It was just a house," Howard said. "It wasn't anything special."

"You spent a lot of time there when we were courting," Patricia countered. "It should have had good memories for you, too."

Howard shrugged. "I spent a lot of time there repairing things for your parents there. Once they were gone, I was there just as much doing repairs for our tenant. I never had to work as hard at our house."

"Our house was newer and we took good care of it," Patricia said. "My parents did their best with theirs, but after a while it got to be too much, that's all."

"I was happy to see the back of that place," Howard told her, "and that's enough for today. Let's go."

Patricia frowned. "Go? But I'm enjoying my chat with Fenella."

"I said it's time to go," Howard replied steadily.

Patricia nodded slowly and then looked down at the cat on her lap. "I hate to wake her," she said softly.

Howard clearly had no such qualms. He reached over and gave the cat a shove that woke her up and made her leap to the floor. He stood up and then held out a hand to his wife. "Goodbye," he said to Fenella.

"It was nice meeting you," Fenella replied politely.

He shrugged and then led Patricia out of the room.

Fenella stood up and looked around the room. The kittens were being passed around and snuggled. The mother cat had found herself another lap and seemed to have fallen asleep again.

"I hope she isn't bothering you," Fenella said again as she walked toward the couple who were sitting with the mother cat.

"Not at all. She's sweet enough for me to forgive her for her willingness to befriend just anyone," the woman replied with a wink.

Fenella was sure her face showed her surprise.

"Sit down and tell me what Patricia had to say," the woman invited.

Fenella slid into a chair and grinned at the woman, who had a friendly smile on her face. She looked no more than sixty, although the man with her was probably at least seventy. "I'm Fenella Woods," she told them.

"Oh, we all know who you are," the woman laughed. "We all knew Mona, of course, although no one here was actually in her lofty social circle."

"I'm not, either," Fenella replied.

The woman laughed again. "Most of that circle is long gone, of course. The island has changed so much in my lifetime that I hardly recognize it now. I'm Jeanne Reese, by the way, and this is my husband, Aaron."

Fenella smiled at Aaron, who seemed to be staring off into the distance. "It's nice to meet you."

"He can't hear you," Jeanne told her. "His hearing is terrible." She reached over and tapped his arm. "Fenella said it's nice to meet you," she shouted at him.

"Likewise," he said, nodding in Fenella's direction before returning to staring into space again.

Jeanne rolled her eyes. "I fell in love with him because we could talk for hours," she told Fenella. "We probably ran out of things to talk about after a few years anyway, so I suppose it doesn't matter. At least we never argue."

"How long have you been married?" Fenella asked.

"Oh, forever," Jeanne said, waving a hand. "Our oldest is going to be forty-five this year, so we've been married almost forty-six years."

"That's a very long time."

"In our day, divorce wasn't really an option," Jeanne shrugged. "Oh, we all talked about being independent women who could live on our own and didn't need men in our lives, but we weren't really that different to our mothers. Once we found husbands, we had lots of babies, and we stayed married."

"I should probably tell you that I know a few of the women you knew years ago," Fenella said hesitantly. She wanted to talk about Mabel's murder, but she was enjoying the conversation she and Jeanne were having. The last thing she wanted to do was upset her.

"Women I knew years ago? What does that mean?"

"I'm taking a class with Donna Cannon."

Jeanne inhaled sharply. Her husband looked over at her. "Is everything okay?" he asked.

Jeanne looked at him as if she wasn't quite sure who he was and then nodded slowly. "It's fine," she said, patting his arm.

"I didn't mean to upset you," Fenella said quickly.

"You haven't upset me," Jeanne countered. "Everyone has been talking about Mabel and the murder since Monday, when the article was in the paper. I've been doing my best to keep my head down and avoid the subject, but it was bound to come up, really."

"I read the article, and Donna told me a bit more."

"How is Donna?" Jeanne asked.

"She seemed fine when we spoke on Monday. I'd never met her before, though."

"The last time I spoke to her she was working her way up in the bank and adamant that she'd never marry. You'd think it would be difficult to lose track of someone on an island this small, but with a little bit of effort, it can be done."

"You deliberately lost track of her?"

"Not just her, there were others. I was married and had children. My life was going in a different direction. Cutting my ties felt like, I don't know, drawing a line between my past and my future. Mabel's murder was a horrible thing and I felt as if I wanted to put as much space between it and me as I possibly could."

"I suppose I can understand that," Fenella told her.

"The police were here. A very polite young inspector talked to me for what felt like hours. It's all brought back so many memories."

"I'm sorry."

"I'm not," was Jeanne's surprising reply. "Many of the memories that have been rekindled have been happy ones. Mabel, Marilyn, Donna, and I were like sisters. We grew up together and shared everything with one another. I cut my ties with them quite deliberately, but now I feel as if I made a mistake."

"Perhaps now would be a good time to reach out to some of them," Fenella suggested.

"I've been thinking about doing just that. I'm not sure how receptive anyone would be, though. It's been a very long time. Tell me about Donna. Did she ever marry?"

"No, she didn't. She became the bank's first female vice president before she retired. She's still living in the same house her parents once owned. We're taking a class together on reading old records."

"She was always the smartest of all of us. She really should have gone to university, but her parents wouldn't hear of it. I knew she'd be successful, but I truly thought she'd marry one day. Perhaps no one else ever measured up to Clyde."

"Clyde?" Fenella echoed.

"Mabel's younger brother. We used to tease Donna because she seemed to fancy him, but she always laughed it off. He was so much younger that I never thought of him as anything other than a younger brother, but he was smart and funny and I hoped one day he and Donna might rediscover one another."

"I understand they had a disagreement at Mabel's funeral."

Jeanne shrugged. "It was a difficult time for all of us. Up until Mabel's death, I think we'd all felt invincible, in that way that young people often do. We were all devastated to lose our close friend and shocked that she'd been murdered. Instead of the tragedy bringing us closer together, it seemed to drive us apart. Clyde was nearly inconsolable and he seemed to be harbouring a great deal of anger or resentment towards the rest of us. I think he was just angry that we were still alive while Mabel wasn't, really. He fought with all of us during those horrible first days after the murder and we were all barely speaking by the time the funeral came around."

"How sad."

"It was sad. If I could turn back the clock, that's one thing I'd change for sure. Of course, I'd also keep Mabel from getting killed in the first place. That would change everything that came after anyway."

"You don't remember what Donna and Clyde fought about specifically?"

"It could have been anything, really. The dress Donna chose to wear to the service or how many cups of coffee Clyde drank at the house afterwards. As I said before, we were all barely speaking by that point. None of the friendships really survived much after that. Oh, I think we all tried, but there was always tension between everyone. We all felt Mabel's absence keenly and tried to ignore it rather than address it."

"Donna said she hasn't spoken to Clyde since the funeral."

"Really? I don't remember it that way, but I suppose she could be right. We still went out sometimes, all of the girls, but now that you've mentioned it, I don't recall Clyde coming along. He used to before Mabel died, not every time, but sometimes."

"And then Marilyn got married."

Jeanne frowned. "Ewan was nice enough, but he felt that once she was married Marilyn's place was at home with him. I suppose that was common at the time, but he didn't even like for her to meet the rest of us for coffee or anything. I suppose it didn't really matter anyway, because she was pregnant not long after the wedding and before long she was on bed rest due to complications. I barely saw her after that."

"What a shame."

"Her mother took over, you see. Ewan liked it when Marilyn was home, but Marilyn's mother was obsessed with keeping Marilyn with her at all times. I visited once or twice, especially after the baby arrived and was so poorly, but I never felt welcome." She sighed and shook her head. "I should have tried harder, I see that now, but I was young and single and it was difficult to see Marilyn suffering so much. It was a real test of our friendship and I feel now as if I let her down badly."

Fenella told her the name of the nursing home where Marilyn was living. "Perhaps you should visit her," she suggested.

"I haven't spoken to her since she lost her second child. Can you tell me anything about her life since then?"

"I met her yesterday, actually. She likes to keep to herself at the home, so Crystal had me take the mother cat in to meet her."

"She's a lovely little animal," Jeanne said, smiling down at the sleeping cat.

"She is, yes." With a knack for charming the very people I want to meet, Fenella added silently. "Marilyn and her husband had a third child, but he had the same medical issues as their first. I don't believe he survived for more than a few months. Her mother remained living with them, however. Marilyn's husband passed away about ten years ago, and not long after that Marilyn was badly injured in a car accident. She's been in a wheelchair ever since, and I believe she moved into the home shortly after the accident. Her mother finally passed away about three years ago."

Jeanne sighed. "I make a point of not reading the death notices in the paper. I stopped when the average age of the deceased started being younger than my age. It's too depressing to read about someone who'd supposedly led a long life and then discover that he was younger than I am when he'd died. I wish I'd known about Marilyn's mother, though. I would have gone to the service for her, if only to make certain that she was actually dead."

"Was she that bad?"

"I'm probably being unfair to her, but I don't think she was good for Marilyn. Marilyn was an only child and I often wondered, in light of the difficulties that Marilyn had having children, if her mother had suffered miscarriages or stillbirths before or after Marilyn arrived. Whatever the reason, she doted on Marilyn, although it might be more accurate to say that she was obsessed with Marilyn. I really think Marilyn agreed to marry Ewan more to get away from her mother than because she cared about him. We always used to laugh about how getting married was the only way she would ever get out from under her mother's thumb."

"But it didn't work out that way."

"No, not at all," Jeanne sighed. "I have four children myself, so I do have some sympathy for Marilyn's mother. It's very easy to become obsessed with your children, especially when they're small and need you for absolutely everything. Letting them grow up and become independent men and women is hard to do and incredibly bittersweet. When my first child was born, I used to sit and watch him sleep for hours. I couldn't tear my eyes off of him. I obsessed over everything he ate, over his sleeping habits, over each milestone. It wasn't until I had my second child that I began to relax a little bit."

She laughed and then patted her husband's arm. "Do you remember how crazy I was when little Aaron was born?" she asked.

He stared at her for a minute and then nodded slowly. "You didn't sleep for months."

"I didn't, and then we had Anna, and I was too tired to keep measuring every bite of food Aaron put in his mouth. I think Marilyn would have been a lot better off if her mother had had more children."

"We don't always get what we want," Fenella said softly.

Jeanne nodded. "As I said, I do wonder if she'd lost other babies. I can't imagine how difficult that must be for women. I fell pregnant easily, carried all four babies to term, and had easy deliveries. I do appreciate that many women, maybe even most women, aren't that fortunate."

"Was Clyde at Marilyn's wedding?" Fenella asked.

"No, although I know he'd been invited. When Marilyn sent out the invitations, she sent him his own, rather than including him with his parents. He was just twenty or twenty-one and still living at home, so she didn't have to send him a separate invitation, but it was a kind thing to do."

"Was that before Mabel died?"

"Yes, but only about a week before. I can remember it clearly, really. Marilyn sent each of us our own invitation, actually, even though we were all living with our parents and she could have included us in the invitations she'd sent to them."

"Mabel lived on her own."

"Yes, and that may be why Marilyn did what she did. She had to send Mabel her own invitation, after all. She may have wanted to make sure she treated us all the same."

"If she hadn't, would that have caused any arguments within the group?"

"I don't know," Jeanne shrugged. "We were all young and silly, really. We bickered amongst ourselves about anything and everything. It was tricky, our foursome. Alliances changed constantly within the group. Mabel always wanted to include Clyde in things, which didn't help. Donna always agreed with her, which caused problems between Donna and Marilyn. At any given time, I was probably only happy to see two of the other three, but which two changed constantly."

"But you worked with Mabel. How was that?"

Jeanne smiled. "That was good, actually. I rarely fought with Mabel. She and I spent a lot of time together and we nearly always got along."

"You didn't mind her inviting Clyde along to things?"

"Not really. He was good company and it was sometimes helpful to have a man in our group. We didn't get as many odd looks in pubs when we had him with us. Women weren't meant to spend time in pubs on their own in those days."

Fenella nodded. "It was only Marilyn who didn't want to include him, then?"

"I wouldn't say she didn't want to include him, it was more that she sometimes wanted to have fun with just the girls. Maybe it was because she was about to get married and she knew she wouldn't get to see as much of us once that happened. I'm not sure, really."

"What else did you all disagree about?"

"Nothing and everything," Jeanne laughed. "None of it was serious, but we could bicker about the weather, politics, religion, what movie to go and see, which actor was better looking. As I said, nothing and everything. The only thing we never fought about was men."

"Really?" Fenella was surprised.

"I know, it's odd, but we had ironclad rules about men. The most important rule was that no man was ever allowed to come between any of us. It wasn't always easy, but we always stuck to the rules."

"You said it wasn't easy. Who had the most trouble with it?"

"Marilyn, although it wasn't her fault. She was beautiful, you see, really, truly striking. We actually developed the rules when we were still in school, after a boy I started seeing met Marilyn and broke up with me the next day. She refused to go out with him, and we worked out the rules from there."

"How often were they tested?"

"In our school days, quite regularly, but once we were out of school, it became less of a problem. Then Marilyn got engaged and it was even less of an issue."

Fenella nodded. They seemed to have wandered far away from the things that she really wanted to discuss, but it was interesting learning more about the group of friends.

"You seem to know a lot about all of my friends," Jeanne said. "What can you tell me about Clyde?"

"I met him yesterday, too," Fenella admitted, flushing. "He's at the same home as Marilyn."

"He is? I suppose I shouldn't be surprised. It is a small island, after all. There are only so many places men and women our age can go. Does that mean he and Marilyn have rekindled their friendship?"

"No, I don't believe they speak to one another."

Jeanne sighed. "I'm not surprised, but it's a shame. How is Clyde, though?"

"He seemed well, although I only met him for the first time yesterday. He never married, either."

"Perhaps he never found anyone as special as Donna," Jeanne said, "or he never found anyone as wonderful as Mabel. She was the standard by which he judged all women, of course. She was pretty amazing, maybe he could never find anyone who measured up to her."

"Marilyn seems to think he knows more about Mabel's death than he's ever admitted," Fenella said cautiously.

"She's been saying that for fifty years," Jeanne laughed. "She also always insisted that Mabel was seeing someone behind all of our backs. I always thought she made that up to make it seem as if she were Mabel's closest friend. That would have garnered her even more sympathy, you see."

"So you don't think Clyde is hiding anything?"

"He might be, I suppose. As I said, we all drifted apart after Mabel's death. I don't know that I spoke to him more than once or twice after the funeral."

"The fight at the funeral wasn't to do with him hiding anything, was it?"

Jeanne sat back and shut her eyes. After a long silence, she shook her head. "I truly don't remember much about the funeral. We started drinking as soon as the church service was over. Donna had a bottle of wine in her car and the three of us drank the whole bottle on our way to Mabel's parents' house. Alcohol flowed pretty freely there, too. The whole day is really something of a blur."

"Was Mabel seeing someone secretly?"

"Not as far as I knew, but I wasn't always privy to all of her secrets. We worked together and spent a lot of time together, but sometimes that seemed to make her less inclined to tell me things. She didn't want me to nag or tease her at work, I suppose."

"If she were seeing someone, who might it have been?"

"That's an impossible question," Jeanne laughed. "It wouldn't have been anyone I knew, I don't suppose. She mentioned once that Mr. Neil, the advocate that we worked for, had asked her to go away for a weekend. When he asked me the same thing, I threatened to tell his wife."

"But the third woman in your office went along with him."

Jeanne laughed again. "Helen was a few years older and worried about becoming an old maid. To be fair to her, though, she and Mr. Neil stayed together for the rest of his life, so maybe she did truly care about him."

The pair fell silent for a minute. Fenella wasn't sure what Jeanne was thinking. Fenella was trying to work out how to bring the conversation around to Howard and Patricia Quinn.

"Did Mabel ever tell you that Howard Quinn had made a similar suggestion?" she asked eventually.

Jeanne looked startled and then shook her head. "Did someone tell you that or are you just speculating?" she demanded.

"No one has said anything to me to suggest that he did anything inappropriate," Fenella said quickly. "It was just something that crossed my mind."

"They live here, you know. I saw you talking to them earlier, actually. Did you know who they were then?"

"They introduced themselves. Howard doesn't like to talk about Mabel."

"He didn't like to talk about her when she was alive. He wanted to sell the house, but Patricia wouldn't agree. Since she was so determined to rent it out, he went out of his way to find a tenant that he knew Patricia wouldn't approve of in the slightest. They put poor Mabel right in the middle of their marriage's power struggle."

"How unpleasant for Mabel."

"She put up with it because the house was nice and it was affordable. Patricia used to drop in unannounced at all sorts of odd times. I'm not certain what she thought she was going to find, but no doubt she was hoping to find something that would have allowed her to throw Mabel out of the house."

"Someone else mentioned her visits to me," Fenella told her.

"She'd come in the middle of the month and demand the rent payment, too. Sometimes Mabel would pay Howard, but he wouldn't tell Patricia and then she'd insist that Mabel give her more money.

When she first moved in, Mabel thought the whole thing was going to be friendly since the Quinns knew her parents so well, but before long she found that she had to get receipts for the rent every time she paid it and that getting things repaired was always an issue."

"Someone told me that Howard handled all of the repairs himself."

"He did, and he wasn't very good at them. I think he repaired the same bathroom tap about six times in three weeks, and I'm sure Mabel was still complaining about it after that. If Patricia had been a little bit nicer, I might have almost felt sorry for her, really."

"But she wasn't nice?"

"She was horrible. She didn't approve of women living on their own. The house was hers and she seemed to be terrified that Mabel might accidentally knock down a wall or start tearing doors off of hinges or something. As I said, she used to visit all the time. I'm sure she'd have been even more upset to find Mabel alone in the house with a man than if Mabel had actually knocked down a wall, though."

"Presumably Mabel was alone in the house with Howard, though," Fenella said thoughtfully.

Jeanne raised an eyebrow. "You aren't suggesting that Mabel had an affair with Howard, are you?"

"Why not?"

"He was older and very married. Mabel could be impulsive and even deliberately shocking, but I can't see her taking up with the man who co-owned the house where she was living. There were plenty of other married men around, after all."

"Including Mr. Neil, although he was older, too, wasn't he?"

"Much older, maybe thirty-five or even forty. At the time that seemed old, anyway. I suppose Howard was only around thirty, but he seemed older. He and Patricia were friends with Mabel's parents, after all. It felt as if they belonged to that generation rather than ours."

"Do you ever speak to them?" Fenella wondered.

"No, although I don't go out of my way to avoid them, either. In spite of appearances today, very few of us actually spend much time in the residents' lounge here. We all have our own flats and we tend to come and go much as we did when we lived in houses elsewhere on the island. Aaron and I were quite happy in our little house in Onchan, but the garden was becoming more and more of a struggle. Our youngest daughter was the one who finally convinced us to move here, and we don't regret the decision, at least not yet."

"I wonder why Howard and Patricia are here."

"Perhaps Patricia grew tired of always having leaky taps," Jeanne suggested. "We have maintenance staff on call here all the time. When we need something repairing, we only have to ring and someone comes and takes care of it within hours. Everything we've had done has been done right the first time, too."

"There was another name that came up when I was talking about Mabel with someone. Do you remember Stanley Middleburgh?"

"It will have been Donna who brought him up," Jeanne said with a laugh. "She was rather obsessed with the poor man."

"Really?"

"Poor man is altogether the wrong way to put things, though. Stanley was incredibly wealthy, but equally, incredibly odd. He lived in the house next door to Mabel's and he used to sit outside and stare at all of us when we were visiting. I always thought he was just a rather sad and lonely man who needed some friends, but Donna thought he was creepy."

"Do you know what happened to him?"

"He moved to Canada right after Mabel died. I think it was Canada, anyway. It might have been Australia. It was somewhere quite far away, anyway."

"Was he a suspect in the murder investigation? The papers never mentioned his name."

"I'm sure his parents paid handsomely on a regular basis to keep his name out of the papers. As I said, I always thought he was harmless, but he did behave oddly from time to time."

"Oddly?"

"He used to go to ShopFast and fill his trolley with just one type of thing, maybe biscuits, for example. He'd fill a trolley completely full with packets of biscuits and then push it to the front of the store. Sometimes he'd pay for everything and then pass out the bags full of biscuits to random people walking past. Other times, he'd abandon the trolley and wander off without paying. I remember one day when I was there he handed me a bag full of cereal boxes. When I got home, I found I had five boxes of the same cereal. It took me ages to get through them all."

"That is rather unusual behavior," Fenella said, wondering what doctors might diagnose the man with if they had him as a patient today.

"I sometimes thought that he was just bored. His father wouldn't or couldn't employ him and I believe he'd left school at sixteen. I don't know what he did all day long, really, but he seemed to spend most of his evenings sitting outside watching Mabel and the rest of us."

"Was he home the night of the murder?"

"I wish I knew the answer to that. The police would never say and I never saw him again after Mabel died. If he was home, he must have seen the killer coming or going, though."

"You don't think he might have killed her himself?"

"I can't imagine any motive for him. As far as I know, he never even tried to speak to Mabel. He certainly never tried to speak to me, not even when I waved to him on my way in or out of Mabel's house."

"Could he have been the man Mabel was seeing in secret?"

"There wasn't any man," Jeanne said firmly. "Anyway, if she had started a relationship with Stanley, she would have told everyone. He was odd, but he was very wealthy. She'd have been bragging everywhere and showing off expensive presents, I'm sure."

"I think we need to start gathering up kittens," Crystal said in Fenella's ear.

Fenella nodded and then slowly got to her feet. "I'm going to have to take her back as well," she told Jeanne, gesturing toward the mother cat.

"Did someone say they were all available for adoption?" she asked. "We could keep her, couldn't we?" she asked Aaron.

He looked startled and then stared at the cat for a moment. "I'm not sure we want another animal," he said after a minute. "I thought we both agreed that once the children were grown we weren't going to have any more dogs or cats."

"But look how adorable she is," Jeanne cooed.

Aaron looked at Fenella and then winked at her. "We'll talk about it," he said. "I'm not making any promises, though."

Jeanne gave the cat a hug and then handed her to Fenella. "It was nice talking to you," she said. "I wasn't expecting the trip down memory lane, but after talking to the police yesterday, I'm starting to feel more comfortable with the subject."

"You should think about getting together with the others again," Fenella urged her. "It might be awkward, but I think you'd all benefit."

Jeanne shrugged. "I'll think about it, but like Aaron, I'm not making any promises."

Fenella decided to be happy with that for now. She carried the cat to her carrier and put her inside. Three of the kittens had already been located, and it didn't take long for the fourth to turn up, as one of the residents slid her foot into her shoes and nearly stepped on the hidden animal.

"Thank you again for your visit," Crystal told her as she walked Fenella and the animals out. "I think we'll have homes for all of the kittens by the time they're ready to leave their mother."

"The woman I was speaking with might want the mother cat," Fenella told her.

"I'm going to ring Mr. Stone later today, once I've spoken to a few of the residents in more depth. If the kittens will be ready to leave their mother next week, maybe you could bring them over on Tuesday?"

"Have Mr. Stone let me know what you need me to do," Fenella told her.

"I will do," Crystal promised.

Fenella climbed into her car and drove slowly away. "Did you hear that? You all might have new homes," she told the cats, trying to ignore the rush of sadness that accompanied her words. She was happy the kittens were going to get good homes, but she was also going to miss them. No matter how difficult they were to look after, they were also sweet, and part of her wished she could keep them all.

It was time for lunch, and she was starving, but she had to take the cats home before she could think about food. After letting them out of their carriers and giving them all some food, Fenella headed back to the car. She'd stop home to see Katie and then order pizza, she thought. Maybe she should grab Chinese on her way to her apartment. With her thoughts focused on food, she slid behind the steering wheel. When someone knocked on the driver's door window, she jumped.

"How many of my witnesses did you meet today, then?" Daniel asked her.

"Howard and Patricia Quinn and Jeanne Reese," Fenella replied.

He shook his head. "Want to get lunch at the pub around the corner?" he asked.

Fenella thought about her answer for half a second and then nodded. "Sure, why not?"

🦋 12 🦋

A s the pub was only a short distance away, the pair decided to walk rather than drive there.

"How are the kittens?" Daniel asked as they strolled down the sidewalk.

"They're good. I'm pretty sure one of them knows how to get in and out of the playpen and maybe even up the stairs, but it hasn't caused too much trouble, so I'm not worrying about it."

Daniel laughed. "Famous last words."

"I know, I'm tempting fate. I may have homes for them, anyway." She told Daniel about the nursing home visits. "I only need each place to take two kittens and I'm done," she concluded happily. "I'm pretty sure Jeanne is going to take the mother cat, but if she doesn't, I'm hoping they'll have her at the Tale and Tail."

"I never thought about that. Maybe they'd take the kittens, too."

"I've never seen kittens there, but if the nursing homes decide against taking them, I may have to ask."

The pub was quiet as they walked into the main dining room. Daniel went to the bar to order their soft drinks while Fenella read through the menu. By the time he was back, her stomach was rumbling.

"Today's special is steak and kidney pudding," he told her as he handed her a glass.

She shook her head. "Chicken casserole," she said firmly. "It was the first thing on the menu that caught my eye and now I can't think about anything else."

Daniel went back to the bar to order as Fenella sat back in her seat. There were only a few other occupied tables scattered around the large room. She didn't recognize anyone.

"Tell me about your day, then," Daniel said when he'd rejoined her. "You told me how things went for the kittens. Now I want to hear what the various witnesses had to say."

Fenella nodded. "I met Howard and Patricia first," she began. The food arrived as she switched to talking about Jeanne. They were both done eating by the time she'd finished talking.

"Interesting," was what Daniel said. "What about pudding?"

Fenella glanced at the menu and then nodded. "The warm brownie with ice cream sounds like exactly what I need."

While Daniel was at the bar, Fenella checked her phone. She'd missed a call from Shelly, who'd left a voice mail message.

"I was just wondering when you were going to visit Katie today. I'm having lunch with Tim, but I should be home after two," the message said.

A glance at her watch showed Fenella that she still had a few minutes before Shelly would be home. That would give her time to enjoy her pudding, then. The walk back to her car was definitely slower than the walk the other way had been.

"What are your plans for the rest of the day?" Daniel asked when they finally reached Fenella's house.

"I'm going to pop home and visit with Katie for a while. That's about all I have planned," she replied, feeling like a friendless loser.

"I have to work until six. Do you want to meet me at the Tale and Tail around half six? You could talk to them about the mother cat and the kittens and we could have a drink together."

"I'd like that, but I won't be drinking, not when I have to drive afterward."

Daniel nodded. "Why don't I collect you here at half six, then? I can drive us both and that way you can have a drink."

"You don't mind not drinking?"

"I'm on call tonight, anyway. I can't even have a drink at home."

"In that case, I'll see you here around six-thirty," Fenella agreed happily. It had been a long time since she and Daniel had gone out together. Maybe tonight would be a new beginning in their romantic relationship.

"Make sure you invite Shelly along," he added as she climbed into her car. "She always has interesting insights into my cases."

Fenella forced herself to keep smiling as she slowly backed out of the driveway and drove away. As she stopped at the stop sign on the corner, she sighed deeply. So much for a romantic evening. Daniel just wanted to talk about the case and he wanted Shelly's perspective.

She let herself into her apartment and then called Shelly. "Do you want to bring Katie and Smokey over here for a change of scenery?" she invited.

"That sounds good," Shelly agreed. The trio was at her door a minute later.

Mona settled into a chair and smiled at Fenella. "This is better. The flat feels empty without you here."

Fenella only just managed to stop herself from replying. Shelly couldn't see or hear Mona and Fenella wasn't ready to tell anyone else about her ghostly roommate.

"Daniel asked me to invite you to join us at the pub tonight," she told Shelly after a brief chat. "He said you always have interesting insights into his cases."

"Do I? I didn't realize. I haven't been to the pub since you've been staying on Poppy Drive. I'd love to come along if I won't be in the way."

"Daniel told me to invite you."

Mona laughed. "You're avoiding the question," she told Fenella.

Shelly narrowed her eyes at Fenella. "But are you okay with that?"

"You know I love spending time with you."

"When it's just me, sure, but wouldn't you rather tonight was just you and Daniel?"

Fenella thought carefully about her answer. "I don't know," she finally admitted the truth. "I was excited when he asked me and then disappointed when he told me to invite you along, but I'm not sure either of us is ready for a proper relationship at this point. Maybe it's better for both of us if we work on our friendship first and then see how things go."

"If I'm coming along tonight, maybe you'd better tell me all about the case," Shelly suggested.

"Yes, there hasn't been nearly enough discussion of the case," Mona agreed happily.

Fenella told them both everything she could about the case and about the various times she met the different witnesses. Shelly took a few notes as Fenella talked.

"I want to know more about Stanley," she said when Fenella was finished. "I know the name, of course, and I've met one or two of the family members. They're all a little bit odd, but as they have so much money, they're eccentric rather than crazy."

"I've always wanted to be rich enough to be eccentric."

"And now you are."

Fenella blinked. "I am, aren't I?" she exclaimed. "I hadn't realized."

Shelly laughed. "You aren't really eccentric, though, or crazy, or anything bad."

"Maybe I should try being eccentric," Fenella mused.

"You aren't the type," Mona told her. "You're too much like your father, sensible and slightly dull."

Swallowing a reply, Fenella grabbed Katie and gave her a hug. "I do miss you," she told the animal.

"Meeroow," Katie replied before wiggling away.

"I talked to Max about Stanley," Mona said, her tone suggesting that she'd learned something interesting.

Fenella looked over at her, trying to look curious, but unable to speak.

Mona stared back at her with an innocent look on her face.

"I'm hoping Daniel will know more about Stanley when we meet with him later," Fenella said eventually. "I don't know how likely a candidate he is, really. It seems odd to me that he wasn't mentioned in the papers or the police reports."

"Things have changed a lot," Shelly laughed. "You've at least as much money as the Middleburghs had back then, and you've been in the local paper a lot."

"Perhaps if I were willing to bribe someone, I could keep my name out of the paper in the future," Fenella suggested.

"I don't think that sort of thing happens anymore," Shelly told her.

"Of course it does," Mona countered. "Although so much spreads through social media these days that staying out of the papers isn't as useful as it was formerly."

Fenella nodded and then turned the movement into a head roll when she noticed that Shelly was looking at her.

"Are you okay?" Shelly asked.

"My neck is a bit stiff, that's all," she replied, glaring at Mona, who was laughing softly.

"I hope you don't mind, but I'm going to take the cats and head home," Shelly told her a minute later. "I have an appointment at four and then I'll need to eat something before our pub visit. I'll meet you and Daniel there around quarter to seven."

Fenella nodded and then walked Shelly to the door. After giving Katie one last quick cuddle, she let them out and then turned to Mona. "Any thoughts on what I should wear tonight?" she asked her aunt.

"Burgundy-colored dress on the right side of the wardrobe," Mona told her. "It's pretty and casual, but still dressy enough for what may or may not be a romantic evening."

"It won't be very romantic with Shelly along," Fenella muttered as she headed for the master bedroom.

Along with the houses, stocks, bonds, and money that Fenella had inherited from Mona, she'd also inherited a wardrobe full of gorgeous clothes. A local designer called Timothy had made nearly everything inside it for Mona. Even though she and Mona seemed to have very different physical shapes, the clothes in the wardrobe all seemed to fit Fenella perfectly.

The burgundy dress was right where Mona had told her to look.

Fenella pulled it out and smiled. It was gorgeous and exactly what she needed. It would make her feel confident and beautiful and Daniel would probably like it, too. She slipped it on and then twirled slowly in front of the mirror. "It's wonderful," she sighed as she undid the zipper.

"All of my clothes were wonderful," Mona told her. "The choices in the spirit world are sadly limited. I've been complaining since I arrived, but no one seems inclined to do anything about the situation."

"Does it really matter what you wear?"

"Of course it matters. Max has very high standards and he likes it when I dress well. That's why he paid for all of the clothes in the wardrobe, of course, but sadly, there's nothing to buy here."

A dozen questions sprang into Fenella's head, but she didn't bother to ask any of them. "That's a shame," she said instead.

"I'm sure I've told you before that I don't think Max truly realizes that he's passed away. He doesn't seem to understand why I keep wearing the same outfits over and over again."

"Perhaps you should try making something yourself."

Mona looked surprised and then smiled. "That isn't a bad idea, actually. Perhaps that's where I've been going wrong. I shall have to go and see what I can do."

"What about Stanley?" Fenella asked quickly before the woman could disappear.

Mona smirked at her. "I wondered when you'd ask about him. Max remembered him and the whole sad story, actually."

"It's a sad story?"

"Not tragic, just a bit, well, unfortunate. It seems Stanley was a bit more than eccentric, actually. His family did their best to look after him, but he insisted on living on his own. At some point around the time of Mabel's murder, though, he apparently suffered some sort of breakdown. Max never got all of the details, but Stanley's father told him that they'd been forced to send Stanley to a specialist facility in Canada because it was obvious that he needed more help than he was able to get on the island."

"Surely there were facilities closer than Canada for him," Fenella said.

Mona shrugged. "I have no idea. The place in Canada may have been particularly good or the family may simply have wanted to get Stanley as far away from the island as possible. Max wasn't certain as to the exact date when all of this took place, but I believe Stanley may have left the island before Mabel's murder."

"Unless he saw or heard something the night of the murder and that's what caused his breakdown," Fenella suggested.

"I suppose that's also possible, but Max seemed to think that Stanley was gone before Mabel died."

"Then why does Donna think he was involved?"

"No one would have announced Stanley's departure from the island, especially under the circumstances. I'm sure the family waited a few days or even weeks to say anything about his leaving."

"I hope Daniel will be able to find out more," Fenella said.

"I did my best," Mona told her.

"Oh, I know, but until I hear otherwise, I'm keeping Stanley on my suspect list."

Mona shrugged. "I've crossed him off mine. I don't think he had anything to do with Mabel's death."

"Did Max remember anything about Mabel's funeral?"

"Not a thing. He wasn't even sure he was there, actually, until I reminded him what I'd worn."

"Did you ask him about Marilyn's wedding?"

"He remembered that, although not well. It was just one of the many events that he attended over his lifetime. He was invited to everything because of who he was, and he hated disappointing people. I can't tell you how many weddings Max went to over the years. It was something of an island tradition to invite Max to your wedding, even for couples with no connection to him whatsoever. Of course, as it's such a small island, many people felt they had a connection, no matter how tenuous."

"What do you mean?"

"Max owned a number of businesses, so hundreds of people worked for him, or rather worked for his company, not him directly. All of those people had spouses, siblings, children, nieces and nephews, and so on. Anyone who used any of his hotels or restaurants for their events would invite Max as a matter of course, too. I could go on and on, but you get the idea. It didn't help that Max's partner, Bryan, was either painfully shy or simply antisocial, I've never been sure which. He never wanted to go to anything, which meant Max had to do all of the socializing for both partners." Mona fell silent for a minute and then laughed. "Of course, Max adored all of it and never complained, no matter how exhausting it often became."

"You went with him everywhere?"

"Not everywhere. Some people didn't always welcome me. Remember that not everyone approved of my relationship with Max or my lifestyle. I also sometimes went to things with other men, leaving Max on his own for a day or a week or a month."

"Did he have other women?"

Mona shook her head. "He never looked at another woman, not from the day we met when I was eighteen."

"Why didn't you ever marry?"

Mona smiled. "I'll tell you one day, but not yet."

Before Fenella could push her for an answer, Mona faded from view. Fenella put the dress and matching shoes into a small suitcase and then headed back to Poppy Drive. She had just enough time for a quick meal before Daniel was supposed to be picking her up for their pub visit.

"You look wonderful," Daniel said when she opened the door to his knock.

"Thanks."

"I feel as if I should be taking you somewhere nicer than the pub," he added.

"The Tale and Tail is one of my favorite places on the island. I'm excited about going there."

Daniel nodded. "It's a pretty special place."

The drive didn't take long and Daniel easily found a parking space along the promenade. As Fenella climbed out of the car, she glanced over at the storage shed. A large dog was walking past it and the animal stopped to bark loudly.

"You don't think..." Fenella began. Before she could finish her thought, a small mouse ran out of the shed and disappeared down the promenade. The dog started to chase after the creature, but was stopped by his leash.

Daniel grinned. "At least when the cat was living in there, they didn't have to worry about mice."

There were only a handful of people scattered around the ground floor of the pub. Fenella glanced longingly at the shelves full of books as she waited for the bartender to pour her glass of wine. From where she was standing, it felt as if it would take her a lifetime to simply read the titles of every single book.

"I heard you're rescuing kittens now," the man behind the bar said as he handed over her drink.

"Not intentionally," Fenella said quickly. "I'm looking after a mother cat and four kittens right now, and I'm doing everything I can to find them good homes."

"That's always a challenge," he replied. "The kittens should be easier to place. You just have to hope that whoever takes them is happy to look after them for twelve years or more."

Fenella nodded. "Kittens are adorable, but they grow up into cats very quickly. It's quite sad how many people decide to get rid of their cats once they get past the kitten stage."

"On a more positive note, we have some wonderful animals here that we never would have been able to enjoy if they'd been kept by their owners."

A quick glance around the room showed Fenella more than a dozen cats of various shapes and sizes casually sprawled all around the room. There were more than enough cat beds for them each to have his or her own, but Fenella spotted three animals curled up together in one bed. Most of the other animals were climbing on shelves or demanding attention from the pub's customers, though. "If I can't find homes for them, would you be willing to take any of them?" Fenella asked.

The bartender shrugged. "We don't take kittens, mostly because they are fairly easy to place," he told her. "They also need more time and attention than we can give them, and they tend to be a bit too active, as well. We can't have kittens climbing up on the bar and chasing one another through glasses and bottles."

Fenella nodded. "And these four would do just that," she admitted. "What about the mother cat?"

"If you can't find a home for her, you're welcome to bring her in for a visit," he told her. "As she was a stray, it's possible she might have problems getting along with others, though. Some strays struggle to share space with other cats."

"She didn't get along with my Katie, but that might have been more about Katie than the mother cat," Fenella told him. "If I can't find a home for her, I'll let you know and set up a time to bring her in for a visit. Thank you."

He nodded, and then she took her drink and followed Daniel to the winding staircase that led to the upper level. Bookshelves covered the walls on this level, too, but there were couches, chairs, and tables scattered around the large center area. Shelly was sitting on one of the couches, sipping a drink with a book in her other hand. She put the drink down and waved as Fenella reached the top of the stairs.

"What are you reading?" Fenella asked curiously.

"A romance," Shelly replied. "I'm doing research."

"Research? This novel writing is harder than I thought."

Shelly grinned. "Okay, maybe it isn't entirely for research. I truly enjoy reading romance novels."

"Good for you," Fenella said. "I read them now and again. Mona had a few, but I prefer a good mystery."

"Maybe that's why you're able to help with my cases," Daniel said. "Maybe all those years of reading mysteries have given you extra insight."

"I don't know about that," Fenella laughed, "but I do enjoy hearing about your cases."

"How much do you know about the case?" he asked Shelly.

"Fenella filled me in earlier today," she replied. "I can't stop thinking about Stanley. I think he's the key somehow."

"He isn't," Daniel told her. "He wasn't on the island when Mabel died."

"Why didn't Donna know that?" Shelly asked.

"His family kept his departure quiet, for a while, anyway. They had reasons for doing so and, as he couldn't possibly have had anything to do with Mabel's death, I'm sure they didn't see any reason to share the information."

"He's definitely out?" Shelly wondered, sounding disappointed.

"He's definitely out," Daniel confirmed.

"Is he still alive?" Fenella asked. "Because if he is, it might be interesting to talk to him. If he really did sit and watch Mabel's house all day long, he may have seen something relevant in the weeks leading up to the murder."

"You're right, of course, but, sadly, Stanley passed away in the late nineties. He never did come back to the island, and he was never questioned about what he may or may not have seen before he left."

"That's a shame. I'm surprised he wasn't questioned fifty years ago," Shelly said.

"He wasn't, um, there were good reasons why he wasn't questioned at the time," Daniel said awkwardly.

Fenella was trying to think of a way to mention what Mona had told her, but she couldn't.

"What does that mean?" Shelly asked Daniel.

He sighed. "Stanley had some mental health issues," he explained. "He was sent to a specialist hospital in Canada for treatment. The doctors there didn't feel that he was well enough to answer any questions about his former life."

"So he may well have been the key to solving the case," Shelly sighed.

"I'm going to be talking to one of his doctors on Monday. A whole team of people treated him during his years in Canada. I was only able to track down one man who is still alive and willing to speak to me, though. I don't expect him to tell me anything, but I'm hoping he might be willing to go through Stanley's medical records to see if Stanley ever mentioned Mabel. It would be too much to hope for to find that he talked about Mabel and some man who kept visiting, or something along those lines, though."

"If we rule him out, we're left with Mabel's three friends and the Quinns as suspects, aren't we?" Shelly asked.

"I would put those five at the top of the list," Daniel told her. "There are others who need to be considered, though."

"Ewan Coleman?" Fenella asked.

Daniel nodded. "At the time he was seen as being above suspicion, because he was a police constable, but I'm not so quick to dismiss him."

"Who else?" Shelly demanded.

"There were eight or nine different men who were involved with Mabel or one of the other three women in the two years before Mabel's death. They're all remote possibilities, but I'm looking at each of them in turn."

"Is that everyone?" was Shelly's next question.

"You didn't mention Clyde," Fenella told her.

"Oh, I forgot about him," Shelly exclaimed. "Surely he didn't kill his own sister, though."

"He's very much still on my list," Daniel told her.

The trio talked about all of the suspects as they worked their way through a second round of drinks. Eventually Daniel began to yawn between sentences.

"I think we need to call it a night," Fenella said when she found herself following suit. "At least it's Saturday tomorrow. We can all sleep late."

"I'm working at nine," Daniel sighed. "One of the other inspectors is on holiday, so I'm taking an extra shift for him."

"In that case, we should have left an hour ago," Fenella said apologetically.

"It's fine," Daniel insisted. "I don't know that we solved the case, but you've helped me work through all of the suspects in my head. I'm going to have to interview each of them again, I think, although I may focus on Clyde."

"Everyone seems to think he's hiding something," Shelly said.

"That wouldn't surprise me. The trick now is finding a way to get him to share his secret," Daniel replied.

"Maybe it's time to get all of the suspects together," Fenella suggested. "As I understand it, most of them haven't seen one another in many years. Maybe if they were all together, one of them would remember something important or could persuade Clyde to talk."

"It isn't my job to engineer a reunion," Daniel told her.

"Maybe I should have a go," Fenella said thoughtfully. The idea was still playing out in her mind as she followed the others to the elevators. Daniel was silent as they drove back to Poppy Drive. Whatever he was thinking about, Fenella was trying to work out how best to persuade everyone to reunite.

"Thank you for an interesting evening," Daniel said on her doorstep a short while later.

"I hope we can help you solve the case," she told him.

"Even if we don't, at least we're spending time together," he replied. He leaned forward and kissed her gently. "Sleep well," he said in a low voice before he turned and walked away.

Fenella let herself into the house and then counted felines. Everyone was in place, so she headed up to bed. With no real plans for the weekend, she crawled into bed still thinking about getting Mabel's friends together.

The cacophonous sound of angry kittens dragged her out of a sound sleep. "It's nine o'clock," she muttered to herself as she headed down the stairs. "I hope you lot are just hungry."

A quick check suggested that hunger was the kittens' only complaint. She gave them several bowls of food and fresh water before she took her shower and got dressed. The day seemed to stretch endlessly in front of her, but by the time she'd done some grocery shopping, popped home to do laundry and check on Katie, eaten a few meals, and watched some television, it was time for bed again.

Her Sunday was broadly similar, with yet another trip to the shops for things she'd forgotten the day before, but fortunately, no additional laundry. Monday was sunny and bright and Fenella rolled out of bed feeling determined. The kittens were due to visit Mr. Stone again, but that was the only thing on her schedule before her class that evening. Somehow, before the class, she had to come up with a way to convince Donna to take part in the reunion she was hoping to arrange. How hard could that be?

"No, I'm sorry, but I won't do it," Donna said firmly. "With the case being back in the newspapers, I've been thinking far too much about the past. Now isn't the right time to see everyone again."

"There might never be a right time," Fenella told her. "I'm going to make the same suggestion to the others. Do you want me to let you know if any of the others agree to meet?"

"No, I'm not the least bit interested," Donna told her flatly.

"I think we're ready to begin," Marjorie said from her seat at the head of the table. "I thought we'd start today with some more letters. These are from the mid-eighteenth century and are between two brothers."

She passed out the photocopies and Fenella stared in horrified fascination at the black scrawl on the paper. "Are you sure this is English?" she asked. "Are you even sure it's meant to be language?"

Marjorie laughed. "I know this man's handwriting is challenging, but that's why I chose these letters. I promise you that once you get your eye in, you'll be able to read it with ease."

An hour later, Fenella had a slight headache, but she also had a neat transcription of the letter. It was an interesting one, as well, full of gossip about one of the writer's neighbors who was allegedly having an affair with the village blacksmith.

"After the break, we'll read the reply from the man's brother," Marjorie told them. "He lived on the other side of the island, so this was all news to him."

"I hope there was something equally exciting happening in his village," George said.

"You'll have to wait and see," Marjorie teased.

She made tea and opened packets of biscuits for everyone. Fenella joined the others at the table, frowning as Donna seemed to deliberately move away from her as she approached.

"I heard you went visiting last week," Annabelle said.

"Who, me?" Fenella asked in surprise.

"Yes, I heard you spent some time visiting with some friends of mine," Annabelle told her.

"Did I?"

"Howard and Patricia Quinn," Annabelle explained.

"Oh, yes, I did meet them," Fenella agreed. "I took the kittens to visit a few of the nursing homes in Douglas."

"Patricia told me she was quite taken with the mother cat."

"Yes, she said she'd like to adopt her, but her husband didn't like the idea."

"Patricia will get her way. She always has. Howard is completely devoted to her."

"Ha," Donna interjected. "He used to complain about her when he was at Mabel's house doing repairs. I sometimes thought he used to come to repair things that weren't even broken, just to get away from Patricia."

"What a horrible thing to say," Annabelle snapped. "I don't know what you're hoping to accomplish by saying awful things about them, but Patricia and Howard have always been devoted to one another."

Donna shrugged. "Maybe they went through a bad patch, then, or something. I just know what I remember. He seemed to be at Mabel's house more than I was, almost, although Patricia used to visit a lot, too. I never saw them at the house together, though."

"With all due respect, that was a long time ago. Perhaps you've mixed things up in your memory," Annabelle said in a sugary sweet tone.

"I haven't, but you may believe what you like about your friends," Donna told her. She moved a few feet away from the others and sat down with her tea.

"Patricia said you were going to visit again this week," Annabelle said to Fenella. "I'm sure she'll have talked Howard around by that time."

"She isn't the only person interested in taking the mother cat, though," Fenella replied.

✔ Annabelle frowned. "I'll have to let her know, just so she isn't too disappointed if you give the mother to someone else. I'm sure Patricia would be the best choice, if you're the one making the selection."

"As her husband was so adamant that he didn't want the animal, I wasn't even considering her," Fenella said. "Mr. Stone will be making the final decisions on where all of the cats go, anyway."

"As I said, Howard isn't a concern. Patricia will, of course, consider his opinion. She is devoted to him, obviously, but ultimately, if she really wants the cat, she'll persuade him that he wants her, too."

Fenella nodded, even though she wasn't convinced. If it were up to her, the cat would go to Jeanne Reese. Fenella had liked Jeanne and Aaron a good deal more than Howard and Patricia.

"Let's get to work on that reply, then," Marjorie suggested a short time later.

After another hour, this time with a much more legible letter, the class finished for the evening.

"It seems like everyone on the island was having affairs in those days," George commented as everyone packed up his or her things.

The second letter had detailed not one, but two different affairs that were taking place in the village where the other brother lived.

"There was little else for people to do in those days besides gossip about one another," Margaret suggested. "It's all speculation, anyway. Neither brother had any proof. The second brother even admitted as much for the one of the affairs he mentioned."

"We have an entire collection of letters between the pair, maybe a hundred letters in total. I'd be thrilled if anyone wanted to transcribe them all for the museum," Marjorie said. "While these two are particularly gossipy, there's a lot of interesting information about life on the island in them, too. We could learn a lot about society and culture if we had the entire collection available for study."

"They're too sordid for me," Annabelle said tightly. "I enjoy learning more about the island's history, but this sort of salacious gossip isn't why I take these classes."

Marjorie nodded. "I thought they would make a nice change from the wills and import and export records we usually study, but they were a bit racier than I was expecting. The research assistant who dug them out for me just told me that they were full of village gossip. She didn't give me any specifics. It was the particularly challenging writing that made me want to tackle the first letter."

"I hope next week we'll be looking at something rather different," Annabelle replied.

"I have the perfect thing for next week," Marjorie laughed. "One of my assistants has uncovered several handwritten notebooks in one of the boxes from one of the churches. I believe they're notes by a former vicar, mostly to do with his sermons."

Fenella exchanged glances with Margaret and then George. They both looked as unexcited about transcribing sermons as she felt.

"That sounds fascinating," Annabelle said.

"Fenella, darling," Robert said as everyone began to stand up. "I hope you haven't forgotten that you agreed to talk to me about your experiences with the police and the various murder investigations of which you've been a part."

"Actually, you must have forgotten that I said I wasn't interested," Fenella replied. "Sorry."

He shook his head. "But I absolutely need your input. You've been involved in some sensational cases. I've already sold the idea of a series about them to the local radio station. More importantly, I've generated a great deal of interest in the project across. A major London station has suggested that they may well be interested in purchasing the finished series."

"I'm sorry, but I'm not going to take part," Fenella said firmly.

"Inspector Robinson seemed to think you'd be more cooperative," Robert replied.

"Then he was mistaken," Fenella said, wondering if Robert had actually discussed the idea with Daniel or if he were simply throwing Daniel's name into the conversation in an attempt to change her mind.

"He's going to be doing a short segment on each case," Robert added. "He was the inspector in charge of most of them."

"If you have Daniel taking part, you definitely don't need me," Fenella said.

"The series is meant to be about how murder investigations operate, seen from different perspectives. Having the police involved is helpful, but you were going to be the voice of the average man or woman suddenly caught up in a murder investigation."

"I'm sure you'll be able to find other average people to take my place," Fenella replied.

Robert sighed. "I'm going to hold out hope that you'll change your mind. I'll be starting to work on the scripts this week, but I don't have to write your part for a while yet. I'll ask you again next week. Please give it some thought between now and then."

"Please do us both a favor and start looking for someone else," Fenella said. "I'm not going to change my mind."

Robert looked as if he wanted to object, but Donna interrupted.

"Being involved in a murder investigation is a deeply unpleasant experience," she told Robert. "I don't blame Fenella for not wanting to talk about her experiences. I've only ever been involved in one murder investigation and that was fifty years ago. I hate talking about it, even now."

While Donna had been speaking, Fenella had quickly finished packing up her things. She was heading for the door before Robert could reply to Donna.

"I'll see you all next week," she called from the doorway, eager to get away before Robert spoke again.

"Wait a minute," Donna said quickly.

She grabbed her bag and followed Fenella out of the room. In the corridor, she took Fenella's arm and led her to the elevators. It wasn't until the elevator doors were shut and they were descending that she spoke again.

"I don't want to see them again, but if you do arrange a meeting, I'd like to know about it," she told Fenella. "If everyone else wants to meet, I may give the idea a little bit more thought."

"I'll call you if anything gets arranged," Fenella promised. "Your number is on the class roster, isn't it?"

"Yes, it's on there," Donna agreed.

At the first class Marjorie had given them each a copy of the class roster, including contact details. She'd suggested that everyone consider sharing rides and also encouraged them all to discuss their transcriptions in between sessions. Thus far Fenella hadn't even looked at the list, and no one had called her. She could only hope that Robert wasn't going to start bothering her about his radio series.

Fenella drove slowly back to Poppy Drive. Donna hadn't exactly agreed to the meeting, but her interest in hearing about anything that might be arranged gave Fenella hope. Now all she had to do was persuade the others to take part.

"There's my favorite cat," Patricia said when Fenella let the cats out of their carriers the next morning.

Patricia and Howard were sitting near the entrance to the large lounge. Howard was reading a book and seemed to be ignoring both his wife and the kittens that were now racing around the room. The mother cat jumped off the table and headed straight for Patricia.

"Hello," Fenella said brightly as she dropped onto a couch across from the couple. "How are you today?"

The mother cat curled up in Patricia's lap and shut her eyes. Patricia began to stoke her back, closing her own eyes momentarily and then sighing deeply. "I'm better now," she said. "I've missed her."

"She seems happy to see you," Fenella replied.

"Don't get too attached," Howard said gruffly. "We aren't keeping her."

"We can talk about that later," Patricia murmured, patting his arm.

"We aren't going to talk about it later," he shot back, pushing her hand away. "We are not keeping that animal."

Patricia looked shocked, angry, and then sad. "She's awfully sweet," she said in a low voice.

"No," was all that Howard replied.

"Annabelle said there were other people interested in her," Patricia said to Fenella. "I hope you'll find a good home for her." As she spoke, a single tear slid down Patricia's face.

"Mr. Stone is actually going to be the one making the final decisions," Fenella told her. "For all I know, he has a long list of interested parties."

Patricia nodded slowly. "I should be happy for her, really."

"I promise you, she'll be going to go to a good home," Fenella replied.

Patricia didn't say anything, she simply sat and snuggled the cat with tears slowly falling down her cheeks.

"I've been talking to a lot of Mabel's old friends," Fenella said eventually. "Some of them are interested in getting together again. Over the years they all seem to have lost touch with one another."

"Isn't it enough that the police are dragging it all back up?" Patricia asked. "Why would we want to see all of those people again?"

"Who is getting together?" Howard demanded.

"I'm not sure yet. I've talked to Donna about it, but it's really just the beginnings of a plan," Fenella told him. "I'm hoping to get Jeanne and Marilyn to agree, and also Clyde."

"Mabel was our tenant, not our friend," Patricia said. "We barely knew the girl."

"But we did know her," her husband countered. "She lived in our home, after all."

"And she paid us for the privilege," Patricia snapped. "I don't know what her friends are hoping to accomplish by reuniting, but it's nothing to do with us."

"Maybe they're hoping to work out what actually happened to Mabel," Fenella suggested.

"She was living on her own, inviting trouble into her life, and it found her," Patricia said. "If she'd have been living with her parents or a husband, she would have been perfectly safe."

Fenella swallowed a dozen retorts. "That makes it sound as if you're blaming her for getting murdered," she said finally.

"We never should have rented my house to her in the first place. We should have found a nice young family who would have appreciated the place and looked after it properly. My parents lived there for thirty-odd years and never had any problems with the plumbing or the heating or anything else that Mabel used to complain about constantly."

"I used to do repairs for them, too," Howard said quietly. "The house wasn't new and it was starting to show its age. We were lucky Mabel wanted to live there, really."

"We could have found more suitable tenants, if you hadn't let Mabel's father talk you into letting her have the house," Patricia argued. "You know I never liked the idea."

Howard nodded and then looked at Fenella. "Nothing like a fifty-year-old argument between spouses, is there? It's the one fight we both feel as if we lost."

"I did lose. You rented the house to Mabel over my objections," Patricia said.

"And then she got murdered there and we had to sell the house at a huge loss," Howard added. "No one won in the end."

"Except Mabel wouldn't have been there if you'd listened to me," Patricia snapped.

Howard opened his mouth and then shut it again. Fenella could almost see him counting to ten in his head.

"I didn't meant to bring up a sore subject," she said, trying to diffuse the tension.

"It was a subject that we'd agreed to leave in the past," Patricia told her. "Sadly, circumstances have brought the topic back into our lives."

"Maybe now the police will finally be able to work out who killed Mabel," Fenella suggested.

"After fifty years, I can't imagine anyone still cares," Patricia replied. "You said yourself that her friends have all drifted apart. Surely, whatever happened to her, the entire thing is best left in the distant past."

"She was murdered. If her killer is still out there, he or she deserved to be discovered," Fenella said firmly.

"I think it's time to go," Howard interrupted. "I need my medication."

"Didn't you bring it with you?" Patricia asked.

"No," he replied sharply. "Let's go."

"But I'm enjoying..." Patricia trailed off as Howard got to his feet. She glanced at Fenella and then shrugged. "Can you take..." she began, gesturing toward the sleeping cat.

"Of course," Fenella said quickly. She moved the cat over to her own lap. Patricia was on her feet, walking after her husband, before Fenella could say anything further.

"Well, darn," she muttered to the animal. The cat stared at her for a minute and then jumped off her lap and began to prowl around the room. Fenella had been so caught up in her conversation with Patricia and Howard that she hadn't taken the time to see who else was present. She was disappointed to find that Jeanne Reese wasn't among the men and women scattered around the room.

"I think everything is going well," Crystal said as Fenella joined her near the room's entrance. "The kittens seem to be enjoying themselves and the residents obviously love them."

"Mr. Stone said you were thinking about adopting a few of them," Fenella said.

"There's going to be a meeting later today about that very topic," Crystal replied. "I'm pretty sure we'll be able to take two of the kittens here and two at the other facility. That solves your kitten problem, anyway."

"Then I just have to find a home for the mother cat," Fenella sighed.

"Maybe I can help," a voice suggested from the doorway.

Fenella looked up and smiled at Jeanne, who was just walking through the door. "Are you interested in taking the mother cat?" she asked.

"Aaron and I talked about it for hours and he's finally come around," she said. Then she laughed loudly. "Actually, I asked him if it was okay and he didn't hear the question. I assume, since he didn't say no, that it must be okay."

Crystal laughed. "I hope this isn't going to be a problem."

"It won't be. He'll love her as much as I do. With my luck, within a day or two she'll decide she wants to be his cat and I'll never get more than an odd glance from her again. I'd better snuggle with her now, before she changes her alliances."

Jeanne walked over to a nearby couch and sat down. The mother cat was curled up in her lap before Fenella had time to excuse herself from Crystal.

"How are you?" she asked Jeanne as she settled into the chair opposite her.

"I'm fine. I'm oddly excited about having another pet, even though Aaron was right. We did agree that we'd stop once the children were out of the house. I find I miss having someone or something to fuss over, though. The children are all on their own, with their own families. We have grandchildren, of course, but everyone is so busy with everything. I don't get nearly enough opportunities to fuss over the grandchildren, that's for sure. This little cat is exactly what I need."

"Patricia Quinn wants to adopt her, too," Fenella said.

Jeanne made a face. "I don't want to fight over her. If Patricia really wants her, and she asked first, she can have her. I can always adopt from one of the local shelters. I know there are always cats and kittens in need of good homes."

"Howard doesn't want the cat."

"And even though Patricia is used to always getting her own way, sometimes Howard puts his foot down," Jeanne grinned. "He can be quite scary when he gets serious."

"Scary?"

"Oh, not really scary. That was a poor choice of words, but he's usually so quiet and almost invisible, really, until he's pushed too far."

Fenella wondered at the woman's words. "Could he be pushed far enough to kill someone?" she asked.

Jeanne frowned. "I would think if he were going to kill someone, that he would have killed Patricia long ago."

"I thought they were devoted to one another," Fenella said dryly.

Jeanne laughed. "He spent a lot of time at Mabel's, ostensibly repairing things around the house. I always thought he was just there because he hated going home. He used to complain about Patricia almost constantly."

"Donna said something similar, actually."

"Did she? I miss her."

"I was thinking that it would be nice for you all to have something of a reunion," Fenella said tentatively. "There's a nice café not far from Donna's house. They do wonderful cakes."

"I know which one you mean. I haven't been there in years. It's a bit too close to the old neighborhood, really. I told you that I deliberately cut my ties. I try to avoid driving through that part of Douglas, as well."

"Would you be interested in seeing everyone, if I arranged it?"

Jeanne sat back and stared straight ahead for a short while. Fenella watched as a dozen different emotions came and went from her face. Eventually, she sighed and then looked at Fenella.

"Yes, I would be interested," she said, "if only because I'm too old to waste time worrying about how awkward it might be seeing them all again. I hope I have a few good years left, but you never know. I'd like to see Marilyn and Donna at least one more time before it's too late."

"What about Clyde?"

Jeanne shrugged. "You're welcome to include him, if he's interested in coming along. He can stand in for Mabel, as she can't attend. It will be very much like old times, really."

"I'll see what I can arrange. When would be convenient for you?"

"I'm pretty much always available, unless Aaron or I have appointments. Now that I've agreed to it, I'd like to do it as soon as possible, really. How about Friday?"

Fenella pulled out her phone and checked her calendar. It was, as she'd expected, empty for Friday. "I hope you don't mind if I come along," she told Jeanne.

"Not at all. We might need a neutral party," Jeanne replied. "After all these years, I'm sure we'll have lots about which to argue."

"I hope not."

"Mornings are better for me. Aaron naps in the afternoon and he can sometimes be a bit disoriented when he wakes up. I like to be with him at home in the afternoons."

They agreed on ten o'clock at the café near Donna's house. "I'll call you if I can't get anyone else to agree to meet," Fenella promised.

"Oh, don't bother. If no one else comes, you and I can have some cake and chat about other things," the woman said easily. "Now that you've mentioned the place, I can't stop thinking about their Victoria sponge. I've never had better, you know."

"So I'll see you on Friday," Fenella confirmed as Jeanne handed her the cat and got to her feet.

"When will you know about the cat?" Jeanne asked.

"Mr. Stone is going to be checking them all over on Thursday. If the kittens are ready to leave their mother, then I may be able to hand the mother over to you on Friday as well."

"I'd like that," Jeanne smiled.

Fenella stood up, putting the mother cat on the floor. She wandered once around the room and then headed for the table by the door.

"I think she's ready to go home," Crystal laughed as the cat jumped onto the table and climbed into her carrier.

"Yes, I think you're right."

The two of them rounded up the kittens and tucked them into their carrier.

"You'll be bringing them back again, won't you?" one of the women asked as Fenella took a kitten from her.

"We might be adopting a few of them," Crystal told her. "They could live in the lounge here and you could all take turns looking after them."

"I'm not interested in looking after them," the woman said sharply. "I just want to play with them from time to time."

Crystal nodded. "If we do adopt a few of them, their actual care will fall to one of the staff. We would just hope that our residents would play with them and give them love."

"Sign me up for that part," another woman said. "We had cats and dogs and hamsters when the children were small. I don't want to clean up after anything ever again, but I love having a cuddle now and again."

Crystal grinned and then walked Fenella back out to the parking lot. "I think this is going to work out," she said. "Three different members of staff have already volunteered to take care of the hard work associated with kitten care, and I sneaked cat food and litter into the entertainment budget, so that's sorted. I've become rather fond of the little guys myself, so I really hope we can keep them."

"I'll see you tomorrow at the other location," Fenella told her as she slid the carriers into her car. "I hope they're as excited about keeping a few kittens as the residents here are."

"They may be even more excited," Crystal replied. "It's the staff there that I'm struggling with, if I'm honest. I can't seem to find anyone who's willing to volunteer to handle their care."

"Didn't you say those residents need more looking after? Maybe the staff there feels more overworked."

"You're probably right. Maybe we could add a part-time kitten caretaker to the staff. I don't suppose you need a part-time job?"

Fenella quickly shook her head. "Sorry, but I really don't."

Crystal shrugged. "I'm determined to make it work. I really feel as if the residents there need the kittens. The men and women here are allowed to have pets in their own apartments if they really want them, after all. Never mind, I'm sure you have enough problems of your own, without worrying about mine."

"You should ask Mr. Stone," Fenella suggested. "Maybe he knows a teenager who loves animals and wants to be a vet. He or she might welcome the chance to look after the kittens for an hour or two each day, or whatever it would take."

"That's an idea," Crystal mused. "I'll ring him."

Fenella drove home with kittens and care on her mind. When she pulled up in front of her house, Daniel was just driving up from the other direction.

"Need a hand?" he asked after they'd both parked.

Fenella was pulling carriers out of the car. She nodded. "You can grab the other one, if you want."

Together, they took the carriers into the house and then released the animals.

"How was your morning?" Daniel asked.

"Good. I talked to Patricia and Howard. They don't want to have anything to do with a reunion. Jeanne, on the other hand, is willing, maybe even eager, to see everyone again."

"What did Donna say last night?"

"She said no, but then said she'd reconsider if any of the others were going."

"What next?"

"I've arranged with Jeanne to meet on Friday at ten, at the café near Donna's house," she told him. "If no one else wants to come, Jeanne and I will have cake and chat."

"When will you see the others?"

"I'm taking the kittens to the other nursing home tomorrow morning. I'm hoping to find time to chat with both Marilyn and Clyde while I'm there."

"I'm going to be at the café on Friday morning," he told her. "I have a feeling you're going to find out things that are important, once you get everyone together again."

"They might not all come."

"They will. I believe everyone in that group is hiding things. They aren't going to want to risk anyone sharing their secrets when they aren't there."

"I hope you're right. The more I learn about the case, the more I want to know what happened to Mabel."

"Any thoughts on the subject?"

Fenella frowned. "I don't like Patricia or Howard Quinn, but I'm not sure I see either of them as the murderer, either."

"Maybe you'd better run through your conversations with everyone from today," Daniel suggested.

"Let's go in the kitchen. We can have sandwiches while we talk."

By the time Fenella was done recounting her morning conversations, she and Daniel had eaten several sandwiches each.

"I can see why you don't care for the Quinns," Daniel remarked as he washed down his last bite with a soda. "Any idea as to a motive for either of them?"

"Patricia hated renting her house to Mabel. Is that enough of a motive?"

"It's impossible to say what's enough of a motive for any one individual. I wouldn't kill anyone over something as simple as that, but then I wouldn't rent my house to someone under those circumstances, either."

"I keep wondering about Mabel and Howard," Fenella admitted. "By all accounts, they were alone together frequently. Could they have been having an affair?"

"He wasn't that much older than Mabel. It's possible, I suppose."

"I suggested as much to Jeanne and she dismissed it almost immediately."

Daniel shrugged. "If Mabel did have an affair with the man, that seems to give both Howard and Patricia motives."

Fenella nodded. "I can't think of any motive for Jeanne or Marilyn or Donna, really."

"Didn't someone tell you that Donna fancied Clyde? Maybe Mabel was getting in the way of that, giving Donna a reason for wanting her dead."

"If she did kill Mabel so that she could have a chance with Clyde, the whole thing backfired quite badly."

"Yes, but she couldn't have known how things were going to turn out."

"We could imagine a motive for Marilyn if Mabel was having an affair with Ewan," Fenella suggested.

"He was interviewed during the investigation and he insisted that he barely knew Mabel. I got the impression, from reading his statement, that he didn't really approve of Marilyn's friends. It sounded very much like he didn't expect them to be still be part of Marilyn's life once they were married."

"That certainly matches up to what actually happened."

"While we're imagining motives, what about Jeanne?"

Fenella frowned. "I can't think of a single reason for Jeanne to want Mabel dead."

"Maybe it had something to do with their jobs," Daniel suggested.

"Maybe they were both having affairs with the boss and Jeanne was trying to narrow the field," Fenella said, laughing.

"It isn't completely outside the realm of possibility, I suppose," Daniel told her, "but it seems unlikely."

"Then there's Clyde. I can't see him killing his sister, I really can't."

"If he had feelings for Donna, then he had as much motive as she did."

"But surely, if he wanted Donna, he could have told his sister as much. Why wouldn't Mabel have supported the idea if they were both keen?"

"I don't know. We're just bouncing ideas around. It probably won't help, but you never know."

Fenella nodded. "I wish we knew whether Marilyn was right or not. If Mabel was seeing someone secretly, then there's a big piece of the puzzle missing."

"I can't believe no one knew," Daniel told her. "Women confide in their friends. All four women claim they were as close as sisters. Mabel would have told one of them about the man in her life, even if she'd then swore her friend to secrecy."

"Surely murder voids such things. If one of my friends was murdered, I'd want to tell the police absolutely everything I knew that might help solve the murder."

"Perhaps the friend doesn't think that what she knows will help solve the case. Maybe the mystery man couldn't have been the killer for some reason or other."

"It's still useful information for the police."

"I hope you'll communicate that to everyone at your gathering on Friday," Daniel told her.

❧ 14 ❧

It was pouring rain when Fenella woke up on Wednesday morning. She frowned and then rolled over and covered her head with a pillow. A moment later a kitten jumped squarely onto her back.

"How did you get up here?" Fenella demanded as she sat up in bed.

The kitten gave her an impish grin and then dashed away. By the time Fenella slid on her slippers and bathrobe and followed, the kitten had disappeared. When she reached the living room, all four kittens were shouting loudly from the playpen with their mother.

"I know it was one of you," she told them all. "You're just lucky I didn't have my glasses on so I don't know which one."

After she'd filled their food and water bowls, she turned the coffee maker on and then took a shower. After both cereal and toast, she felt more like facing the day, rain or not.

"I didn't even have a late night," she told the kittens as she bundled them into their carrier. "I had frozen pizza in front of the television, all alone."

One of the kittens meowed sympathetically at her as she shut the carrier's door.

"Come on," she told the mother cat. "We've people to visit again."

A short while later she was on her way, windshield wipers going as quickly as they could as she drove.

"What a terrible day," Crystal said as Fenella dashed into the foyer of the nursing home with one of the carriers. "Do you need help?"

Fenella looked at the woman's immaculate cream-colored business suit and shook her head. "It's a mess out there. I'll get everything myself."

"Oh, I wasn't going to go myself," Crystal laughed. "I was going to send one of the maintenance staff with you."

"Never mind. By the time someone gets here, I'll be back with everything else."

Fenella was soaked through by the time she'd made it back through the door with the second carrier and the various supplies the animals needed. Crystal had someone hold the door for her, at least.

"Right, let's see how everyone feels about the kittens today," Crystal said brightly as she led Fenella into the main lounge area. A dozen men and women smiled eagerly at Fenella as she put the carriers on the table. As soon as the kittens were released, voices began calling to the animals. Fenella smiled as the kittens began to race around the room, reveling in the attention.

"I wonder if you'd like to take the mother cat to visit Marilyn Coleman again," Crystal said. "She's been talking about her since your last visit."

"I'd love to," Fenella replied, trying not to sound too eager.

Crystal led her down a long corridor to Marilyn's room. "Marilyn? Fenella is here with her cat again," she called as she knocked on the door.

"Come in, then," Marilyn's voice called.

Crystal opened the door and then gestured for Fenella to enter. "I'll be back in half an hour," she told Fenella before she let the door shut.

"Good morning," Fenella said brightly. Marilyn was in bed, sitting propped against several pillows, a scowl on her face.

"They won't let me out of bed," she complained loudly. "I had a little fall yesterday and now they're insisting that I stay in bed for twenty-four hours."

"I am sorry," Fenella said, setting the cat on the edge of the bed.

After a quick look around, she headed up the bed and curled up in Marilyn's lap.

Marilyn gave her a few pats and then sighed. She sat back against the pillows and began to stroke the animal's back. "This is better than any therapy out there," she said after a minute. "I can't stay mad at the world, or even my doctors, when I'm petting this cat."

"I'm glad I brought her in, then," Fenella said.

"Have you found a home for her?"

"I think Jeanne is going to take her."

"Jeanne? Not Jeanne Richardson?"

"She's Jeanne Reese now, and yes, that Jeanne."

"When did you meet her?"

"Last week, on Thursday," Fenella explained. "I met her and Howard and Patricia Quinn."

Marilyn made a face. "I bet Howard didn't like the cat."

"Patricia wanted to adopt her, but Howard said no."

"And Patricia didn't argue? She never let Howard tell her what to do, not back when I knew her, anyway."

"She argued a little bit, but Howard refused to even consider the idea."

"It sounds as if the dynamics of their marriage have changed, then, over the years. I suppose that isn't surprising, really, given how long they've been together."

"It's probably quite normal," Fenella agreed.

"I wonder how things would have changed in my marriage if things had been different," Marilyn sighed, "if we'd had children to keep us together or drive us apart or if my mother had left us to work out our problems rather than adding to them."

"I'm sure your mother tried to do what she thought was best," Fenella said diplomatically.

"She did what was best for her," Marilyn countered. "She and my father had a difficult relationship. Being with me gave her an excuse to be away from him. She used me to escape from her own marriage, never mind that it destroyed mine."

"I'm sorry," Fenella said, feeling as if the words were inadequate.

Marilyn shrugged. "Maybe Mabel was the lucky one. She died

young and we all remember her as beautiful and full of life. She never got beaten down by harsh reality."

"Maybe you'd feel better if you talked to some of the others," Fenella said. "I told Jeanne I would try to set up something of a reunion for you all, if you're interested."

"A reunion? How very American of you. I'm not sure that any of us are interested in reuniting, not after all these years."

"Jeanne is interested, and Donna might come if the rest of you are coming."

Marilyn fell silent, petting the cat and staring into the distance. After several minutes, she broke the silence. "Where and when?"

"Friday at ten at the café near Donna's house," Fenella said, wondering if Marilyn would know where she meant.

"I haven't been there in years," Marilyn said softly. "They used to do the most delicious Victoria sponge."

"I've been told they still do. Maybe you should find out on Friday."

Marilyn shrugged. "I'll think about it, but I'm not going to promise anything. I may not be allowed out of bed by then, of course."

"Whether you decide to come or not, I do hope you'll be feeling better."

"Yes, well, at my age better is somewhat relative."

"I think that's true at any age."

Marilyn gave her a small smile. "You could be right. How old are you?"

"Forty-nine," Fenella winced, trying not to think of the birthday that was looming at the end of the year.

"I remember when that felt old to me. Make sure that you enjoy it. Seventy-five is only a few days away, or so it seems to me."

"I'm doing my best to enjoy every day," Fenella assured her. While that was very true, she was also less worried about what would be coming next now that she'd spent so much time with Mona. Being a ghost seemed like a pretty good way to spend the rest of eternity.

"And now I need rest," Marilyn announced. "Do you mind taking her away?"

"Of course not." Fenella picked up the cat and then helped Marilyn remove some of the pillows from behind her head.

"That's much better. I believe a rest will do me some good."

Fenella left Marilyn alone for her nap, letting herself out into the corridor and then wondering what to do next. Crystal was supposed to be coming back for her, but she was nowhere in sight.

"Clyde Gross was hoping the cat might visit him, too," a passing nurse told her. "I can tell Crystal that you've gone to see him."

"That would be great," Fenella said happily. The nurse gave her Clyde's room number and directions to his room. A few minutes later, she knocked on the door.

"If you've brought me a feline visitor, you can come in, otherwise, go away," a voice called.

Fenella laughed and then pushed the door open. "It's my lucky day," she said brightly as she put the cat down on the floor.

Clyde was sitting in a chair by the window with a book on his lap. The cat jumped up and shouted loudly at the offending paperback. Clyde grinned and then put the book on the table in front of him. "Sit down," he told Fenella. "Make yourself comfortable. I'm hoping for a long visit with this little lady."

Fenella took the chair across from him and sat back. He was rubbing the cat's tummy with a satisfied smile on his face.

"I wish I could keep her," he said after a minute. "I can't look after her properly, of course, but I wish I could. She's incredibly sweet."

"Jeanne Reese might be taking her," Fenella told him.

"Jeanne Reese?"

"She was Jeanne Richardson when you knew her."

Clyde nodded. "I knew she'd married, but I didn't remember her married name. She's four years older than I am. I suppose I should be happy for her if she's still capable of looking after a pet."

"Patricia Quinn really wanted to take her."

Clyde frowned. "I hope you told her no. She's much older and not at all suitable."

"Her husband said no before I got the chance."

"Howard," Clyde said in an odd tone.

"Yes, that's right."

"Did you see Marilyn again today?"

"I did, and I saw Jeanne yesterday and Donna the day before."

"You really are pushing yourself into Mabel's past, aren't you?"

"It isn't intentional," Fenella told him, "but I am trying to arrange a reunion of sorts for you all. Every one of you seems sad about how you've lost touch with one another. I thought you might like a chance to talk again."

"One last time, you mean."

"I wouldn't say that. I'd like to think that you might rekindle your friendships and have many more gatherings after this one."

"You've actually arranged something?"

"I've arranged to have tea and cakes with Jeanne on Friday. Anyone else who wants to come along is welcome."

"Tea and cakes? Where?"

"There's a little café near where Donna lives."

Clyde frowned. "That isn't far from where we all used to live. I haven't been to that part of Douglas in many years."

"Well, you're more than welcome to join us at ten o'clock. Marilyn may be there, if she feels up to it. Donna said she might come if everyone else is attending."

Clyde nodded. "Anyone else?"

"I don't know if Jeanne's husband might come along. I mentioned it to Patricia and Howard, but they weren't interested in coming."

Clyde stiffened. "I won't come if they might be there."

"They aren't going to be there. I never even told them where we were meeting or when. I told them a reunion was being discussed and they both told me they weren't interested in attending."

"I should think not," Clyde said in a low voice.

Fenella swallowed the questions that sprang into her mind. "I'm sure everyone would love to see you," she said instead.

"I'll think about it. It's been a long time. There were reasons why we stopped seeing each other, though. Those reasons are still in place."

"Maybe it's time to work through everything," Fenella suggested. "You were very close once."

"They were close. I was always on the outside, looking in," he sighed. "They were like sisters, and I know Mabel was always slightly disappointed that she didn't have a real sister. I was something of a disappointment to her."

"Everyone I've spoken to has said that she adored you," Fenella countered.

"I adored her," he countered. "She put up with me because I was all she had, but she would have preferred a sister, someone with whom she could share her secrets and her problems. I was a poor substitute, even though I tried my best."

"I'm sure it wasn't like that."

"I know it was exactly that. She and the other three women, they were close, almost as close as sisters, but not quite. Mabel kept secrets from them and from me." He sighed. "I'm sorry, but I'm tired and this conversation is upsetting. I'd like you to leave."

Fenella got to her feet reluctantly. "If you'd like, I can just sit here quietly while you enjoy your time with the cat."

Clyde looked down at the sleeping animal. "I'm beyond enjoying her company right now. Just take her and go, please."

As if she'd recognized her cue, the cat woke up and jumped into Fenella's arms. Fenella turned and headed for the door, feeling oddly guilty about upsetting him.

"Friday at ten?" he asked. "I may be there."

"I hope you are," Fenella replied.

She walked back to the main lounge and found Crystal chasing kittens.

"There you are. I was just going to go and look for you. I think the kittens are dangerously close to overstaying their welcome right now."

Fenella put the mother cat into her carrier and then helped Crystal find the last kitten. "Does this mean you don't want any of them?" she asked worriedly as she picked up the carriers.

"I don't know. I think we still want them, but they were hard work today. We can't afford to take on a full-time member of staff to deal with the kittens. It might be better if we try to find them all homes at the other center. Those residents are allowed to have pets, after all. If all of the kittens went to individual homes, I wouldn't have to worry about them."

"Let me know what you want to do," Fenella told her. "I believe they'll be ready to leave their mother by Friday."

Crystal smiled tightly. "Yes, let me know," she said faintly.

It took Fenella three trips in the heavy rain to get the animals and their things back into the car. Sighing deeply, she pulled away from the home.

"What did you guys get up to back there?" she demanded as she drove. "They were ready to give you a good home and now they're not. You must have caused a lot of trouble."

Her question was greeted with silence. When they got back to the house, Fenella found all four kittens fast asleep. Whatever they'd done, they'd clearly worn themselves out.

"They're ready to leave Mum, but I'm not sure Crystal is going to take any of them," Mr. Stone told her the next day. "Apparently they weren't exactly well behaved yesterday."

"I never did hear the whole story," Fenella replied. "When I got back to the lounge, Crystal was packing kittens into the carrier as quickly as she could."

Mr. Stone laughed. "I didn't get the whole story either. She just told me that they were harder work than she'd anticipated and that she didn't think that particular home could accommodate them. I understand she's still considering taking one or two for the other home, but I think she'd rather individual residents adopted them than have the home take on the responsibility for them."

"I hope you have some other ideas for them, then," Fenella said. "I really don't want to keep them for much longer."

"I'm sure we can find them somewhere to go," he told her. "Don't worry about it for today. I'll talk to Crystal again tomorrow. It will all work out."

Fenella didn't share his optimism, but she didn't argue. "The mother cat has been offered a home," she told him, explaining about Jeanne. "Are you okay with her going there?"

"I'd like to see the mother cat going to a home where she'll be kept indoors," he replied. "If your friend is prepared to keep her indoors, I'm happy with her if you approve of her."

"I'll talk to her tomorrow and see what she says. I can't imagine her not keeping the cat indoors, really, but we didn't discuss it."

"I'd like to keep seeing her, too," he added. "I've grown rather attached, really, but I can't make that a condition of her adoption, obviously. Just let her new owner know that I'll give a substantial discount if they bring her here."

Fenella nodded. "I know what you mean. I'm rather fond of her myself."

Daniel paid her a visit that evening. Fenella had just finished her dinner and was popping popcorn in the microwave to go with a movie.

"I have popcorn in the microwave," she told him as she let him in and then dashed back to the kitchen. The popping was just slowing down, and she counted three seconds between pops and then pulled the door open.

"Scorched popcorn is horrible," she explained as she dumped the steaming hot treat into a large bowl.

"I can't argue with that," he laughed.

She put the bowl in the middle of the table and then offered him a drink.

"As much as I'd love to share a bottle of wine with you, I'm on call tonight and things are a bit hectic at work at the moment."

"Oh?"

He shrugged. "There was a large drug bust yesterday in the wee small hours of the morning. Tomorrow's paper will be full of the story. We're concerned that it might just be the tip of the iceberg in terms of what's being brought into the island. I've been pulled off the Gross case to help the drug and alcohol unit with their investigation."

"Oh, dear. That sounds serious."

"It is serious, and it's disappointing because I truly think we're getting close to a solution to Mabel's murder."

"Does that mean you won't be at the café tomorrow?"

"I'm still hoping to be there, but I may have to make it an early lunch break rather than anything else. Depending on what else happens between now and then, though, I may not make it. Please be careful if I'm not there."

"We're meeting in a very public place," Fenella reminded him. "Even if someone says something they shouldn't, nothing is going to happen in the middle of a crowded Douglas café."

Daniel nodded. "If I can't be there, I'll send a constable. It may not be anyone you'll recognize, but there will be someone there, and he or she will be listening to your conversation very closely, but hopefully, very discreetly."

"That sounds good," Fenella told him.

"Who's going to be there?"

"Jeanne is the only one who has actually agreed to come, but I suspect the others may well show up, even though they're all being noncommittal."

"Who is least likely to attend, do you think?"

Fenella thought for a minute. "Donna was most insistent that she wouldn't attend, but when I rang her and told her that Jeanne was going to be there, she seemed to soften considerably. I think Donna will be there. I think Marilyn will be, too, if her health permits. I suppose Clyde seems least likely, but he also seemed to feel as if he was less welcome. He said something about always being on the outside of the group."

"Do what you can to get them talking about Mabel, but don't upset anyone. I'm planning on interviewing them all again soon, assuming I can wrap up what I'm doing with the other case quickly."

"Maybe just seeing one another again will be enough to bring back a few memories. If any of them are keeping secrets, I hope they realize it's time to share them with the police, even if they still want to keep them from the others."

Daniel glanced at the clock and then sighed. "It's been a very long day. I'd really like to stay and talk through the case with you again, but I'm out on my feet. I need to get some sleep. Tomorrow isn't going to be any easier."

Fenella walked him to the door and then let him out. He looked as if he was considering kissing her, but in the end he took a step backward and then walked away.

"And that's me on my own again," she grumbled as she headed back into the kitchen. The popcorn was gone and the movie no longer sounded interesting. She grabbed a book and headed up to her room to read. When she fell asleep in the middle of chapter two, she didn't wake up until morning.

By nine o'clock she was pacing around her living room, making the kittens crazy. "I'm sorry," she said as she nearly tripped over one of them. "I'm just a bit anxious about this morning. I'm not sure if I'm hoping they all turn up or that none of them do."

She sat down and petted the mother cat until she was feeling calmer. "Here goes nothing," she told them all as she headed for the door a short time later.

The café was mostly empty, so it didn't take Fenella long to spot Jeanne sitting by herself at a table in one corner. As Fenella crossed the room, she noticed Daniel at the table next to Jeanne's. He was sitting facing the back of the room and wearing a hat. If she hadn't known him so well, she might not have recognized him. The man across from him was no stranger, either. Fenella nodded at Mark Hammersmith, another Douglas police inspector, as she passed their table.

"Good morning," Jeanne said as Fenella slid into the chair next to hers. "I've been here for at least twenty minutes. I'm unbelievably anxious about all of this. Is anyone else actually coming, though?"

"I certainly hope so. Everyone said maybe, at least," Fenella told her. "I think they all want to come, but I wonder if nerves might stop at least one or two of them."

"They nearly..." Jeanne trailed off, her eyes on the door.

Fenella looked up and then smiled as Donna walked into the café. She waved and Donna nodded and then began to walk toward them.

"It's Donna, isn't it?" Jeanne whispered in Fenella's ear. "She looks the same, really, just older."

"Jeanne," Donna said when she reached the table. "I wasn't sure about this, but it is nice to see you."

"It's nice to see you, too," Jeanne replied politely.

"Donna, do sit down," Fenella urged after an awkward silence.

Donna seemed to hesitate before she pulled out the chair opposite Jeanne and sank into it.

"You look wonderful," Jeanne told her friend.

"I'm old now," Donna countered. "We both are, of course. Some days I really feel my age. Today is one of those days."

The café door swung open and Fenella felt as if the other two women were both holding their breath as Marilyn was wheeled into the room.

"Marilyn," Fenella said brightly. She waved again and a moment later caught Marilyn's eye.

"She looks terrible," Donna hissed to Jeanne as Marilyn's companion pushed her toward them.

"Living with her mother for all those years must have been diffi-cult," Jeanne suggested.

"Good morning," Marilyn said.

Fenella got up and moved one of the chairs out of the way so that Marilyn's wheelchair could be pushed right up to the table.

"I'll be back in an hour," the young woman with Marilyn told her. "You have my mobile number if you need me sooner."

Marilyn nodded and then turned and seemed to study Jeanne and Donna. "You look good," she told Donna eventually, "and you look happy," she added, nodding at Jeanne.

"I am happy," Jeanne replied. "I ended up marrying a truly good man. We've had a good life together."

"You were lucky," Marilyn said.

Jeanne nodded. "I was, at that. I went out with more than my fair share of unsuitable men. Aaron was the first one I actually considered marrying."

Marilyn and Donna both laughed. "You forget how well we know you," Donna said. "You would have married just about any man, given the opportunity."

Jeanne flushed. "I don't think that's true."

"You were almost as bad as I was," Marilyn interjected. "I was desperate to get married, of course, because I wanted to get away from my mother. You weren't quite desperate, but we all knew you were really hoping to get married sooner rather than later."

"I don't remember it that way," Jeanne replied with a shrug. "It was a long time ago, of course."

"Fifty years," Donna said, sounding surprised. "Mabel died nearly fifty years ago. I can't quite get my head around it. She was only twenty-five, which means she's been gone for twice as long as she was alive. That doesn't seem possible."

"I still miss her," Marilyn said. "I've missed both of you, as well."

Jeanne nodded. "I've missed you both, too. It all just felt overwhelming at the time: Mabel's death, the funeral, your wedding. I felt as if I were just going through the motions and not truly understanding what was happening. It seemed easier to pull away from all of you than to deal with everything."

"I think we all felt that way," Donna said. "Mabel's death was the most horrible thing that had ever happened in my life. Even now, at seventy-five, I can say that it was the most horrible thing I ever went through. Losing my parents was easier in many ways."

"Losing my children was the worst thing I ever lived through," Marilyn said bitterly, "but losing Mabel was the next worst. Everything about it was awful."

Jeanne nodded. "When I close my eyes, I can still see her lying on the kitchen floor. I've never managed to get that image out of my head, in spite of the years that have passed."

"It wasn't just Mabel's death, though, it was the aftermath. She was murdered and for months I kept expecting her killer to come after me next," Marilyn said. "It would have been a lot easier if the police had discovered her killer."

"I always thought I was going to be the next victim," Jeanne said. "I thought for sure Mabel was killed because of Mr. Neil."

"Mr. Neil? Why would she have been killed because of him?" Donna asked.

Jeanne shrugged and then looked down at the table. "Maybe we should get some tea and cake."

Fenella looked around and caught the eye of the waitress.

"Are you waiting for anyone else?" she asked as she pulled out a small order pad.

"There may be one more, but we'll order now anyway, if we can," Fenella told her.

"Whatever you want," the girl shrugged.

She was back a few minutes later with four slices of Victoria sponge and four cups of tea. "Let me know if you need anything else," she told them after she'd unloaded her tray.

Fenella took a large bite of cake to stop herself from asking Jeanne to explain further. If one of the others didn't ask, though, she would.

"I still want to know why you thought Mabel was killed because of Mr. Neil," Donna said after she'd swallowed her first bite.

Jeanne sipped her tea and then sighed. "We all know Mabel was no angel. None of us were, really, were we? When I first started working for Mr. Neil, Mabel was having an affair with him."

Donna nearly choked on her tea, coughing violently for several seconds.

"Are you okay?" Fenella asked as Donna's breathing returned to normal.

"I think so," Donna told her. "I was just taken by surprise, that's all."

"I knew about it," Marilyn said, a touch smugly.

"Mabel knew you wouldn't approve," Jeanne told Donna. "She insisted that I not tell anyone. I didn't even know that Marilyn knew."

"Mabel was terrible at keeping secrets from me," Marilyn said. "We used to talk on the phone every night because my mother wouldn't let me visit Mabel all that often. Mabel would tell me all manner of things during those chats, things she'd then swear me to secrecy about."

"What else did she tell you?" Donna demanded. "I'm starting to feel as if I barely knew her."

"Mostly she talked about Mr. Neil. The affair didn't last long, but she was able to use it to get more money out of the man for less work. It wasn't exactly blackmail, but it was close," Marilyn said.

Donna shook her head. "I didn't know Mabel at all," she said sadly.

"She didn't see it as doing anything wrong," Jeanne said quickly. "She was just having fun. If Mr. Neil had called her bluff, she would have found another job rather than tell his wife about the affair. She wasn't interested in him. She just thought it was exciting to be involved with a married man."

"How long did the affair last?" Fenella asked.

Jeanne shrugged. "Not long. I know they were together when I started working there." She stopped and flushed. "That was how Mabel got me the job, actually. Mr. Neil didn't really need three secretaries, but he hired me anyway to keep Mabel happy."

"You started working there at least a year before Mabel died," Donna said. "Was she still seeing him for that entire year?"

"Oh, no. I don't think the affair lasted more than a month or two after I was hired," Jeanne said. "It wasn't much more than a month after I started when Mr. Neil asked me to have dinner with him, anyway. We went out a few times, but I wasn't willing to sleep with him, so he moved on to Helen fairly quickly."

"Helen was the woman he was with the night Mabel died?" Donna asked.

Jeanne nodded. "That's right. She and Mr. Neil started their affair at least six months before Mabel died. They left the island together once everyone found out about it."

"If you thought you'd be a target because of Mr. Neil, did you think it was his wife who'd killed Mabel?" Fenella wondered.

"I didn't have any idea who killed her, but I couldn't think of any reason why anyone wanted her dead. Thinking that it was something to do with her work seemed better, somehow, than thinking it was just something random," Jeanne replied.

Fenella opened her mouth to ask another question but stopped when she saw the color drain from Donna's face. Donna was staring at the door and Fenella looked over to see Clyde making his way toward them.

❧ 15 ❧

"Hello," Fenella said when he reached the table. "Have a seat." He looked around the table and then nodded slowly. "Thank you." There were empty seats between Jeanne and Donna and between Marilyn and Fenella. After a moment's hesitation, he sat down next to Fenella.

"I'm sorry I'm late," he said slowly. "I wasn't sure I was going to come, then I thought you all would probably appreciate some time to talk without me around."

"We were just talking about Mabel," Marilyn told him.

"Some of us didn't know her as well as we thought we did," Donna added, sounding angry.

Clyde looked at her for a minute and then nodded. "She had secrets. I didn't find that out until it was too late."

"You knew she was having an affair with a married man?" Donna asked.

Clyde frowned. "I've done everything I can for the last fifty years to keep that quiet," he said tightly. "My sister's reputation matters."

"She was the one who chose to have the affair," Marilyn replied. "I don't think she was as concerned with her reputation as you were."

"I won't have you talk about her in this way," Clyde said, getting to his feet. "I've kept Mabel's secret for fifty years, in spite of everything, to protect her reputation and her memory. I don't know how you found out about her and Howard, but I won't sit here and listen to you discuss it."

"Howard?" Donna echoed. "Mabel was having an affair with Howard?"

The three women exchanged glances. "Not that I knew of," Marilyn said after a minute.

"She never told me anything about Howard," Jeanne added.

Clyde flushed. "You didn't know," he said angrily.

"She had an affair with Mr. Neil," Jeanne told him. "That's what we were talking about."

For a minute Fenella thought the man was going to storm out of the room, and she was sure Clyde thought the same thing. After several deep breaths, though, he sank back down into his seat. "She had an affair with Mr. Neil?" he asked, sounding defeated.

"Just a short one," Jeanne told him, clearly trying to make it sound less significant.

"And you all knew about it?" was his next question.

"I didn't," Donna said sharply.

He stared at her for a minute and then nodded slowly "She wasn't who I thought she was," he said sadly. "I thought losing her was the worst thing that ever happened to me, but this feels like a betrayal."

"What about Howard?" Jeanne demanded. "She was having an affair with him?"

"I thought he'd forced her into it or something," Clyde said, sounding confused. "I thought he'd taken her innocence. She was so upset, sobbing even, when she told him about the baby. He didn't believe her. He said she was trying to trick him into giving her money." He stopped and then put his head in his hands.

Fenella patted him on the back with one hand while she dug into her bag for a tissue with the other. After what felt like an hour, he looked up.

"I'm sorry," he said. "I'm going to have to go to the police and tell them everything I know."

"Tell us first," Jeanne demanded.

Fenella glanced over at Mark and Daniel. It was clear that they were hanging on every word Clyde was saying. Fenella was worried they were going to interrupt, but neither man moved as Clyde spoke again.

"I went over to see her that night, the night of the engagement party. I wanted to ask her about..." he stopped and glanced over at Donna. Blushing brightly, he shook his head and then continued. "That part doesn't matter. When I got to the house, the windows were all open. It was a hot day for June. I walked around to the back, to let myself in through the kitchen, and then I heard voices."

Daniel was on his feet now, but he still didn't interrupt.

"What happened next?" Jeanne demanded when Clyde stopped speaking.

"Mabel was arguing with Howard. It took me a while to work out what they were fighting about, and once I did, I didn't want to believe it."

"They were having an affair," Jeanne said softly.

"Mabel wanted Howard to leave Patricia and run away with her," Clyde said. "She told him she was pregnant."

Fenella felt a tear trickle down her cheek. What a shock for poor Clyde, who'd been so devoted to his sister.

"And Howard wasn't interested?" Donna asked.

"He told her he didn't believe her," Clyde replied. "He told her that he couldn't have children. He'd had mumps as a child and it had left him unable to father children. Apparently, Patricia didn't know and he didn't want her to find out, but he told Mabel to get her to stop pretending."

"Was she pretending?" Marilyn wondered.

"I don't know. I never saw the autopsy report. My parents did, and they never said anything about it, but they wouldn't have told me if she had been pregnant. They would have wanted to protect Mabel's reputation as much as I did."

"What happened next?" Donna asked.

Clyde shrugged. "I ran away. I was shocked and confused and I couldn't quite believe what I'd heard."

"Howard must have killed her," Donna said. "You should have told the police what you'd heard. They could have arrested Howard fifty years ago."

"Just because he and Mabel had a fight that night doesn't mean that he killed her," Clyde said. "I've spent the last fifty years wondering if I'd almost been a witness to Mabel's murder. Obviously, I never expected anything bad to happen to her or I never would have run away."

"Why didn't you tell the police?" Marilyn asked.

"A lot of people said that nice girls didn't live on their own. Mabel was a nice girl and I hated it when people suggested otherwise. I would have done anything to protect her reputation. I've kept quiet for fifty years to protect her good name and her memory."

"And let her murderer go free," Jeanne added.

Clyde shrugged. "If I'd known for certain that Howard killed her, I would have told the police, but what if he left right after I did and someone else came and killed her? If I told the police the whole story, Mabel's reputation would have been ruined and Howard's marriage would have been destroyed. I saw what happened to Mr. Neil. It was horrible."

"If Howard didn't kill her, Patricia did," Jeanne said. "Maybe she paid one of her unannounced visits and found Howard and Mabel in a clinch."

Clyde winced. "Or maybe it was a random intruder," he suggested. "The police have never really considered that, as far as I can tell."

"We have, actually," Daniel interjected. "We've considered many different things, but having had a great deal of information withheld from us, we've never been able to find the solution. Perhaps, in light of everything I now know, I'll be able to get closer to working out what really happened to your sister."

Clyde had tears in his eyes as he followed Daniel out of the room a short while later. Mark stayed behind to organize getting all three of the women down to the station to make their own statements.

"We'll need a statement from you, too," he told Fenella. "Daniel said to tell you that he'll visit you later at home."

Fenella nodded and then watched silently as Mark escorted the three women out of the café. She paid the bill for everyone's tea and cake, including paying for the two police inspectors, who'd clearly forgotten to do so in all of the excitement. She was back at her apartment before noon, feeling very much at loose ends.

"Patricia killed her," Mona said a short while later, after Fenella had told her the whole story. "She must have arrived a short time after Clyde left and found Mabel and Howard together."

"I'm pretty sure one of them killed her," Fenella replied. "I'm not certain which one, though."

"I hope you can get Daniel to give you a peek at the autopsy. It would be interesting to know if Mabel truly was pregnant."

"If she was, I wonder who the father was," Fenella added. "If Howard couldn't make babies, who did?"

After thoroughly discussing the case with Mona and then visiting Katie, Fenella went back to Poppy Drive feeling slightly better. When she spotted Daniel's car in his driveway, she hoped that meant he'd be over to talk to her soon.

She'd only just finished giving the cats their dinner when he knocked on her door.

"How about dinner at the pub?" he suggested when she answered.

"Can we talk about the case over dinner?"

He sighed. "I'll tell you everything I can now, before we go."

Fenella nodded and then led him into the living room. He sat down and then leaned back and shut his eyes. "I haven't been sleeping well," he told her. "Or rather, I haven't been spending enough hours in bed."

"Let's just order a pizza, then," Fenella suggested. "We can talk about the case while we wait for the delivery and then, after we eat, you can go home and get some sleep."

"That sounds great," Daniel agreed without opening his eyes.

By the time Fenella ordered the food, Daniel was snoring softly on the couch.

"I shouldn't wake him," Fenella told the mother cat. The kittens were nowhere to be seen, even after they'd spent most of the day chasing one another through the living room. The mother cat shrugged and then leapt into Daniel's lap. He jumped and then grinned at her.

"Did you tell her to wake me?" he asked.

"Not in so many words."

"Right, you heard what Clyde said at the café. He mostly just repeated that back at the station. He still seems to think that he did the right thing by not telling us years ago. His sister's reputation seems to mean more to him than finding her killer."

"It was all he had left to protect," Fenella suggested in a low voice.

Daniel nodded. "I spent the afternoon talking with both Howard and Patricia Quinn."

"I'm sure that was interesting."

"I can't tell you anything that was said, of course, but the case is still wide open at this point."

"I was hoping one of them might be shocked into confessing."

"So was I, but they've both spent fifty years keeping secrets. They aren't going to give them up that easily."

Daniel's phone blasted an annoying ringtone into the room. He frowned as he pulled it out of his pocket. "I'm on my way," he said a moment later.

"What's wrong?" Fenella asked.

"I'll explain later. Maybe not today, though," he replied as he headed for the door.

Fenella ate the pizza on her own, refrigerating the leftovers. She was still watching old movies when someone knocked on her door just after one in the morning.

"You look completely exhausted," she told Daniel when she opened the door.

"I was hoping there might be some pizza left," he replied. "I wouldn't have knocked if I hadn't seen lights on, though."

"Come on into the kitchen and I'll reheat your pizza."

"I can eat it cold," he offered.

"Sit and relax. It won't take long to reheat."

Daniel didn't argue. He slid into a chair and rested his chin on his arm.

"Can you tell me what's happening?" she asked after a minute.

"Howard and Patricia are dead," Daniel told her.

Fenella felt dizzy for a minute. "What?" she asked, grabbing the back of a chair for support.

"You've gone very pale," Daniel said, getting to his feet and guiding Fenella into a chair.

"I'm okay. What happened?"

"They both overdosed on sleeping tablets. Apparently, Patricia was prescribed them years ago and, from what we can determine, she's been getting the prescription filled regularly but not taking many tablets."

"That's odd."

Daniel shrugged. "Her doctor speculated that the couple were stockpiling them in case one of them became incapacitated and wanted to end things. Apparently this wasn't the first time he'd seen such behavior."

"They both committed suicide?"

"That remains to be determined. It might have been a case of murder and then suicide."

"Who died first?"

"Again, still to be determined, but also, it won't necessarily be conclusive."

"One of them killed Mabel, then."

"Howard left a note," Daniel told her. "I can't reveal the contents, but I can tell you that we'll be closing the investigation into Mabel's death."

Fenella swallowed her frustration. Daniel had to follow the rules, no matter how much she wanted to know what was in the letter. She fed him pizza and then sent him home, finally crawling into bed many hours later than normal.

On Monday she took the mother cat and kittens to visit Jeanne.

"Can I keep her?" Jeanne asked as she cuddled the mother.

"Mr. Stone wants her to be kept indoors at all times."

"I have no intention of letting her out. She's had a hard enough life outside. She'll have a wonderful life in our little home now."

"In that case, she's yours," Fenella replied. "That's one down and four to go."

The pair deliberately avoided discussing anything that had happened with the case or with Howard and Patricia. Fenella ran into Crystal on her way out.

"I was going to ring you," Crystal said. "We've had something of a shock here, and that's upset everything."

"I heard."

"We've decided we want all four kittens, though," Crystal added. "We're hoping that they'll serve as a distraction from everything else that's happened."

"They're a long-term commitment, not a distraction," Fenella said sharply.

Crystal nodded. "I do appreciate that. I promise you that they'll have a good home here. You're welcome to come back and visit them at any time."

Fenella might have argued further, but one of the home's residents walked past and then stopped and came back over. "Have you brought the kittens again?" he asked. "We're all hoping they'll stay one of these times. My wife never leaves our room except when the kittens are here, you see."

Before she could second-guess herself, Fenella handed the carrier to Crystal. "I'll bring the rest of their things over tomorrow," she said as she headed for the door.

"Thank you," Crystal called after her.

Moving back to her apartment felt like coming home. Fenella happily collected Katie from Shelly and then unpacked.

"You need to get a local paper," Mona told her a short while later. She faded away before Fenella could argue.

The headline was shocking enough to make Fenella do a double take in the shop. "Suicide Note Confession to Double Murder," it read. Fenella paid for the paper and then rushed home to read the article.

"Douglas native Howard Quinn sent his suicide letter to us here at the *Isle of Man Times*," the article began. After a short paragraph about Mabel's murder, the paper printed the confession in whole.

"He confesses to killing Mabel because she was threatening to tell Patricia about their affair," Fenella told Mona, who'd reappeared as soon as Fenella had returned with the paper. "He also confesses to killing Patricia so that she would never know what had happened."

"I still think Patricia did it," Mona replied.

"Howard wrote the letter."

Mona shrugged. "You can believe what you like. I knew Patricia and Howard. He didn't have the courage to kill anyone, and Patricia would have done it without batting an eyelash."

Daniel rang later that evening as Fenella was getting ready to go to her class.

"I assume you saw today's paper," he began.

"I did. I was shocked but not shocked, if you understand what I mean."

"I do understand. It's all very sad, anyway."

"Do you really think he killed Patricia so that she wouldn't find out what had happened?"

Daniel sighed. "You mustn't repeat this to anyone for the next twenty-four hours, but we've had a handwriting expert go over the suicide note. The paper has done the same, and they've had the same results. Expect another shocking headline tomorrow. The note that was sent to the papers had been signed by Howard, but the note itself was written by Patricia."

Fenella gasped. "So she did know."

"It seems so. I don't think we'll ever really know which one of them killed Mabel, but at least we can close the file now, one way or another."

Donna was quiet throughout the class that evening. When it was over, she stopped Fenella.

"I just wanted to thank you for having us all get together again," she said. "I'm glad the police have finally worked out what happened to Mabel, even though I'm shocked and saddened by what's been revealed."

Fenella nodded. "It's all terribly sad."

"We're meeting again this Friday," Donna added. "We may even try making it a regular thing. Just the girls. Clyde doesn't want to see Marilyn or Jeanne right now. He and I are having dinner together tomorrow, though."

"How nice for you. I hope you have a pleasant evening."

Donna nodded. "I hope so, too."

ACKNOWLEDGMENTS

Thank you to my beta reading team – you know who you are and how much I appreciate you.

Thank you to my wonderful cover artist, Linda, at Tell-Tale Book Covers. She continues to be a joy to work with and has become a friend.

Thank you to my editor, who has always worked incredibly hard to make these books better. Your efforts are greatly appreciated.

And thank you, readers, for continuing to spend time with Fenella and Mona. I love sharing their stories with you.

LETTERS AND LAWSUITS

Release date: October 18, 2019

Along with everything that she left to her, Fenella's aunt Mona left instructions for her own birthday party. Doncan Quayle, Fenella's advocate, is in charge of arranging the party, following Mona's detailed plans. He gets a little sidetracked, however, when a woman turns up on the island claiming to be Maxwell Martin's daughter.

Max had been Mona's benefactor for most of her life. He'd showered Mona with gifts, and now Rosemary Ballard is demanding a share in Mona's estate. She claims to have letters that prove that Mona had blackmailed Max for years. When Rosemary turns up dead, Fenella is the number-one suspect.

Inspector Daniel Robinson has to keep Fenella at arm's length, no matter how he feels about her. As Rosemary's family threaten to continue with the planned lawsuit, Fenella finds herself trying to prove her innocence in the murder investigation, and to find evidence that Rosemary was lying about her parentage.

Mona, Fenella's ghostly roommate in her luxury apartment, is insistent that the letters are fake. As she reveals more to Fenella about her relationship with Max, Fenella works to find a way to protect her fortune and find a killer.

Is it possible that Mona badly misjudged Max? Who else besides Fenella had a motive for wanting Rosemary dead? Mona is sure that Max's sister is behind the whole thing, but proving that might be an impossible task. As Mona's birthday party gets closer, Fenella begins to wonder if there is actually going to be anything to celebrate.

ALSO BY DIANA XARISSA

Aunt Bessie Assumes

Aunt Bessie Believes

Aunt Bessie Considers

Aunt Bessie Decides

Aunt Bessie Enjoys

Aunt Bessie Finds

Aunt Bessie Goes

Aunt Bessie's Holiday

Aunt Bessie Invites

Aunt Bessie Joins

Aunt Bessie Knows

Aunt Bessie Likes

Aunt Bessie Meets

Aunt Bessie Needs

Aunt Bessie Observes

Aunt Bessie Provides

Aunt Bessie Questions

Aunt Bessie Remembers

Aunt Bessie Solves

Aunt Bessie Tries

Aunt Bessie Understands

Aunt Bessie Volunteers

Aunt Bessie Wonders

The Isle of Man Ghostly Cozy Mysteries

Arrivals and Arrests

Boats and Bad Guys

The Isle of Man Romance Series

Island Escape

Island Inheritance

Island Heritage

Island Christmas

ABOUT THE AUTHOR

Diana grew up in Northwestern Pennsylvania and moved to Washington, DC after college. There she met a wonderful Englishman who was visiting the city. After a whirlwind romance, they got married and Diana moved to the Chesterfield area of Derbyshire to begin a new life with her husband. A short time later, they relocated to the Isle of Man.

After over ten years on the island, it was time for a change. With their two children in tow, Diana and her husband moved to suburbs of Buffalo, New York. Diana now spends her days writing about the island she loves.

She also writes mystery/thrillers set in the not-too-distant future as Diana X. Dunn and middle grade and Young Adult books as D.X. Dunn.

Diana is always happy to hear from readers. You can write to her at:

Diana Xarissa Dunn
PO Box 72
Clarence, NY 14031.
Find Diana at: DianaXarissa.com
E-mail: Diana@dianaxarissa.com

215
132
83

Made in United States
Troutdale, OR
05/19/2025

31517612R00130